# THE
# GUARDIANS

Vol. 1 (PHL)

Johnny Duncan

MK Publishing
San Antonio, TX

MK Publishing
P.O. Box 760031
San Antonio, TX 78245

Publisher's Note: This is a work of fiction. Names, characters, places, and incidents are a product of the author's imagination. Locales and public names are sometimes used for atmospheric purposes. Any resemblance to actual people, living or dead, or to businesses, companies, events, institutions, or locales is completely coincidental.

Ordering Information:
Quantity sales. Special discounts are available on quantity purchases by corporations, associations, and others. For details, contact the "Special Sales Department" at the address above.

The Guardians Vol 1 (PHL)/ Johnny Duncan. -- 1st ed.
ISBN 978-1-943711-08-6

# CONTENTS

*To Malakai, my first born. Always stay true to your heart and dreams. Stay hungry. Stay foolish.*

# CHAPTER 1

**B**obby Celliva strolled into his job at the Thomas Jefferson hospital. There was a quick, yet relaxed pace in his strut as he hummed to the annoyingly catchy song that his car radio played, minutes before he parked. As much as he wanted to strangle the teenage star and her incessant whining, he couldn't resist playing the song over and over in his mental playlist. Although still relatively new at the hospital, he was finally getting the hang of the processes as he distanced himself further away from the "new kid at a new school" feel that haunted him in the beginning.

The past month had been absolute hell for him as he learned to envy all of the newbies with their new job jitters and fears of leaving a bad first impression. Unlike Bobby, the fresh faced rookies all had one thing in common: they actually belonged there. They had endured long hours of studies, grueling tests, lost sleep and thousands of dollars in pursuit of achieving that one sheet of paper that would validate them as qualified medical experts.

Bobby, however, had no such degree. Before his first day, all of the information he received on being a nurse came from those popular medical shows that made everyone feel they could get a medical degree just by watching them. He never spent a day or took a course on anything medical related, and yet his entire career relied on passing himself off as a qualified medical professional.

Everyone got to know him as Bobby Century, as well as his cover story and any element that might come up in conversation or a background check. Concealing the fact that he secretly worked for the CIA was top priority, and any lie he had to tell, or role he had to play was acceptable. Although deception was never in his nature, he understood that his position was instrumental to saving countless lives. No award, medal, or key to the city was in store for him, but then again, if he was doing it for the fame and glory, he never would have signed up for the CIA in the first place.

Working for the CIA was like a wild dream turned reality. Growing up, Bobby desired to be part of the Central Intelligence Agency. Making a difference in people's lives and positively impacting the world almost excited him just as much as gaining access to privileged information. Even as a young child, he sought out the truth of things that didn't make sense to him. By the age of eight, Bobby had uncovered the truth of Santa Clause and the Tooth Fairy, and by the age of twelve he became fascinated with the history of American government and the system's recurrence to lie or withhold a great deal of secrets from the public.

He sympathized that in most cases, the secrets were for the greater good, but he still wanted to be part of the "in crowd" with informational flow. In that moment, Bobby decided to join the CIA, and never wavered from that ideal. This childhood dream was the only thing he clung onto when his first mission went south. He was savagely beaten, tortured, and all but guaranteed to die that night.

In High School, Bobby was naturally smart and found pride in not needing much study time to achieve good grades. With more free time than a good portion of his struggling peers, he joined the basketball and football team, which earned him popularity points and the nickname, "The Smartest Jock." He never consulted with a guidance counselor or took a personality assessment, because he was clear on his path, and refused to allow anyone to derail him. This rule also prevented him from attending parties and gatherings that had any potential for alcohol or illegal substances.

Transitioning to college life didn't change many of his ideals as he stuck to the straight and narrow path while enrolled in University of Nebraska. Pursuing first his Bachelor's degree and then Master's degree in Criminal Justice, the more he learned about the criminal world around him, and the more he wanted in. When the time was right, he applied and was accepted in to the CIA, which inherently was the best day of his life.

The unprecedented challenges of agent training drained Bobby mentally, physically, and emotionally on a daily basis. All of his hard work and accolades meant nothing as he constantly felt like a below average recruit barely scraping by. However, even in his darkest of days Bobby clung onto his goals, and as colleagues dropped and flunked out, he hung in there. Concepts of friendship were once again dismissed as he doubled and tripled his efforts to succeed. Top marks in all of his classes and zero social life earned him his second nickname: "Poindexter."

Towards the end of training, a cheating scandal broke out and instructors went scrambling for the truth. Twelve class-mates were rumored to have shared answers for their final exam, which rocked the whole integrity of the system. They needed the culprits removed as expeditiously as possible, and in unison the instructors agreed there was one person perfect for the task: Bobby. Within a week, he had completely reversed every predictable attribute as he made friends, went to parties, and voiced his concerns on the mandatory redo test they were going to impose on every recruit.

He lied about how he studied like a mad man and yet barely squeaked by the first time, and was certain he didn't have it in him a second time to pass. In little time, his cries landed his on target audience, and he had the names of everyone involved in the scandal from ringleader to pion. Bobby informed the instructors, and in turn, four recruits were reprimanded, two landed in jail, and six in total were removed from the acad-emy. He was revered by instructors, but hated by peers, which earned him his third and final nickname: "The Rat."

Jokes and rumors circled the newly aliened classmate, which followed him all the way up to graduation. As the agents ea-gerly awaited the details of their first assignments, they were equally anxious to find out which ones would have the great misfortune of being assigned with Bobby Celliva.

The CIA worked hard to accommodate their wishes on initial locations, and sighs of relief were shared as they came through for the majority of agents. Much to everyone's sur-prise, the most anticipated person was one of the few without an assignment listed. Instead of a displayed city, state, and point of contact, the space next to his name instructed him report to a remote building later that day.

He reported in, and what seemed to be a computer glitch turned out to be a life changing meeting, vastly altering the career path he was headed in. Two agents sat him down and pulled out records, which appeared to be his academic file. However, once opened they took turns talking about some of his past actions in which he never gave a second thought about. They talked about his unwavering dedication and integrity, even when he was thoroughly criticized and isolated.

They brought up a couple of instances in which he followed the strictest rules knowing it would lead to isolation and ridicule.

Before Bobby had time to inquire where any of this was going, one of the agents placed a stack of papers in front of him and instructed to start signing. The agent explained that the paperwork was for disclosure of Top Secret information and if any of it was leaked, Bobby would be facing federal charges that would easily land him in prison for the first of his life.

The punishment wouldn't end there; not only would he be in prison, but solitary confinement, so he could never tell another soul, and whomever he told would share the same fate. Being considered a terrorist in that moment, Bobby would no longer be considered a U.S. citizen, which meant neither he nor his confidant would receive the luxury of a trial or jury.

As Bobby combed through the paperwork, there were many redundancies as he acknowledged the importance of safeguarding information and the severe penalties involved with breaking protocol. By the time he reached the end of the stack, he rubbed and rotated his sore wrists. While other agents transferred to various locations to begin their new careers, Bobby learned about the most secretive and elite branch of the CIA, in which most agents would spend an entire career without hearing a rumor about.

Exposing one truth after another, each blow came equipped with undeniable proof and footage to back it up. Bobby was exposed to pieces of a puzzle that he never knew existed, and in essence the game was changed forever. The program was called Project 4G; an organization within the agency that was not only viable but essential to the nation's success. After learning the truth his whole world felt different and smaller.

Like Neo from The Matrix, Bobby, as well as most Americans, had his blinders on and he injected his "blue pill' of reality. It was silly to think that only a handful of people like Jeffrey Dahmer and the group that framed Timothy McVeigh were the only ones with the knowledge and willingness to successfully inflict mass casualties against U.S. citizens on American soil. It was naive to believe that only a handful of people like Steve Koresh, Jim Jones, and Charles Manson had the charisma and warped reality to influence droves of followers to kill and go against authority.

These numbers, just like the ones of disillusioned copycats that attempted to shoot up schools, or foreign terrorists that came close to making 9/11 look like a drill were drastically underestimated. In that moment, Bobby was shown that these occurrences happened in a frequent enough period to petrify even the most grounded individual. Project 4G was well aware of the true threats as opposed to what made it to media, just like they knew that only one force could stop these imminent threats, while avoiding mass hysteria and anarchy: The Guardians.

Guardians are four person teams that exist all over the nation in major select cities, and Project 4G exists solely to fund and physically assist the Guardians any and every way to get the mission done. Guardians serve as protectors, and their job is to eliminate threats before the general public catches wind, or that would inflict too much damage on other responding agencies if they didn't get involved. Injected with a serum at a very young age allowed these Guardians to accomplish some unimaginable feats, unrivaled by any individual.

Unlike the layers of hierarchy in the CIA, Project 4G was much more simplified with only four ranks: G1, G2, G3, and G4. Bobby's concern for growth potential was immediately squashed when he realized that the lowest ranking G1 still made about what was equivalent of the director.

The weeks that followed the post graduate of both UNL and CIA answered questions from both written and practical scenarios, which consisted of virtually unimaginable situations. Although he responded to every question, each and every test left him wondering if he passed or failed. Eventually, he sat down with the director and was informed that he was the newest member of Project 4G.

The next day, the newly anxious G1 agent embarked on his first mission, despite the limited details given. The objective was simple: retrieve some important documents from Langley, Virginia, and transfer them to an intelligence office in ⬚ New York. "Pinnacle Force" was the password needed for him to hand it off. He wasn't sure what any of this had to do with Guardians, but he was determined not to fail on such a simple task, having no clue that it was his final test as a 4G candidate. Within twelve hours, what was supposed to be an easy job would objectively become the hardest challenge in his adult life.

For his travels, his supposed handlers issued him a Black Chevy Tahoe with bulletproof tinted windows, a travel credit card, and credentials.

Bobby wasted little time to acquire the briefcase and hit the road in route to his destination, making sure to abide by every traffic rule given to include speed limits. He made it to ⏾ his destination a little after 8:00pm but much to his surprise, the entire area was desolate. He was expecting some sort of corporate office or secured compound, but instead he was led ⏾ to what seemed to be an abandoned warehouse.

Bobby entered the vacant space, looked for his next step, and walked on the balls of his feet to minimize any potential noise. He turned around the corner of a concrete wall and moved into a large open bay. Soiled oil stains contained a strong musty stench in the air. The room had open crates, and cardboard boxes were scattered around in the middle of the room, two men sat in folding chairs while playing cards on a cheap wooden table. They wore matching black suits with white shirts and long skinny ties, and also had a similar muscular build, as both men appeared extremely fit.

Bobby stood in silence for a few seconds as he alternated glances between the men and the briefcase. The entire area gave off a shady feel worthy of any bad guy drug deal scene in a cop movie. Before Bobby could take a step back and reconfirm the address, one of the men looked up and immediately placed down his cards. He stood to his feet and walked towards Bobby, as the second man followed.

For the past couple of hours Bobby's stomach growled and his eyelids grew increasingly heavy. Harboring a desire to rest and relax was an understatement, and all that was left was the password....which never came. The men continued to walk towards Bobby without a word said, and when within six paces of him, he instinctively moved a few paces backwards toward the door, which in turn encouraged the man on the left to crack a smile.

"Hang on there, hoss." the slightly taller man spoke up in a deep southern accent.

"We're on the same team here. Why else would I be stuck here in this dump?"

Bobby's eyes narrowed and shifted between the two men for a second, and responded with a one word question, "Password?"

Without hesitation, the man responded, "Never-ending journey." As Bobby flashed a quizzical look, the man threw his hands up as he gave a loud exhaust through his mouth.

"All right kid, you got us.

Truth is we were in a rush and completely spaced out on learning what the new password is. I'm guessing you're new, because we do this type of stuff all the time, and no one gives a crap about the password. Honestly, the main reason why they have us running around like this is because we're the decoy for the bigger boys, and they want us to at least seem important. But we all have our bosses to answer to, right? Anyway, I guess I'll take that off your hands...."

Bobby remained silent, and as the man reached for the briefcase, he took two steps back.

"If you want this, contact your superiors. I'm not giving this up until I have the required password."

The man's eyes widened and he pursed his lips as the second man spoke up. He had a surprising New York accent, and equally surprising question, which informed Bobby that playtime was over:

"What if we just took it from you!?"

New York rushed towards Bobby, but briefly halted once he pulled out his 9MM Beretta pistol, firing a shot towards the ground without hesitation. He lifted the pistol, and the barrel alternated between the two men, as Bobby maintained his distance.

"Back up! Back the hell up! I'm leaving with this briefcase, and unless you want a bullet in your skull, I recommend you consider this one a loss!"

Bobby slowly inched backwards toward the door, while remaining focused on the men, and prepared for any abrupt movement.

"You don't have the balls to shoot!" exclaimed New York.

He stormed towards Bobby a second time, which made his heart unexpectedly jump up a few extra beats. The man sped towards Bobby as the pistol barrel stared straight at him. Bobby jumped in response but made a point to no show fear when he spoke up.

"Wrong answer, genius!"

He aimed his muzzle toward the man's right leg and pulled the trigger.

Much to Bobby's surprise, the gun didn't go off. Instead of being greeted with a loud boom and squirts of blood, the gun gave off a loud audible click. He had loaded his full magazine earlier that day, so he quickly racked the slide and watched a bullet eject allowing a fresh one to enter the chamber. As he pulled the trigger for a second time with the same result, New

York reached for the case only to be met with a swift pistol whip to his right cheek, which sent both the man and the gun flying. His wingman took advantage of the opening and landed a hearty sucker punch on Bobby's jaw. He instantly hit the ground and wallowed in pain, as the briefcase flew out his hand and landed to the side of him.

Blood dripped from Bobby's mouth as he sat momentarily dazed, but quickly shook it off and tactfully rolled towards the briefcase just in time to avoid the man's impending foot stomp towards his chest. With briefcase cradled in his body like a delicate newborn, he went to a knee, and waited for the men to respond. Stationary and with his head hung low, New York took the seemingly easy opportunity to kick him again, which he anticipated.

Bobby waited for the man to get a running start and launch his foot at Bobby's eye level and towards his face, before he ducked out the way and shoved the case into the New York's sternum. Bobby quickly stood to his feet and connected a wild swing on the man's face, which sent him flying as Bobby regained his balance.

As he gained the upper hand in a situation where he didn't expect anything more than a simple hand off, he gained a sense of empowerment. Yet, even with the impromptu call to action, and weapon malfunction, he stood tall.

Unfortunately for Bobby, this small victory was short lived as the disregarded partner struck the back of his hand with something hard. He wasn't able to detect whether it was a pipe, stick, or one of the many other tools lying on the ground before he hit the ground hard and the briefcase flew away from his hand again. As he turned his body to lie on his back, Bobby closed and opened his injured body part a couple of times and felt a sense of relief that it wasn't broken.

He placed both hands underneath his butt and pulled his legs towards his abs. The muscle memory from his numerous combative courses were in full throttle, and there were too many stories of agents that were knocked down and never given the opportunity to stand up and defend themselves. If this could turn out to be the case for him, a rigorous bicycle kick just may be his saving grace, as they wouldn't be able to get close enough to land any solid hit on him.

New York stood up to join his comrade and both men tactically moved on the opposite side of him to attack simultaneously.

Bobby fought valiantly, but it didn't take long for one of the men to attack a blind spot and render him ineffective.

A couple minutes later, the two men sat a defenseless Bobby in a nearby chair in the middle of the room and used industrial rope to tie him up When secured, both men dusted themselves off and dabbed the spots of blood that Bobby had caused, but neither tended to his swollen eye or the blood that dripped down from their nose and busted lip. When satisfied and composed, New York walked towards the case while the other picked up a nearby brick and forced the case open. After a few good swings, it flew open and both immediately scrounged through the contents, which contained a folder with a few sheets of paper.

A smile flashed across the southern agent's face, and he enthusiastically moved a chair to face Bobby and sat down in front of him with folder in hand.

"See, I tried to tell you, kid....all of this trouble, and you were nothing but the test monkey."

One by one, the man held the three pages in front of Bobby, giving him time to read and sink it all in. Page by page, Bobby read what seemed to be transcribed from a cookbook. There was no code to decipher, and no possible anagram that he could come up with. The pages contained nothing more than cooking instructions; the first page for making pancakes, the second for French toast, and the third was Denver Omelets.

The man silently waited for Bobby to look away before he sat them down underneath his chair and continued in a calm and rational voice.

"Sorry, kid. At this rate, we probably know more about your organization than you.....which is fine. We all have a job to do, but we're not bad guys. There's no reason to keep you so we're going to let you go."

He began to untie the ropes as New Yorker watched, unaffected. Moving closer, he looked at Bobby and raised his index finger in the air.

"Oh, one more thing before you leave. We already know about your organization, except for the official name. What is ⬚ it so we don't have to keep calling you guys Project X?"

Bobby looked up at him, and looked towards the ground. The southerner stopped untying and chuckled softly.

"He makes a good point. Don't worry, we're not asking for any details of your operations. I'm sure there's nothing you can educate us about anyway, but I suppose we should know the name of y'all."

Bobby looked up at both men and quietly announced, "I can't tell you that."

"You're serious....are you freaking serious right now!? Just tell us the damn name or I will..." New York started until his partner put his hand up.

New York stopped talking and stormed away, leaving Bobby and the southerner to talk. The man still showed patience and restraint, but Bobby could see that it was running thin. What they asked was a simple request, but he was given strict instruction not to divulge any information unless given permission....which even included something as simple as a title. Before the man spoke up again, Bobby repeated that the name of their organization was private, but they could continue to call them Project X.

The man's eyes widened and glared at Bobby with anger. He was already shown that he was lied to by his people.....that his mission wasn't as important as it seemed, and most importantly, Bobby was the one being held captive and yet he sat defiant and gave them instructions.

"You...pompous little shit...."

The southerner watched New York storm back towards Bobby and ball up his fists. This time he sat back in prideful silence as he punched Bobby hard in the face.

"How about now!? No!?"

The man backhanded Bobby with an open hand, but equal amount of force.

"How about now!?"

Regardless of the anger and embarrassment, Bobby kept his mouth shut. He refused to tell them what they wanted to know, and any compromise would only enrage them more. The seconds turned into minutes, and the minutes into hours. What started as a simple question evolved into a battle of submission and respect. Every part of his body ached; his ribs were bruised and his legs felt like linguini. New spots of blood emerged all around his face, as well as his left eye which was rapidly swelling shut.

Concepts of diplomacy had escaped them long ago, and all that was left was rage in their quest for dominance. In and out of beat downs, Bobby found refuge within his mind which often sent him off to some faraway beach, or eating double blueberry pancakes at IHOP with his parents. As time progressed, the potential for escape seemed more and more bleak. They appeared equally as determined to learn a simple name as much as he didn't want to give it, and every hour that passed made matters worse.

He began to hope that this would all turn out to be some big test or misunderstanding, because that would surely be the only way out this situation. The more he allowed the thought to mature, the harder he desperately clung on to the idea.

Another hour had passed and it seemed that the two men were at their breaking point. The southerner sat down in the chair in front of Bobby again. He took a second to catch his breath after his latest rounds of hits as Bobby tried to focus and fought the urge to pass out completely.

As the man began to speak in the same calm and rational voice as before, he reached out and grabbed Bobby's right hand. He carefully went through every finger, giving each one a light tug and squeeze as if he was inspecting it. Bobby found it extremely awkward, but so was getting punched repeatedly. Like it or not, he was at their mercy.

"I think I'm starting to understand the problem. Maybe you think this is a game, and since we're asking for something small you can just toy around with us. It's not really about the damn name, but it's the principle of the whole thing. You're being a stubborn jackass for a small price to pay for freedom. That's just outright disrespectful and my friend already thinks we should just end you for wasting this much of our time! So maybe you think this is all a game....or maybe some kind of dream. If so...it's time..... for you to wake the hell up!"

Suddenly Bobby heard a loud snapping sound, like the sound of a hollow twig breaking, followed by the most excruciating feeling he had ever felt. The sharp pain sent his mind in a frenzy as he looked down and saw his pinky bent in the most unnatural position. He wasn't a doctor, but one look and he knew the finger was broken.

"Who the hell do you work for!? What do you call yourselves!?"

In that moment, Bobby had accepted that this was not a test. There was no pause button, and backup was not coming for him. Maybe they would've authorized for him being roughed up a bit for the sake a loyalty, but they have now upgraded to broken ligaments which he feared was just the beginning. Bobby looked at both men glaring down at him as they waited for him to speak. Bobby began to pant heavily and his eyes began to water from the pain, as both men smirked.

"Okay! Okay! I'll tell you, just please....don't hurt me any-more."

Both men stood in silence momentarily, then the southerner spoke in his cool, calm and collective tone.

"Then tell us. Who do you work for? What are you called?"

Bobby lowered his head, speaking in a low and somber tone. "I work...."

His throat was dry and his voice was quivering. He closed his mouth, swallowed some saliva and tried again. "I work....for your mom. She told me to buy some condoms because we ran out last night. I was supposed to tell--"

The man backhanded Bobby's face hard, almost losing his balance in the process.

"Who the hell do you work for!? Why were you—"

Bobby returned the favor of cutting him off.

"Call her and ask her! She's at home, butt naked, making me grits right now!"

The New Yorker cocked his fist back, prepared to punch Bobby the face.

"Stop! That's enough!" emerged a female voice from near the entrance.

New York stopped immediately and dropped in hands directly in front of Bobby. The two men looked at each other and nodded in agreement as Bobby looked at them both in shock and tried to turn his head to look at the stranger in the room. Without saying a word, both men moved away from Bobby and out of sight. In walked a butch woman that appeared to be in her late forties. She wore a black dress with pearl earrings, and had a short hair with black and grey strands all brushed to the side. She stood over him for a second as if she was a lab professor and he was the new science experiment.

"Drug him, and let's move him out."

Without hesitation, southerner returned with a needle in hand and instantly injected Bobby in the neck.

Within a couple of seconds, his entire world went black, and that was the last he saw of the warehouse.

Bobby woke up in the bed of what seemed like a high class hospital room, reserved for investors, patrons, and their spoiled rich kids. He laid next to a large glass tinted window, and the exposed drapes showed that it was bright and sunny outside.

The bed was more soft and plush than the one he had at home, and the spacious room was aesthetically, pleasing with the mounted large screen television facing him in the middle of the room. The front left corner was occupied by a leather sectional, and the right corner had a green plant standing tall beside a fish tank that consisted of various exotic and colorful fish.

Noticing the bathroom on the left ignited Bobby's desire to go as he rotated his body to kick his feet off the bed, but quickly found himself restricted. His right wrist was shackled to one of the bed posts, and a couple of reactionary yanks showed he wasn't going anywhere, but he remained calm as he laid back into position.

His wounds were treated, to include his finger which already had a splint on it. He still ached somewhat, but he felt leagues better than the night before. There was no point in getting riled up at this point; there was no point in going through all of the trouble to fix him, only to break him again...or at least he hoped.

Someone had to put him there, and surely someone had to be monitoring as well. He took a more detailed look around and faced the once-overlooked camera pointed directly at him from the ceiling. Confirming his suspicion, Bobby gently nodded his head and closed his eyes. Surely, whoever monitored him was on their way so he figured he might as well enjoy the silence before being badgered with whatever questions or demands they had left.

Bobby had his eyes closed for less than three minutes when the door opened and in walked the same woman from the night before. She wore a black business suit, small gold earrings, and the same distasteful hairstyle.

Grabbing one of the plush chairs on her way in, she pulled up next to Bobby and sat down at his eye level.

"Good morning, Agent Celliva. Don't worry, you're safe. Everything that happened last night was your final test and you passed marvelously. You are exactly what we need in Project 4G."

She ignored his skeptical facial expression and continued.

"My name is Cecilia Smith and I'm the director of 4G. If I'm not mistaken the password we told you to use was Pinnacle Force? During your training, your main handlers were agents Lee and Whiteman, and the only reason why you're still handcuffed is for your benefit.

A few years back, I came in to congratulate another agent, and the crafty shit decked me and stole my gun before I could get a word out. He ran out and held one of our workers hostage."

"Took us an hour to calm his crazy ass down." she muttered to herself as she shook her head.

"So, what about you kid? Do you think you can contain yourself to not attack your new boss while we have a chat?"

Bobby slowly nodded, and she stood up and pulled the keys from her pocket to uncuff him.

"I don't want you pissing your pants or anything, so why don't you head to the restroom and join me on this couch over here once you're done?"

Bobby nodded his head a second time, agreeing with the assertive yet pleasant woman as her slight southern twang made her sound even more hospitable. Bobby shut and locked the door, and while enjoying the best pee break in history, the idea of running crossed his mind on whether or not to run. The exit door was literally adjacent to the bathroom, and it would take no effort at all to make it out. The woman was much older than him and wasn't remotely close to his physical fitness level, so he could lose her.

Their conversation played back in his mind as he finished up and washed his hands, finally realizing none of it mattered. She knew way too much already to require any information from him and if she wanted him harmed, she had countless opportunities. She had to be telling the truth, which meant she would be the one he would ultimately decide the fate of his livelihood from duty, to money, to location.

Bobby washed and dried his hands and stood in front the mirror to try and fix his "bum living off the street" appearance. A seconds later, exited the bathroom to sit in a chair across from the patiently waiting Director Smith. With head and shoulders high, she was busy jotting down information in her organizer. As Bobby sat down, she closed the book and placed her palms atop her crossed leg.

"I'm sure you have a lot of questions, but even though we may have embellished some rules for the sake of training, the basics are still vital to follow. By now you should know about our ranking system from G1 to G4, which are all responsible for a different mission for Guardians. Like everyone else has, you're starting at the bottom as a G1, and can build your way up. In case you weren't told, this is your starting salary."

Smith handed Bobby a small white sheet of paper with so many zeros it made him want to jump for joy and kiss the unattractive butch woman on the lips, tongue if she pleased. According to the pay scale, his salary would be higher than what most agents grinded their entire careers to attain, if they were lucky. The last time he saw the numbers, he was certain it was a typo, but this time he was convinced.

"As you can see we treat our agents well, but we also require a great deal from you. Loyalty is everything in this company, and we had to put you through that unfortunate test to check yours. No matter what instructions you are given, you're expected to follow them to the bitter end. Besides your little death wish, you did pretty well, and that's the only reason we're having this conversation.

But cross us one time, and all of this will go away! In case you don't think we are that serious about a simple title or you telling your occupation to a loved one...we are! We will send you and whoever you blabbed to away in a heartbeat and replace you like used bubblegum! Do you understand!?"

Bobby nodded his head and silently responded, "Yes, ma'am."

In a matter of seconds, Bobby went from feeling empowered to guilty, but her message was brilliantly clear and he understood every word. If they had put him through hell within the past twenty-four hours to simply test his resolve, he could only imagine what would happen if he slipped up. Every U.S. citizen was subject to a slew of laws created, but government agencies had their own set to pile on top. He could only imagine what juicy fine print lurked in the books of secret government rules, and he had no intention of finding out.

Director Smith finished up with her threats and warnings and immediately switched back to her original peaceful and congratulatory mode.

"Well, after the crazy night you had, I bet you must be starving."

She instructed him to shower and change and said there would be a buffet breakfast waiting for him in the cafeteria. Twenty minutes later, Bobby decided not to ask how there was a perfectly tailored suit waiting for him, as well as the added accessories that were all in his size and taste. Instead, he remained thankful for the consideration and more importantly to get out of his stinky, bloody, and tattered clothing.

Cleaned up and refreshed, he headed to the dining area and was greeted by thirty people in an otherwise empty room. Engaged in their own conversations, Bobby approached the room of strangers and the first person to make eye contact immediately stood up and began to applaud.

Others followed suit until everyone stood and faced Bobby with big smiles affixed on their faces. Islands of white gold ⬚ domes with steam underneath were lined up to the side of the long table, and the guest of honor was led to start off. One by one, Bobby grabbed the handle and removed a dome to discover a new hot and freshly cooked food item lying underneath. A detailed amount of yogurts, fruits, juices, and pastries were also beautifully displayed on the countertops, and with a full plate of food, he sat down at the center of the table.

There were twenty-one men and nine women, and the majority were in great shape and relatively good looking. The 4G employees took turns to introduce themselves and carry on surprisingly interesting conversations about life, family, and hobbies. Amongst the thirty were the two men that assaulted him for the majority of the night, whom were the first to congratulate him. Both men were kind and approachable as they took turns to apologize and brag about how well he resisted.

As both men shook his hand, Bobby desperately fought every urge he had to run in the opposite direction.

After breakfast, Bobby met back with Agent Smith so she could explain exactly what his real job assignment would be. She explained that a G1 was responsible for Guardian candidate testing, and hand selecting future Guardians throughout the country. She also informed him he would be working at the last place he would imagine: a civilian hospital.

Bobby listened to her instructions, constantly battling every desire to interrupt her with a resounding, "Are you serious right now!?"

With his pinky finger as a friendly reminder, he knew at this point he had two options: walk away completely, or follow every instruction without question. There was no in-between; in that moment, he decided to be all in. More importantly than the pay being retirement worthy, he was making the world a better and safer place.

However, he could see why this group had to be so secretive. If the public caught a hint on what he was going to do they would dedicate a whole year to the story.

Many people would see what needed to happen as immoral and a violation of almost every right entitled to a human beings, but if Director Smith was telling the truth, it was necessary.

# CHAPTER 2

For weeks, Bobby regularly worked shifts at Thomas Jefferson Hospital, all while trying his hardest to pass off as a nurse, but more importantly....as part of the team. The lies were made easier with practice, but his motivation dwindled. Why was he in the hospital in the first place? The thought resonated in his brain and the voice grew louder and louder as time passed. He did what was asked and injected every newborn inside the hospital with a strange serum, knowing the FDA, medical staff, and media would crucify him if they ever found out.

The drug was named Genotransphinemorphadine, nicknamed "Genesis," and according to the G1 agents, roughly every one out of one hundred babies would be affected by the serum, hence turning that chosen one into a Guardian Candidate. "I was just following orders" had never worked historically for lowly peons from Nazis of WW2 to the U.S. Army of Guantanamo Bay, and everything else in between. What if he were to get caught? How much backup could he really expect from one of the most top secret agencies in history? Surely they would simply deny involvement and paint a picture of "Bobby: The Rouge Psychopath." Certainly, the CIA had done much worse than that before.

Bobby would've happily dismissed all of these concerns and risk factors if he could at least get some results; there had to be some reason he was taking such a huge risk in the first place, and that it was all for the greater good in the end. His doubt began to show in his work and ethic, and for the first time in history, Bobby debated on calling in sick a couple of times without any more than a scratchy throat.

Bobby always looked for a proverbial lighthouse to bring him back to shore when his thoughts and actions were lost in a sea of confusion, doubt, and fear. In this case, his guiding light came by the name of Rachael Newsby.

Like Bobby, Rachael was a new employee, and being new to the city meant she was also without friends or family.

She worked at the hospital cafeteria and before she came along, the shift at lunchtime was dominated by an old bitter woman named Olga. Olga was originally from Eastern Europe, but she lived in the U.S. for the past few decades. Bobby didn't bother to learn anything more than that about her life due to her consistently bitter attitude and resting bitch face. Regardless of his attempts, no level of charm or charisma would win her over. Cheerful greetings and warm conversation openers were met with silent glares followed by declaration of the amount owed.

He witnessed all he needed to in his first week when a brave young male nurse seemed determined to make the old woman crack a smile. He stood in front of Bobby in the checkout line and greeted Olga with a wide grin as if he had just discovered the winning lottery numbers.

"Good morning, ma'am! How are you today!?" the nurse said, while she tallied up the man's order.

"$5.80, please."

With a smile still on his face and a twenty dollar bill in his hand he stated:

"This food smells good. Do you ever try any of it? Actually, you all probably have the really good stuff in the back to eat, huh?"

The man softly chuckled as Olga gave a blank stare and snatched his money from his hands.

"Your change, sir. Thank you."

She began to tally the next order, just as expressionless as she was with the nurse. Quietly admitting defeat, the nurse walked away with tray in hand to the cafeteria benches. Olga did not discriminate in the slightest. It didn't matter if you were old, young, local, foreign, male, female, medical, or maintenance. She was only focused on three things: processing your order, paying you out, and getting you the hell out of her line as quickly as possible.

Bobby had hoped for leniency one day when he was twenty cents short, but she showed none. As he stood at the checkout line with his tray of food, he asked for a pass. She gave him her trademark look and repeated the amount owed until he placed an item back. She expressed an emotionless "thank you" as he rolled his eyes and stormed off to find his seat.

He didn't care if she could or couldn't allow it, but there was a little something called customer service that was missing. Saying something like "Sorry, but I have to follow policy set in place," or even a simple, "I can't," would've been better than her actions, especially knowing that she spoke perfect English. He had better communication with Chinese and Korean employees that barely spoke the same language. In time, Bobby accepted that her bitter attitude was going to be the inevitable hurdle to jump when eating lunch in the cafeteria, until the day he met Rachael.

At this point he was programmed to grab his food, checkout, and pay without so much of expressing a look of content to the cashier. The line of paying customers was deadly silent as he jumped in and followed suit. While checking over his choices, he slowly inched forward to the checkout line to pay. The changeless daily routine had taught him many things about timing to include the exact moment in which he needed to pay without looking up. With one glance at the packets of butter, Bobby instinctively pulled out his wallet and began to pull out his cash.

"Good afternoon, sir. How are you doing today?" a young, female voice emerged from the cash register. Not only was the voice friendly and unfamiliar, but it happened to be one of the loveliest voices he heard in a while. His eyes immediately shot up to face his greeter, and for a second he was frozen in time, unable to speak or move. The aggressive throat clearing from the man behind him yanked him back to reality.

From that first encounter, he was absolutely mesmerized by Rachael. She was twenty-three years old with long, flowing red hair, light brown eyes, the cutest little button nose, and full lips. She had a short stature, standing about five feet two inches, and a small frame.

She wore tight blue shorts and a loose fitted Beatles t-shirt, with one sleeve hanging down and exposing the black bra strap she had on. She also wore a long necklace with a peace symbol near her lower torso. As he returned her greeting, he tried hard to think of something witty to stand out amongst all of the other customers, but felt the pressure under such short notice.

"Good afternoon, things are good. Of course, it will be much better if you can look the other way for a minute, so I can get this meal for free."

Rachael softly giggled. "Yeah, right, I'm already in enough trouble on my first day." Rachael responded to Bobby's perplexed look by gently tugging on her shirt.

"Not exactly the required uniform around here, but I forgot mine at home."

"Just please don't get fired just yet. I'd much rather see you every day, because the usual one makes me feel like I'm doing a prison sentence. Of course knowing my luck, you're probably related or something."

"Actually, she's my only living relative. My beloved grandma."

"Great."

She looked at his face and laughed. "No, I don't know anyone here because I just moved to the city." Bobby smiled and was about to respond, but the man behind him exhaled a loud audible breath as tapped his tray on the chrome rails used to move them along. Bobby and Rachael shared a look that it was time to end the conversation. They said their goodbyes as Bobby walked to the benches and Rachael rung up the next customer.

In the days that followed, Bobby took every chance to visit Rachael without letting it interfere with their jobs or giving off any sort of stalker vibe. Eventually he asked her out, and she gracefully accepted. The more time they spent together meant the stronger his infatuation grew, even though there were many things about Rachael's personality that was polar opposite of his own.

She was a twenty-three-year-old self-proclaimed modern day hippie, and unlike the majority of her peers, she had no interest in his professional career and academic achievements. She rarely asked him anything about work, which in turn made him extremely happy. For the first time in a while, he could be perfectly candid instead of being forced to lie and make up stories like normal. She cared far more about his musical inspirations, having fun, and debating on subjects like vegetarianism and politics.

They may not have been the ideal pair that others would imagine, but they were perfect for each other. By the time Bobby reached his two month mark at the hospital, the two were inseparable and barely a day went by without them spending time together. He found peace in the fact that he was sent on a pointless and time-consuming task.

Not one of the injected babies showed any symptoms, and knowing the people he worked with, they probably never would. However, he was close to hitting his two hundred fifty mark and not one reacted any different than the pain of some monster sticking them with a needle of God knows what. He knew what he was told, but he also knew his employers centered on progress and lies. His recently healed pinky reminded him how he couldn't put anything past them, but then again, he felt that way about any government agency.

However, the more time he spent with Rachael, the more his concerns melted away. He would still do what was asked of him, but he no longer gave a crap if he would ever find a candidate, or if he was ever supposed to in the first place. One way or the other, he was already in it now, and all it meant for him would be administrative work and more time in the office. He'd much ⸮ rather enjoy the company of his beautiful and witty girlfriend, and the fact that the government was paying him a handsome sum to take her out and play pretend.

One day shortly after, his entire outlook was flipped on its head as Bobby stood face to face with his first candidate. The day was otherwise normal, and from an earlier conversation, he agreed to meet Rachael at a play that started twenty minutes after his shift. She really wanted to see it but kept missing the showings, and the night was the final showing in the city. With such a small window between his shift and the show time, Rachael admitted defeat. Bobby, however, told her he could do it, and promised to be there on time.

Two hours before his shift ended, Bobby learned that a young woman was in the middle of giving birth and everything should be done within the next half hour or so. He casually strolled to his Postpartum unit, and checked his watch. He still had plenty of time to finish up with work and make it to the play.

It helped that he was his own boss and could come and go and he pleased, as long he produced the right quota for the month. It didn't take much for his schedule to mirror Rachael's, as long as he kept up with the sporadic times in between where he had to come in and do his business. Even then with practice, he could be in and out when need be.

Soon after Bobby had arrived to his unit, the woman had given birth. Her name was Marie Andrews. She was twenty-two years old, recently married, and had no idea what she was doing.

Her equally clueless husband, Samuel, stood by her side and the ward filled up with staff members that took turns to greet the new family.

The couple had strolled in hours prior and Dr. Choi was the first to meet them and give them an initial tour. He was only a resident but was on top of his game, and like many times before, he led the charge for all deliveries during his shift. The friendly and personable five foot Asian tried to ease the minds of his nervous guests, as he showed all the amenities available and encouraged any questions they may have had. Dr. Choi made sure to be one of the first ones to congratulate the parents afterwards as well.

Every prospective new parent came equipped with a sea of questions, and he made sure to keep his distance, knowing that they would certainly be his biggest threat when it came to being ousted. The slightest contradictory remark was all that was needed for an already suspicious and protective person to challenge everything he had to say, which was horrible for someone basing his actions on improvisation.

Things would be substantially more risky when the patients brought an entourage of family and friends for support like half of them did. In those cases, there was always an overbearing person in the group, calling all the shots and hell-bent on making sure everyone knew their loved one was the priority. Surely, those personalities would also be top notch on sniffing ⬚ out an imposter.

Bobby was relieved to find that Marie had only brought Samuel, and that they decided to actually listen to the Lamaze instructor that warned them not to freak out when her contractions started. Nine centimeters dilated was the magical number for birthing and no matter how quickly they would get to the hospital, pain and waiting were inevitable. Unlike many couples before them, Marie and Samuel stayed home a while longer.

Marie endured the pain while propped up on her couch and watched TV with Samuel until the contractions were timed closer. Doing so, she avoided the fate of many others that spent eight hours in a hospital bed before they could even start. By the time they visited the staff, it was time to deliver shortly after.

With practice, Bobby's observations had transformed into a science, and after confirmation of the newborn, he started the actions he had done many times over.

He knew that a birth meant "go time" for the staff and they would take turns introducing themselves while being friendly and congratulatory. Some were genuinely happy and excited for the parents, while others couldn't care less. They were destined to see dozens of these little rugrats, and the more that popped out only meant more work for them.

Sometimes, they would have to alter a planned break or work overtime, which always didn't sit well with some. However, when it was "go time" and they had to do their portion of the procedures, they always made sure to put on a happy face. No matter how stupid or redundant a question was, they were thoroughly trained on how not to give attitude, verbally and nonverbally.

Bobby knew exactly when to make his appearance, and knew to never be the first or one of the first to introduce himself. There was a possibility that inquisitive new parents could ask him medical questions beyond the realm of general knowledge that they had forgotten to ask the charge nurse. He constantly visualized exaggerated scenarios in which he would thoroughly screw up a simple medical question that even the lowest GPA averaged graduate could answer, which would lead to the parents yelling "Imposter!" over and over again until he starts to run, only to be chased by the entire staff.

The husband, built like O.J. Simpson in his prime, would easily catch up to him, and dishes out the most devastating beating of his life before turning him in. He watched the inbound and outbound traffic of the usual parade of nurses and doctors, walked down the hallways towards his office, opened the door using his specially designed key, and locked it behind him. Only a few people had a copy, which in his opinion was a few too many, but unavoidable.

Refusing people like the janitor or the building custodian could only draw suspicion, which could lead to more people asking questions. Besides those two, he made it a point not to share with anyone else. Whenever Project 4G moved their agents into a hospital, they always would make sure to coordinate with the Board of Directors within that area.

Explaining current situations with half-truths, they would openly admit to being CIA, and that there was a threat. However, the threat was a made up potentially deadly flu string that affected infants, but was easily prevented if detected early.

The story actually coincided with their target numbers, as they openly explained how one out of every one hundred children could be affected in only a handful of carefully selected cities in the U.S. Typically, the board was easily convinced under the pretense that 4G were mere observers and the chances that even one citizen would be remotely affected was highly unlikely.

The board granted Bobby a working space within the hospital, which was very small but effective. The pristine and organized room contained a laptop computer, desk, two office ⊠ chairs, small FM radio, baby bassinet, two landline phones, wall mounted TV, and a hospital bed. The room also came equipped with accessories used to blend in from thermometers and pulse readers to diapers and baby wipes.

The walls were even decorated with baby instructional posters, informing new parents how developed a child should be from week one up to their third year of existence. He knew that no parent would ever walk in to ever see it, but he felt compelled to play the part, just in case.

Out of all the tools and visual effects, there was only one item in the room that he actually cared about, and it was the only thing not in plain sight, nor could be stumbled across by mistake. Unbeknownst to the rest of the staff, including the directors and janitors, there was a removable tile on the otherwise sturdy floor. Bobby walked to the portable desk near the far wall, rolled the office chair out the way, disengaged the ⊠ wheel locks of the desk, and grabbed the front.

He looked at the position of the front left wheel, and rolled it two tiles backwards and three to the right. Bending down in front of the tile, he used both hands to carefully place the only removable one aside. The exposed area showed a square shaped, key coded safe that was custom made to fit perfectly within the small gap. If an erroneous code was entered twice, the entire system would seize up, and no regular locksmith would be able to open it. In fact, there were only a few technicians in the world that could accomplish such a task, and the majority were on the 4G payroll.

Bobby carefully punched in the code and waited for the green lights to blink twice at him, in conjunction with the soft beeps that informed him his entry was correct. He only heard stories about the long steady red light that informed that the wrong entry was entered. He pulled the lever of the door, opened it, and allowed it to swing over the top the adjacent tile. Faced with a steel handle and casing, he rotated the thick six inch bar counterclockwise and lifted the contents underneath. He pulled until two circular trays were fully exposed and Bobby's face was brightly illuminated with a bright blue glow, forcing him to squint.

The trays stood a few feet off the ground, and Bobby turned the bar clockwise to lock them in place.He quickly looked over the sealed glass vials that filled the trays and the small amounts of blue liquid inside them that made his face look like a Smurf. He grabbed hold of one of the forty vials and used the loaded locking mechanism to release it.

With the vile in hand, he lowered the trays, locked the safe, and repositioned the floor tile and desk as if they had never moved in the first place. He raised the vile to his eye level and examined it, making sure it was the normal color, glass was intact, and that there were no outside objects that somehow made it inside.

As a group the vials were a bit overwhelming, but individually, they often reminded him of small blue fireflies. He was never instructed to do this, but it always put his mind at ease and he felt more like a trained professional, as opposed to some dude that was picked off the streets. Regardless of potential, the serum was designed to be inherently harmless and undetectable, but it made him feel better.

Bobby sat at his desk, unlocked the bottom right drawer, and exchanged the vile for a black binder that he placed on the desk in front of him. He rotated the chair and his body to log onto his computer and access the medical database, which provided the majority of the information needed. As information of the new guests displayed on screen, Bobby flipped the binder's index tab labeled GENISIS in bold black letters.

He checked the month and day before thumbing down to find the next unused number slot, which was number sixty-one, and transcribed Marie and Samuel's information. He picked up the vile again to copy the eighteen-digit control number, and left the binder open, still in need of the time of birth and lastly the child's name.

He carefully checked the date created and ensured the vile was labeled "SHOT G" in bold letters. Satisfied, Bobby broke the seal and reached for a fresh syringe located in the left drawer. He unloaded the contents into the syringe, removed the air, secured the needle, and tossed the vile in a specialized biohazard bag.

He stood up and walked towards the door, but took a moment to quickly glance in the mirror and made sure that his game face was on point. In a minute he would be thrown into the role of the caring nurse again, in which failure wasn't an option. He made sure his scrubs and nametag were intact and quietly exited the room and walked down the hallway. As Bobby walked into the room, a soft orange glow emitted from a small lamp from the otherwise dark room.

Marie lay in the hospital bed with her head propped up while Samuel was on the seemingly uncomfortable adjacent couch. It looked like they had both been through hell and were losing the battle of resting as the young child was in the process of waking up. The newborn innocently whimpered and was seconds away from completely unraveling the poorly engineered swaddle created for him.

"Aww. So cute," Bobby whispered quietly as he hovered over the wooden mobile bassinet in the middle of the room.

"Hey, little guy. Are you giving mommy and daddy a hard time?"

Both parents looked up at him, smiled with tired eyes, and nodded their heads in unison.

Bobby returned their gaze with a warm smile and said, "Hi, I'm Nurse Century. If you don't mind, I need to take this little guy away for a few minutes and do a couple of tests. You should have him back in no time."

He turned his attention back to the child and said, "What do you say, little man? Want to let mommy and daddy sleep for a few minutes? What's your name, huh? What's your name, little guy?"

"Chris," Marie answered softly.

Bobby found it both confusing and annoying when people would eagerly ask a baby questions, knowing full well the answer would come from the parents. He was sure that the last thing a mother wanted after hours of child birth was to play ventriloquist to some random stranger, but he had seen too many professionals do it to not play the part.

He was fully prepared to answer any questions in depth, as far as what he was doing and where he was going, but just like most cases, there was no need. Especially with adding the small nugget of hope that they could squeeze in a few moments of sleep, they were sold almost instantaneously.

A few minutes later, Bobby was back in his office, with the ⬚ basinet in the middle of the floor.

At this point, the young baby Chris was awake and his unraveled swaddle had him seconds away from full-fledged crying. This was an ideal situation for Bobby, since he was seconds away from injecting the baby with a needle anyway. He preferred not to wake a newborn up only to harm them, and with as much practice as he had, he'd become quite the swaddle expert. Bundling a newborn just right with blankets would avoid hours of unnecessary cries and stress, so in a way he thought he was doing them a favor.

He allowed for Chris to cry as he wrote his name in the ledger, along with the time of birth and retrieved the already prepped syringe. He smirked as Chris had already opened the blankets that he usually had to unravel like a complex tamale. He wasted no time in opening the onesie, then held the bare foot and exposed the web between the baby's big and index toes. Bobby injected him with the needle and pushed until all of the substance entered his body. He quickly disposed of the syringe and snapped Chris back up in his onesie.

The next step was simple: he would observe the child and look for any changes. If nothing abnormal happened within a minute, that would mean the baby was not a candidate. Just like he did for every other newborn, he began to wrap him up so he could send him back to his parents.

Sometimes he felt generous and held onto them a little longer than needed, just so the parents could at least get a power nap in. However, today was not the day for that, since he had a date he wouldn't dare be late for. Not to mention, he was a little burned out from screaming babies from the week. He looked forward to some much deserved adult interaction and Rachael was more than capable of providing that.

When he first started the injections, he brought a stopwatch to count every second so he could know exactly when a minute had passed. As patients increased and complacency set in, he came to the conclusion there was no point. In fact, he was overqualified to time a minute of nothing, but he did it anyway.

At about the thirty second mark, Bobby casually grabbed his pen and binder to document the same as all of the others, but heard a sound that made him rush back. After the shot was given, there was a normal cycle in which the newborn went from crying to whimpering to quiet, if not sleep. Like normal, Chris cried from the needle, but unlike anything Bobby had seen, he went to a stage that didn't resemble pain or peace.

If Bobby didn't know better, it sounded like pure rage, but that was impossible. Chris hadn't even reached his twelve hour mark of being in this world, and yet he sounded like a man forced to endure and not ready to give up. Bobby's eyes widened as he rushed towards the bassinet, listening to the heavy pants and occasional low growls.

Bobby hovered over Chris and his jaw automatically dropped. His heart pounded faster and faster as he trembled uncontrollably. For the first time since the night he thought he would be executed, Bobby felt fear. This feeling wasn't fear of death or any sort of imminent danger, but the unknown. His trainers advised him to stay opened minded and told him on multiple occasions exactly what to expect and see in this very moment. In theory, he was prepared and trained to know exactly how to react, but the entire landscaped changed when he witnessed it for himself.

Bobby stood frozen in time, unable to move or think, as his eyes remained fixated on the newborn. Chris's eyes were transformed to be completely black and as he continued to kick, it seemed to be with a purpose. He began to kick harder and faster as the growls continued on, as if he were full of rage. Thirty seconds later, his eyes and movements suddenly returned to normal. Immediately afterwards, Chris began to doze off and in no time, he was fast asleep.

Petrified from the sight, Bobby didn't move a muscle until Chris was sound asleep. He lingered a few extra seconds to process what just happened. He tapped his face a couple of times to get his head back in the game, and followed his instructions. Bobby felt thankful for all of the training that he felt redundant at the time.

If he didn't know any better, he would be convinced the baby was possessed or cursed and would've probably bolted to the nearest chapel and waited for the end of days. The truth was that fate had finally introduced him to a Guardian Candidate, and it was just as surreal as people tried to warn him about. Bobby swaddled the baby, walked to a nearby phone in the room, and wiped off the dust before he picked up and dialed out.

With two rings, someone picked up on the other end. "Ming Garden, home of authentic cuisine. How can I place your order?"

"Genesis Package 628," Bobby declared.

"Go ahead with package."

"Location: Philadelphia; Thomas Jefferson Hospital."

Bobby recited what was drilled in his head perfectly, which surprised him because he never had to use it before. If he had deviated at all, they would've hung up on him and traced the call. They would confirm Bobby was an authorized caller but was an idiot, which he didn't want. The authentication code changed weekly and "628" was the most recent. With these measures, erroneous calls were virtually impossible..

Typically, he would only need to update the ledger and turn in a weekly report, but now he was following a different set of rules since he'd come in contact with a candidate. The speaker on the other end grilled Bobby about his observations, and asked questions about the natural vs. transformed eye color, full name, parent's names, address, phone number and whatever else information that was deemed pertinent.

The female on the end of the line remained assertive and concise, which gave Bobby a new sense of calm. She instructed him with a list of items to find out about the new baby's family information and to report back to her within the hour. He hung up the phone and took one more glance at Chris before returning him back to the parents. The fear had subsided and was replaced with amazement and curiosity.

This kid could actually become a Guardian one day. He could be a protector and savior of the city, and it was Bobby's efforts that made it all possible. In that moment, Bobby felt empowered and reenergized. During his tenure, if at least one kid turned out be a Guardian, that would make every minute spent in the hospital, lying and deceiving everyone around him, well worth it.

Although great sacrifices would be made, he was a proud member of Project 4G as a G1 agent. With the baby safely returned to his parents, Bobby made it back to his office and ⬚ checked to make sure the room was sanitized before he would look further into Marie and Samuel. He walked to close his notebook and froze mid-step.

"Oh, crap!" Bobby said in a loud whisper.

He glanced at the clock on the wall, stormed to a nearby phone and quickly began to dial.

"Hey, baby, I know what I said and I'm really sorry...but there's no way I'm going to make it tonight. I still have a lot of work to do after all."

# CHAPTER 3

## 19 YEARS LATER

66 Bzzzzzzzzzzzz." The cell phone vibrated and illuminated in the dark room as Chris slept five feet away in his bed. With every vibration, the phone repositioned itself closer to the mirror and the enhanced rattle against the glass was almost impossible to ignore. He grabbed the pillow next to his head and formed an impromptu feathery sandwich for his head to block out the sound. When the sound had stopped, Chris placed the pillow next to his head while keeping his eyes closed. A victorious smirk emerged on his face, only to transform to a frown when the phone began to buzz again.

Chris exhaled a loud grunt as he kicked the covers off his feet and hopped out of bed. Like a cruel joke, the call ended within moments of him being able to answer. As he looked in the mirror with tired eyes, he shook his head with disapproval. If he had remembered to put the phone on silent or turned it off, he would've been in bed, asleep.

Chris picked up the phone and took a second for his eyes to adjust so he could read the time: 8:05am. This was one of the few times he would get to sleep in, but there was no point in continuing where he left off. He was awake and there was no going back at this point, which meant he wouldn't see his dream play out. Typically, he either dreamt of nothingness or couldn't remember if he had when he woke, but this rare one remained vividly embedded in his memories.

In the dream, he was on a beach sipping margaritas, when

he ran into a group of people whom he immediately befriended. Out of nowhere, a tropical storm emerged to break up the party. Within the course of the storm he stopped a crazed killer, ran away from a vicious dog, and made out with a supermodel. He was helping cops transport the killer to jail when the buzzing of his phone connected his dream to reality.

As he entered the missed call section to get the name of the person who interrupted his big bust, he tried to think of what movie or show made him conjure up such an outlandish dream in first place.

"Jasmine" was displayed on the small, older phone. Friends and coworkers always felt the need to tell him about the benefits of upgrading to a phone that was much faster and that he could do simple tasks on, but he refused. He found no point in paying an outrageously higher price for the latest and greatest in technology.

He had recently switched to an Android phone for the first time, but that didn't stop people from giving their unsought advice about moving up again. The conversations, however, quickly showed him how a good portion of people in society are like sheep. He had seen how consumers would crave the latest trend, not because they needed the new features, or even knew what they were, but the product was brand new and they had to have it.

With phone in hand, Chris pushed Jasmine's name display to call her back and she immediately picked up on the other end.

"Hey, why didn't you answer the phone a minute ago?" she greeted.

The question hit him like a defibrillator jolt and he was now wide awake. She had called twice, both calls were back to back, and no more than five minutes had elapsed when he called her back.

"Huh? What do you mean?" Chris stalled as he checked his phone list to see if she called the night before or even earlier in the morning, and to see if she was being serious. He confirmed his assumption as she repeated her question, slightly more abrasive than the first time. Two minutes had passed since the missed call, and yet she felt entitled to confront him. He pulled the phone away and shook his head while flashing a baffled and disgusted look.

He was aware that she couldn't see any of it, but it made him feel better as he tried to process the fact that this question didn't come from a family member or girlfriend, but some girl he met once, only three days ago! Even then, it wasn't a blind date or some magically cataclysmic bout of circumstances that would forever link them, but a ten minute conversation in a park.

Getting to Fairmount Park was about a twenty minute commute for him if he used public transportation, but it was a great place to jog. He could always jog around his neighborhood, but there was something special about heading to the park and running next to the Schuylkill River. It may not have been the cleanest river, but the fact that his jogging path was next to a body of water and was full of trees and smiling faces from different walks of life made him feel inspired.

If he looked close enough, he could catch a glimpse of his past, present, and future as he always spotted the obese just starting out, average types like himself, and the impressive gods of fitness that made him feel both motivated and depressed at the same time.

He spotted Jasmine for the first time on the bus on his way to the park, and she immediately stood out to him. Not only was she one of few wearing workout clothes besides him, but she also looked absolutely gorgeous with minimal effort. Her pink and black jacket was perfectly coordinated with her form fitting pink t-shirt and black pants.

Her black shoulder length hair was pulled back into a ponytail and no makeup was needed to complement her flawless caramel skin. She was short in stature with a sexy well-toned body, which hinted that she worked out all of time. In that moment, he felt inspired to work harder and run farther than usual. He consciously reminded himself not to prolong his admiring glances for too long, so they weren't mistakenly translated into awkward gazes.

The last thing he needed was for her to go on the defensive before he would even make an attempt, especially since they were probably getting off at the same stop. His eyes wandered around the bus and outside the window, but continuously landed a gaze back on her, until eventually their eyes met. She returned his smile, which gave him confidence, and a couple of stops later he made sure to be in speaking distance as they both exited the bus.

Chris had a strong philosophy that many people made it a habit of blowing a situation out of proportion in their minds.

If you want something in life, within reason of course, then go for it. That was his philosophy at least, and made a point not to overthink things in which the worst case outcome wasn't such a big deal. In this case, he wanted to get to know this girl before they went their separate ways and knowing the worst case scenario was simply for her to dismiss him, he went for it.

Even if she were to turn him down, the attempt would be ten times better in his head than playing the "what if" game that he always tried to avoid.

"So, looks like you're going to take advantage of this nice day too," he said from behind as she shimmied towards the front of the bus.

"Yup. I figured I should burn off that half a pizza I ate last night," she responded cheerfully.

As the two exited the bus, they continued the conversation as they walked towards the start of the jogging trail. By then, they managed to exchange names, share a couple of laughs, and subtly declare themselves as single. They agreed to exchange phone numbers, and when Chris pulled out his phone, she immediately began to laugh.

"Whoa there, Fred Flintstone. Is that really a Universe 2 phone!?"

He shrugged his shoulders and flipped it towards the back where it showed "Model Version: U2." Jasmine shook her head as she showed her phone, which displayed U5 on the back. He figured that it must have been a Universe 5, the latest model of the line, and just as quickly he realized he couldn't care less. If the phone did everything he needed it to, why would he care or need to upgrade?

However, the fact that Jasmine was so amused by it was a different story. Was she cynical about a lot of things, or was she just a big phone or tech head? He quickly changed the subject back to getting to get her phone number and asking her out. They agreed to meet at a newly established club called Club Envy on Saturday, three days away.

When he made plans to meet late Saturday night, he never thought she would call him first thing that morning, but there he stood with his agitated future date on the other end. Chris stood in the darkness of his room, analyzing the seriousness of her voice and contemplated his desired response. He had a naturally friendly, yet sarcastic personality, and after making sure this wasn't a joke, he actively held back every indicating remark that she was acting like a crazy person.

He had yet to go on a first day with her, so maybe restraint wasn't the worst thing at the moment.

"Well, it's kind of hard to get the phone when I was asleep, but is everything okay? We were supposed to meet tonight, right?"

"You were still asleep!? It's like, 9:00am!" she exclaimed.

Chris narrowed his eyes as he momentarily stood there in silence. Her lack of tact and sincerity astounded him. Almost as if she was reading his mind, Jasmine spoke before he could respond:

"You better not fall asleep when you're out with me tonight. What time are we meeting up?"

Part of him wanted to call the whole thing off, but couldn't find the words to say it. Maybe she was having a bad day or something, and she would be able to cool off and apologize later that night. Maybe he should at least go on one date with her, but completely dismiss her afterwards. They agreed to meet at the front entry of the club at 10pm and hung up the phone, leaving Chris to start his day.

He put down the phone, stretched his muscles, and headed to the bathroom. His initial plan was to sleep longer, especially with him closing on most nights at One Stop Movie Shop. Typically, he couldn't step foot in his apartment any earlier than 1:00am, and that alone was enough reason for his mom to feel the need to constantly check up on him and gradually ease him into quitting. After all, she had big plans for him to go to college. She didn't care what degree plan or career path, as long as it required some type of higher education.

Chris had recently finished up a semester at Temple University, and although he received good grades, he knew that his degree plan wasn't even close to what he wanted to do in life. In fact, he wasn't even sure that his ideal job required a degree; he had yet to figure what that ideal job was. At the time, his path to success wasn't his own. The roads were cemented with abundant outside influence and societal subtexts like "college graduate or loser for life."

This would've been fine if he was still a kid, trying to learn all of the tools and traits of being a man. But he was grown and his destiny was reserved for himself and God to forge. He took a break from school, funded by student loans, which he often referred to as "educational loan sharks, "and started working at the One Stop Movie Shop, where he could raise money until he figured out his next move.

The moment he decided to leave was the moment his mom

tried everything for him to see the light and come back.

Unlike his coworkers, Chris was hardworking, dependable, and took the job seriously. Within six months he was promoted to manager, and as he diligently saved his money until he could figure out his next move, the significant pay increase helped. However, he was forced to work a lot more hours, especially with a lazy staff that wasn't getting any more dependable.
He had looked forward to his one morning to sleep in and not worry about an alarm clock. Turning off his phone didn't even register, since he rarely got back-to-back calls in the morning. As Chris got ready for the day, he chuckled at the irony.

His neighborhood was relatively safe, especially compared to rougher areas in the city. Like any other place outside of Sesame Street, Bandera Heights wasn't completely safe. In the past few years, the area had seen sporadic cases of domestic abuse, larceny, and gang violence, but nothing consistent enough to show legitimate concern.

This of course didn't stop his mom Marie from thinking the worst, as she remained concerned for his safety. However, this didn't surprise him, she was always a pro at taking situations out of proportion. Witnessing two distinct revelations of this during childhood encouraged him to purposely withhold information as an adult, for his own sanity.

During grade school, Chris was generally a normal kid. He rarely was the one to cause trouble or give anyone a hard time. Not having physical or mental handicaps allowed him to blend in with the masses. Like most kids in elementary school, his student body loved to publicize anything that was out of "the norm" and stood out to them. His fourth grade class was the most abusive.

For example, Tim became the center of attention when his new glasses made him look like a nerd and he was picked on until they moved to Angela, with her shoes that were too old. Unlike Tim, Angela didn't take it well. As she wore the same shoes, the jokes grew and lingered for days. On the third day, Chris couldn't stand the abuse and decided to help her by willingly becoming the next target. In class, they read a popular American novel and when the teacher sought out volunteers to read, Chris immediately raised his hand.

All was normal until Chris began to stutter halfway down his passage. Knowing he had a very small window to correct himself, he passed the threshold of time until he finished the passage. Classmates immediately started to crack jokes, which the teacher swiftly put an end to. Chris, however, knew that it was only the beginning and as expected, he became the center of negative attention in the days that followed. He happily accepted, knowing that Angela was off the hook, and that unlike her, he could take it.

On his second day of ridicule, Chris wearily returned home to find his mom home early from work, at the dining table reading a newspaper.

"Hey, baby. I had an appointment, so I got off a little early. How was school?"

She talked while her eyes remained focused on the paper, which encouraged Chris to reply with a simple "eh" as he headed for his room, thinking it was more small talk than it was an actual question.

"Boy, you get back here! I asked you a question."

He quickly returned to the dining room, where Marie had already placed the paper down and took a sip of the tea she had next to her.

"It was okay, Mom."

"Okay? Why just okay? Don't tell me you think you're too cool for school."

Chris cringed at the phrase.

"No, I just think I'm too cool to deal with immature classmates."

She frowned as she leaned forward and looked at him more intensely.

"Are they picking on you? Because I can say something to...."

"No, Mom! They're just being silly, but it'll all blow over in a couple of days."

After a few minutes of question and answer, she relaxed her expression and dropped the subject all together. She nodded her head silently as Chris pleaded for her not to intervene and was happy when she moved on to talk about dinner.

The following day, Chris thought nothing of it when his mom offered him a ride to school instead him taking the bus. She was in good spirits as she explained how she had to sign some form at the school before she would head into work. During the car ride, they had a pleasantly generic conversation, and when they arrived at the school, the final bell had just rung. As Chris flashed a worried look that he was going to be late, his unaffected mother responded:

"Don't worry about it. I already told my job I had to come

here first, and you'll be excused from your class. Now, come on, let's go."

She exited the car, and Chris did the same as he followed her inside. He assumed they were going to the principal's office, ⏷ but instead she led him straight to the nurse's office, which ⏷ only added mystery to his already multi-layered enigma.

The only time anyone would see the school nurse was when there was no other option, and it was usually during classes. He hadn't had as much as a slight tingle in his throat for the past month, let alone felt sick. In his opinion, there was no desire or purpose to see her, and he was tired of playing this guessing game. He spoke up to get answers, but he only got as far as "Why are we...." before he was stopped in his tracks by one of his mom's signature "now is not the time" looks.

He had seen it many times, and it wasn't a look of happiness or willingness to talk. It was one of concern and intense focus, and he had previously learned the hard way to keep his mouth shut in moments like these.

He followed her directly into the open doors of the nurse's office and immediately greeted the relatively young woman ⏷ typing away at her computer. She looked equally surprised to see Marie as she stood up from her desk to greet her.

"Good morning, Nurse...Jackson," Marie said pleasantly as she looked down at the bronze nametag on the desk. They shook hands as the nurse glanced at the young perplexed boy and then back to Marie.

"How can I help you?"

Marie instructed Chris to wait outside while they talked for a minute, and he quietly obeyed, shutting the door behind him. He sat in the waiting room for about a minute and when she walked back out of the office, she told Chris to wait with ⏷ the nurse while she took care of something. She didn't bother waiting for a reaction or response as she stormed down the empty hallway.

Nurse Jackson invited Chris into her office and it seemed ⏷ that they were both silent and in an awkward impasse. It was obvious that she hadn't exactly planned for her shift to start as a babysitting gig, and she began to ask generic questions about school and life. He was still confused about why he was there in the first place, but it didn't take a nuclear physicist to see that she was doing his mom a favor.

Therefore, he decided not to make it worse by being diffi-⏷

cult and ask questions she was obviously clueless about. He put on a fake smile and went along with small talk as they talked about his favorite school subjects and analysis of his favorite superheroes.

Marie returned about ten minutes later and appeared lot more content as she thanked the nurse and took Chris back into the hallway.

After they shut the door and walked a few feet towards the entrance, she paused and stooped down to his eye level.

"Okay, honey, you can head off to class now. If your classmates give you any more trouble, let the teacher know or tell me about it as soon as you get home."

The reality hit him like a heavyweight boxer's knockout blow, and as she hugged him goodbye, Chris said softly:

"Mom...you didn't...."

"You don't worry about that! Just focus on your education, and let me know if anyone tries to bully you."

She gave him a second hug and departed the front entrance, as Chris continued to walk down the hallway. He had walked them countless times before, and yet he never recalled the walk feeling so long and tedious. It was evident that she spoke on behalf of someone, but the question was what was said and to whom.

His imagination ran marathons and his worst case was he would be viewed like an overgrown crybaby that ran straight to his mommy. Even the most disciplined emotional wreck of a child knew not to resort to such measures unless an absolute last resort, since it would typically make matters worse.

Chris opened the door to the classroom; he kept his head low as he walked in and found his seat. As Mr. Bravinder wrote on the chalkboard, he hoped that the abnormal silence and feeling that his peers were virtually burning a hole in his soul was all in his head.

Mr. Bravinder finished writing his sentence and greeted Chris with a wide smile and a cheerful persona, which felt a little too over-the-top for him. Chris's heart jumped as he didn't bother to question his tardiness and as he focused on the blackboard, his peripheral vision showed eyes of anger and disappointment looking his direction.

"Class. Class! Eyes up here; I need you to focus!"

Chris was relieved for the assistance, but was unable to relax, knowing the victory would be short lived.

Immediately after the lesson ended, one of the ringleaders

walked up to him and said, "Hey, mama's boy." Chris flashed the most puzzled look he could muster on short notice, but he knew what would happen next. Now that he was considered "off limits" he was a prime target when the teacher wasn't around. The assumption that he ran to his mother only made them more encouraged to see him break.

Not only did they continue to crack jokes, but patronized him by saying, "Uh, oh! Be careful, he's going to run and tell him mommy again!" Even neutral parties pulled him and explained how it wasn't a good idea to get his mom involved and for her to address the whole classroom.

There was no point in explaining the reality of the situation, for the perception was too far embedded and much more entertaining. Chris endured the extra days of ridicule until they grew bored and moved onto another hot topic.

Chris was upset at his mom's reaction, but not completely surprised. As a single mother going on three years, she was empowered to raise and protect him at all costs. She often responded in ways that felt overly dramatic and over the top. He had let it go in the past, accepting that it was just the way she was, but he never thought she would take it this far. He decided to consciously withhold from her any information that would only make matters worse in the end.

In the years that followed, he kept her out the loop about every fight and argument that didn't concern her, until one faithful day as a high school freshman. The sun shone brightly in the late afternoon as Chris had just reached his halfway mark of the typical twenty minute trek to his home, when two bigger and older boys called out to the lanky ninth grader.

With one glance, Chris could tell that they had bad intentions, but struggled to maintain a cool and calm exterior, even though he felt anything but. The black Land Rover cruised down the empty road from behind Chris and then hopped the curb and blocked Chris's path.

Both boys jumped out of the car and walked towards him, with the driver yelling out, "Hey! Let me talk to you for a second!" Although Chris didn't know it at the time, the two had every intention of robbing him that day. Later, he would want to kick himself for not following his instinct to run in the opposite direction when things didn't feel right to him. Instead, he didn't want to give off the appearance of playing the part of the wimp and stood his ground.

He had never met either one of them, and for all he knew,

the two overzealous teens simply wanted directions or to pass on a message from a mutual friend. As they walked up on him, the driver stood a few inches in front of Chris and his partner positioned himself behind and off to the side.

Chris quickly glanced around, secretly hoping for witnesses, but there was no such luck.

There were no other cars passing by, no couples out for a stroll, or owners walking their dogs. The only exception was an older gentleman walking the opposite direction with his walking stick, but he was almost out of Chris's line of sight, and had no reason to turn around. Chris was alone with the two strangers blocking his way. The driver stared him down with a malicious grin on his face while his partner stood perfectly still with arms folded.

"Don't you know my girlfriend Stacy?" the driver asked.

This threw Chris off completely as he tried to recollect meeting anyone named Stacy. With a puzzled look on his face, he shook his head.

"What grade are you in?"

"Ninth grade," Chris quietly responded.

"She's in the eleventh grade," the driver said, and then briefly explained what she looked like. Afterwards, the driver looked at his friend as if he forgot his line in a play and didn't know the next move. Chris was about to continue his walk when the man spoke up again. "How much money do you have?"

There was no time to react before the passenger shoved him down. Chris's body scraped against the hard pavement, and he was immediately forced on his belly as his hands were placed behind the small of his back as if he was about to be handcuffed. As the passenger held him down, the driver went through all of his pockets, only to find a library card and a ball of lint. The driver let out a sound sigh of disappointment, and both jumped off him and Chris instinctively scrambled to get to his feet.

Suddenly he felt a sharp pain from the back of his head, which sent his body crashing back down to the pavement. A wave of sleepiness hit him as the two hopped back into the vehicle and sped away. His head was throbbing and when he reached back for the painful area, his hand retuned with a small spots of blood.

It wasn't enough to cause any major concern, but just the

right amount to take it easy for the rest of the day.

With eyes swelled and tears rolling down his cheeks, he returned to an empty home, which he was extremely thankful for. He had time to pull himself together and assess how bad his condition was before his mom would get involved. Chris headed straight for the bathroom, locked the door, and grabbed paper towels.

Facing the mirror, he began to blot out the blood and applied pressure to his head. The plan was simple: if the blood continued to flow, he would have no choice but to tell her. If it stopped, then the situation was under control and the only real damage would be his hurt pride, which could be handled internally. Within fifteen minutes, the pain had subsided and the blood stopped.

When his mom entered the house, Chris was in the living room doing his homework with the TV playing in the background. He immediately greeted her and after the usual "how was your day" back and forth exchange, she entered the bathroom. After a loud gasp, she stormed back out, dangling a bloody paper towel from her hand. With eyes wide and mouth ajar, she began her inquisition.

After his best efforts of playing it off as nothing, she eventually learned the truth. Marie was initially upset with him for trying to hide it from her, but it quickly transformed into retribution and she instructed Chris to get in the car so they could search for the culprits. This was the last thing he wanted, but recognized that he was in no position to make demands and entered the car.

The odds of finding the two boys standing at the same spot reliving their glory days of finding the "magical lint ball" were non-existent. Yet, Chris was forced to retrace his steps as if his mom was a top-notch detective hell-bent on uncovering the truth and bringing the assailants to justice. As she drove through the neighborhood, Marie kept reminding Chris to look for anything suspicious and it was no surprise to him for their first stop to be "the scene of the crime."

Like he suspected, neither the road nor sidewalk provided any answers, but Marie refused to give up. She aimlessly drove from block to block, repeating questions about the vehicle, appearance, and what they wore. Not only did he get beat up, but he also had the added bonus of talking about it in excruciating detail with his mommy!

Half an hour later she eventually gave up on the search and

headed back home.

When they arrived, Chris was thankful for three things: the next day was Saturday and there was no school, they never found the guys, and that they could finally put the whole matter behind them. He could only imagine what would've happened if he actually spotted them. Would she have forced them to apologize and bring their parents into it? Would she report them to a teacher or principal?

It wasn't like they lived in a horrible area where they had to fear for safety on a regular basis. They lived in a middle class, relatively normal community, but even so, sporadic bad things occurred there like anywhere else. He was certain this whole incident was isolated, and was more than happy to just forget about it. He was finally given that opportunity to do so as he went to bed...or so he thought.

His Saturday morning began not by the smell of breakfast cooking or the sounds of birds chirping, but the ring of a doorbell. Chris was still in bed at the time and voluntarily transitioning in and out of consciousness as he revisited the dream fragments that generally had a positive outcome.

A couple of times he even ran into the two bullies, and heroically responded in every way that he wished he had. The ringing doorbell subsequently became his wake up call for the day, and as he rose he could hear his mom open the door, greet the individual, and let them enter. Chris didn't bother to find out who it was, or why they spoke in a low volume that was a notch above whispering.

He walked out his room and went across the hall into the bathroom. After relieving himself, flushing the toilet, and washing and drying his hands, Chris opened the bathroom door to find himself face-to-face with his mom. She produced an awkward and weary smile as she said, "Good morning, Chris. You have a visitor in the living room."

She didn't wait for a response and instructed Chris to join them. An older gentleman stood in the middle of the living room and shook Chris's hand as he entered. He was a balding white male that appeared to be in his 40's, with no facial hair except for his bushy mustache. He was also extremely tall to Chris, which made him slightly intimidated as he shook his hand. Marie quickly excused herself from the room.

"Hi, Chris, I'm Detective Glenn. I heard you had a situation last night."

Instantly, Chris was hit with a wave a varied emotions. From anger to embarrassment, from betrayal to regret, and one solution became crystal clear to him: perseverance. It didn't matter who they were or what status they had in society, his level of compliance or withdrawal would depend on the situation. This cop wasn't going to get a shred of truth. He felt that there were numerous reasons to go to a cop: if there was a murder, rape, or an assault that caused serious bodily harm, he would've been the first to stand up and provide whatever information needed.

However, with the effects of his attack already a distant memory, he felt that police intervention was pointless. He was annoyed by the officer's presence, but he was irate that he ⍰ had been blindsided by his mother without so much as a heads up that he was on his way.

Detective Glenn stared at Chris and waited for him to speak about the incident. After a minute of silence the detective spoke up again, this time sounding a little more assertive and impatient.

"So, do you want to tell me about the assault that took place last night? I heard that there were two men? What did they look like?"

Chris immediately shrugged his shoulders and said, "I can't really remember."

Detective Glenn squinted his eyes and crossed his arms.

"Well, kid, I really would like to find these two guys so something like this won't happen to someone else. Anything you can remember would be a great help to finding them. How tall were they at least?"

His memory was intact, but his mind was clear. His mom wouldn't have felt justice was served until the two were tossed in a jail cell for a few years and only see the light of day through a window or chain gang duty. Even though the punishment wouldn't be that severe, he still refused to go that route.

Surely, karma would catch up to them without any help from him. Five minutes later, the detective summed up by saying: "Okay, so two males. One black and taller than you and his counterpart was white. The both wore blue jeans and were driving a black or blue car or SUV? That's all you remember?"

Chris nodded his head as the detective rolled his eyes and forced a card into his hand.

"I probably won't find them on that information, but take

my card and if you remember anything else, let me know."

The detective stormed out the house and didn't bother to speak to Marie. As he drove away, she came from the laundry room.

"Oh, he's leaving already? Did he get enough information?"

Chris took one look at her concerned face and he could no longer be angry with her. She obviously did what she felt was right in effort to protect him. Although he strongly disagreed with her methods, he couldn't argue her intent. Chris nodded his head.

"Yeah, I gave him a lot to go on, so he said he's going to keep looking until they find them."

Marie immediately smiled and said, "See? And you probably would've thought this was a waste of time." Chris forced a smile back to her and kissed her on the cheek before he walked away to get his day started.

Instead of wallowing in pain and fear, he sought solutions and began taking martial arts and self-defense classes. Although he became a quick study and proficient student, he decided to never use what was taught unless an absolute last resort.

As soon as he graduated high school, Chris eagerly moved out of the house, fully prepared to enter a new chapter of adulthood. However, this didn't stop Marie from tossing in her opinion of every action she didn't agree with, regardless if he asked or not. Throughout the years, Chris remained closed, but always made sure to spend time with her.

As Chris stood in the kitchen of his apartment, fully showered and dressed, he decided to give her a call while he fixed a quick breakfast. They talked for fifteen minutes, and as they discussed plans for the day, he decided to leave out all details about Jasmine.

Opening that door would surely lead to a through investigation with questions that no man, short of an obsessed psycho, should know on the first date. After another coming of age lesson from her, he decided not to ever tell his mother of a romantic interest unless the girl was without a doubt someone special. They agreed to meet for lunch as they hung up the phone, and after finishing his breakfast, Chris left the house to run errands.

Later that night, Chris checked for all of the items he would need for his date.

Although he never cared about luxuries for himself, he always strived to be an awesome date. During the day, he went to the ATM to withdraw enough money for the both of them. He had been on quite a few dates in the past, and financial responsibilities, as far as what he was expected to pay for, were just as confusing as they were on his first date.

He was never a cheapskate, nor was he a pushover. He had no problem paying for the girl, but he despised the types that demand a to do list of activities and felt entitled to be covered without as much as expressing a "thank you." He had no problem paying, but only if the girl was at least willing to pay partially and show a little gratitude if he did.

Regardless of her expectations, he would be prepared for it.

Chris looked at the mirror one last time, making sure he didn't overlook anything before heading out. He already replaced his black worn out sneakers with dress shoes, khaki shorts with loosely fitted blue jeans, and his green t-shirt with a long sleeved striped collared shirt.

After dabbing cologne on his neck and brushing the hair of his fresh cut, Chris left the apartment and headed for the nearby bus stop. Getting to Club Envy would be about a thirty minute commute by bus, as opposed to the ten minute taxi ride. Although he had the money, Chris didn't mind the extra time, knowing the money could be better used for other purposes.

As the bus arrived Chris hopped on, paid his money, and found an empty seat. Being relatively empty, Chris took his time to spot a good seat, knowing they were headed downtown and that the bus would soon fill up. He pulled out his iPod, placed earbuds in his ears, and listened to music.

Although Chris decided to stay optimistic, he didn't have many hopes for Jasmine. He had been on a few dates since he lived on his own. A string of epically short-lived relationships, if they even made it past the first date, just about convinced him he was cursed. Bumping into emotionally and spiritually damaged girls seemed to be his new specialty. He was physically attractive to many, but not nearly all.

He may not have been supermodel quality or was conceited enough to believe he would've had a definite shot. He had met enough beautiful women that either saw him as stunningly handsome or butt ugly, which made him mutually intuitive and humble.

He was amazed how men twice his age never learned basic

principles of how to treat women, especially with childhood concepts like respect and honesty.

He felt like a rare breed and was often surrounded by hordes of men who were immature and disrespectful asses to women. Often times it seemed that his reward was to date the most incompatible women on the planet. As a vigilant optimist, he refused to give up, knowing that she could literally be around the next corner.

The bus filled up with people and he began to focus; he watched as the riders entered and exited. Some people saw riding the public bus a daunting necessity, but Chris didn't mind it. He rather enjoyed the thought of strangers coming together to accomplish a goal, and in this case, it was getting to whichever destination they had to get to.

As the bus filled, his curiosity soared as he imagined where his band of fellow travelers was coming from and headed to. Some were easier to point out than others. An obese lady sat with two enthusiastic primary school aged kids a few rows away. They jumped up and down and playfully hit each other as the woman attempted to command their attention long enough to calm them down.

There was an antisocial, mentally drained old woman with a sack of groceries and a walk that felt like slow motion of a drawn out movie scene. A vibrant group of young teenage girls endlessly chattered about school, boys, and everything in between, while a middle aged man in his business suit somberly discussed the results of his job interview on his cell phone. As many times before, Chris's thoughts transformed into his "what if" game, and he looked around for the shady characters of the day, which were never hard to find in public transportation.

The bus stopped and picked up a man seemingly close in age to Chris and mad at the world. His sagging blue jeans were barely on his waist and his dark blue hoodie concealed part of his face as he paid his fair and found a seat. The game was in full effect as Chris began to conjure up hypothetical scenarios. "What if he just went irate and began attacking and threatening people?" "What if he had an accomplice and they both pulled out guns?"

By the time he made it to his stop, his head was flooded with various things he could've and would've done if the improbable situations ever became a reality.

Although he liked to pretend, he was thankful his mental

challenges remained just that. Pretend.

As the bus slowed towards his stop, Chris stood to his feet, rolled up his earbuds around his iPod, and placed both in his back pocket. The time was 9:45pm and he was conveniently located about two blocks away from Club Envy, which meant he had fifteen minutes; plenty of time to meet Jasmine on schedule. He exited the bus and began walking down the crowded downtown sidewalk towards the club.

Although it was his first time in the area, the closer he would get, the more he knew he was going the right direction. He had heard about the two colossal spotlights that lit up the sky, and he followed them like the North Star until he saw the lights perched on the front corners of the building.

From five hundred feet away he could hear the loud, popular song playing inside, while the thumping bass rumbled and vibrated his core. In the front of the building, two massive doors were swung open and held in place with chrome velvet rope stands. Four bouncers dressed in all black stood outside the door, as people stood in lines on both the left and right of them. The line on the left side was much smaller, and Chris quickly identified it as VIP, as they stood on a red carpet and were expedited. The much longer line on the right consisted of at least twenty-five people that all waited to gain entry.

Chris walked towards the line to get a closer look, and look for Jasmine, when he saw a man being yanked out the building by bouncers that were inside. When at the threshold, one of the bouncers shoved the seemingly intoxicated partier, which almost made him lose his balance. His friend trailed out of the club while the inside bouncers turned their attention to their coworkers outside.

"This guy is out! Don't let him back in!"

All four of the big men nodded their heads, as the other two returned to their stations inside.

"Oooooooh!" emerged from some of the people standing in line.

One of the guys in line turned his attention to the drunken man, as he regained his balance.

"Dude, you just got punked in front of everybody!"

The drunk man flashed an angry look at the crowd while his less intoxicated friend tried to pull him away.

"Let's just go home!" the friend said.

"Give me a minute!" responded the drunk man.

More voices emerged from the crowd. "That's right, don't let those bouncers do you like that!" yelled another male voice from the crowd.

Suddenly a female chimed in to say: "You better be a man and hit one of them back. Don't be afraid; he's just a man like you...or are you a man?"

A loud "ooooooooooooh!" errupted from the crowd again as the angry drunk turned his attention to one of the bouncers, which happened to be the smallest one.

As members of the crowd egged him on, and all four turned their attention to the one man, Chris realized the female's voice was Jasmine!

His eyes scanned and it didn't take long to spot her wide grin as she enthusiastically watched the drunken man and the pending chaos that she helped create.

Two of the bouncers assertively directed him not to do it, and repeated instructions to walk away, but he stood his ground, sneering as he gently swayed back and forth. He balled his fist and took a swing and within seconds was pummeled by the duo. The crowd roared with excitement and laughter. Among them stood Jasmine, who jumped up and down while maintaining her wide grin.

In that moment, her eyes met with Chris's and she waved him over. Completely turned off by her immature and insensitive behavior, he was ready to end the date before it started, but his manners wouldn't allow it. Even so, he was convinced that the date could only go downhill after this point. No round of "what if" could've possibly prepared him for what was to come.

# CHAPTER 4

By the time Chris and Jasmine entered Club Envy, the line to get in was a third longer than when they started. The doorman at the front door allowed Jasmine to pass, but made sure to pat Chris down like every other male going through. As they passed the threshold, they stood in a beautifully decorated entryway with newly laid red carpet, dimly lit lamps hanging off the walls, and an elegant décor. An extended velvet rope split the lobby in half; the left lane remained clear for people trying to exit, while the right side directed people to pay the cashier. With a scowl on her face, the cashier skipped past the pleasantries and said:

"One or two?"

Chris pulled out his wallet to pay for both as Jasmine responded "one" with cash in hand. As Chris and Jasmine paid for their own ways, he gave her points for independence, still aware of her deficit from the outside immaturity. Chris followed her through the velvet entry drapes and instantly witnessed how packed the place really was. The massive dance floor was cluttered with people; they were also lined up against the sidewalls.

They ranged in all different shapes, sizes, and age groups, but the theme seemed to be "young and sexy." As hordes of people talked and gyrated to the loud and fast tempo of the popular club song, Chris looked around the impressively decorated interior. Big neon signs pointed him towards the bathroom located in the corner, and a lavish bar and chill lounge sat next to the dance floor.

Under the dim lights, people sat on beautifully decorated chairs and couches. Two stairwells sat on opposite ends of the room, which led upwards. As they explored, Chris quickly learned that each floor within the four level building was designed the same. The only real change was the distinct difference in music each DJ was playing on their floor.

Each floor surprised them both with the amount of people and high energy; there was no floor in which the bulk of people congregated to and declared the "fun level."

There had to be thousands present, and it seemed that every DJ fed off the energy of their people, matching the excitement, high energy, and desire to be there. The place was packed without the annoyances that usually accompanied a crowded place. There weren't droves of people standing in line to place a drink order, nor those maneuvering from one point to another and bumping into many in the process.

There wasn't even a need for people to sacrifice their personal space to earn a spot on the dance floor. Seats for the public were scattered all around the different lounges, as opposed to making them available to the select few willing to pay over four hundred percent market value for bottle service.

After exploring, Chris and Jasmine headed to the ground floor dance floor and danced for an hour before they found a seat in the adjacent lounge. As Jasmine relaxed on the plush white leather couches, Chris grabbed a couple of beverages and joined her.

He found her physically attractive, and from the random glances of admiration from the guys around him, he knew he wasn't alone in this thought process. Her feeling towards him seemed mutual, which made him even more willing to talk to her. He tried to shake his initial reactions about her, as she seemed rather sincere and nice.

Everything about her screamed independence, and Chris had no doubt that Jasmine would always speak her mind, regardless of the setting or consequences involved. They sat on two facing couches and talked about whatever came to mind from their day, to pros and cons of family living in the city, to future ambitions. The more time that passed, the more at ease Chris felt around her, as he saw the down to earth and friendly side of her. They smiled, joked and laughed at one another as Jasmine playfully tapped him with every opportunity that presented itself.

With the various features that helped Envy stand out from its competitors, the club was also fully equipped with the typical cast of characters that any owner and promoter would love to avoid. First, there were the relentless hunters on a continuous prowl to find the right target; an attractive person that would give them the time of day.

The gangsta wannabes were present, ever ready to prove their toughness by fighting a random stranger for even the vaguest of reasons; like mistakenly stepping on their shoe or talking to a mutual interest. Chris observed the list of characters from afar, not knowing he was a few minutes away from coming face to face with the unwanted guest that would alter the course of his night: the drunken idiot.

Chris was finishing a funny story about growing up with his mom that involved a curious kid stumbling across a pack of "water balloons" oddly placed in her bedroom drawer. As he explained his confusion over how his mom could get so upset over an impromptu water balloon fight with his childhood friend, he paused when he saw Jasmine's shocked expression.

She slowly shook her head with mouth ajar, as her shock turned into a look of disgust. In that moment, Chris's mood swiftly shifted from humor to embarrassment, which Jasmine quickly picked up on as she let out a soft chuckle.

"No, not you. I was looking at the girl behind you. The drunk skanky one."

Chris slowly turned around to see a tall, slender woman with long blonde hair, a short slinky red dress, and matching high heels walk towards them. She seemed to be in her early 20's, almost as tall as him, and extremely intoxicated, as her beeline towards them looked more like a modified zigzag. In other circumstances she would be pretty cute, but her lack of control and near inability to stand made her the opposite.

As she stumbled her way towards them, it was obvious that they were her intended destination, and the two shared confused looks as the stranger approached them. Chris moved to the cushion next to Jasmine and watched the new center of attention as she moved in closer. Every few seconds she would be distracted, either by bumping into someone or dancing with one of the guys pulling her along.

At one point, Chris cringed as a man aggressively pulled her along to dance and held on to her as she smiled and reciprocated. Regardless of if she accepted a free drink, apologized for her clumsiness, or grinded on one of the random guys on her path that showed attention, she continued to periodically glance over towards Chris and Jasmine, almost to say "I haven't forgotten about you; I'm coming."

The woman eventually made it to her destination, and while Chris's face was full of confusion and wonderment, Jasmine's consisted of annoyance and disgust.

Completely oblivious to the fact that she was already dis-
liked, Red Dress plopped down directly in front of Jasmine
and occupied Chris's previous seat. She maintained the same
cheerful attitude as she spoke in a loud and screechy voice,
slurring her words in the process.

Chris was thankful for the loud music and crowd that
partially drowned out her voice, which made it more bearable
to listen to. To him, she personified the image of a bumbling
valley girl in which many foreigners and locals alike loved to
make fun of.

"OMG, girl, why didn't you join me!? I can't believe you just
sat here all night!"

Red Dress looked around the club, and noticed Chris next
to Jasmine. Before she could open her mouth, Red Dress spoke
again to say, "Oooooh, now I see why. He's hot! What's his
name...and where are his friends?"

"Ummmm...who the hell are you?" Jasmine asked sharply.

Oblivious to the fact that she was being addressed and more
importantly not well received, Red Dress continued to look
around the club when she asked another question. "I am so
beat. Let's get out of here! You ready!?"

Jasmine's eyes grew bigger and she looked around her in
disbelief. She crossed her arms and narrowed her eyes at the
woman as she scowled.

"Maybe you didn't hear me. I said who the hell are you, you
dumb drunk bitch!"

This finally got her to focus her full attention on Jasmine,
which made her mouth fly open. As she instinctively placed a
hand over it, her eyes widened.

"You're not Stacy. I'm so sorry, I thought...you were someone
else. She was sitting here...right here, like ten minutes ago.
Right? Have you seen her? She's wearing a dress like yours, has
brown curly hair...."

"No!" Jasmine interrupted.

"Maybe she went to the bathroom?" Red Dress asked.

"Yeah, maybe she went to the bathroom. Go find her!"

The woman failed to notice that Jasmine's harsh words were
almost to the point of being threatening as she continued to
look around almost as if waiting for some kind of sign or hint
on what to do next.

"I'm sorry, think I drank too much and I need to go home.
She's my ride. She even has my cellphone and house keys and
she said she would be right here. What should I do?"

Jasmine immediately rolled her eyes at the worried woman and remained silent as she shook her crossed right leg vigorously.

"She said she would wait in this area for me, but maybe she went looking for me on the dance floor? I don't know. I don't really want to...."

"Yeah, you should look for her on the dance floor! Go!" Jasmine interrupted.

Red Dress gave her another look of shock and seeing her eyes, she immediately looked away as she stood up.

"Sorry. I'm sorry to have bothered you. I guess it's not your problem."

Chris pulled out his cellphone to offer it to her, only to find that it was dead. Jasmine had a phone and he contemplated asking to borrow hers but hesitated. This action would catapult her to a whole new plateau of pissed off, and he surely wouldn't hear the end of it. Red Dress seemed to be significantly more worried than five minutes ago; she was no longer concerned with cute random strangers, cranberry vodkas, or dancing to her Top 40 hits.

She was focused as the possibility of being ditched with no ride or phone, a very real and partially sobering moment. She introduced herself as Kate and humbly apologized for interrupting their date. She excused herself and headed to the bar. A few seconds later, she walked into the crowded dance floor as she took gradual sips of her plastic cup of water. As she joined the people on the floor, Chris let out an annoyed exhale as he put his phone away.

Not only didn't he speak up when the poor lady was getting bashed by his date, but he made no effort to help her get home. Sure it could've caused an argument later, but he didn't even try to get Jasmine to lend her phone out.

As quickly as the woman left, Jasmine went back to being calm and relaxed as if the last few minutes never existed. Chis was amazed on how effortlessly she was able to disregard the concerns of others and in some ways, he even envied her. He didn't have it in him to only worry about himself, but also the people he knew. If he did only worry about himself, life would certainly have been easier for him.

No matter how hard he fought it in the past, he couldn't just let matters be, just like with Kate. He watched Jasmine forget and move on as she asked for Chris to continue his story. She sat comfortably in her chair as he forced out every word of the story. Unlike before, however, he couldn't focus and continued to distract himself as he glanced around the building. He tried to remind himself that Kate was a grown woman, and she made her own choices to put herself in the situation. He was on a date and deserved some relaxation without worrying about the people around him. However, the resistance only lasted a couple of minutes before he asked the inevitable question: "Shouldn't we help her?"

Just like he predicted, Jasmine instantly snapped as her anger turned back on as effortlessly as flipping a light switch.

"Why should I feel obligated to help out this girl!? I don't even know her and whatever dumb ass decisions she made, those were hers to make! It's not like she's a little girl!" Jasmine looked surprised from the sharpness in her speech, and took a pause before she spoke. She lowered her voice and appeared calmer.

"It doesn't matter, anyway. I'm sure she'll find her friend in a minute and everything will work out. We shouldn't get involved, because we don't have a reason to. We don't even know her."

Chris listened to every word and thought of his next move carefully and he compared what he wanted to do to what needed to do. Whatever the action, it would dictate how the rest of his night would go. Part of him screamed to just let it go as Jasmine had made strong points that he owed this girl nothing. Why waste the time and effort? Jasmine was beautiful, could be fun to be around, and was obviously into him. She also had a bit of a temper and possibly a jealous streak.

He repeatedly glanced over at the dance floor and as expected, all types of men lined up to pounce on their self-proclaimed easy prey, thanks to her earlier free spirited actions. He continued to watch as the retired party girl searched for her friend and struggled to maintain a balance between declining dance offers while simultaneously being polite about it.

While some understood and walked away from "no, thank you," others connected her friendly attitude with previous wild girl actions and figured she just needed more persuasion. Kate displayed every sign of disinterest, and yet some of the more dedicated hunters found it appropriate to grab her hand or pull her closer by her hips as she tried to get past them.

Chris made his final decision when a guy she danced with earlier blatantly slapped her ass after she declined his advances and tried to walk past him.

She turned and flashed him a glare, then shook her head as she continued to walk away. Showing no remorse, the guy zealously reported back to his three friends that were standing nearby. As he talked to the trio, he consistently pointed in her direction and soon afterwards, all four walked towards the direction in she had headed.

At this point, Jasmine recognized that his heavy concentration had nothing to do with her, and she intentionally cleared her throat. He caught her angry glare as she stared at him with crossed arms and legs, waiting for Chris to come back to reality. Instead of allowing her to state the obvious, he spoke up first to plead his case.

"That girl, Kate I think, needs help. We can at least let her borrow a phone or get her a cab."

"You're on a date with me! Why are you so worried about some other chick!? Oh, I get it; since she's slutty, you figured you might as well go for the easy one! My God, how desperate are you!?"

The thought highly offended Chris, and he chose his next words carefully as he desperately tried to keep his emotions in check while speaking his mind.

"She's all alone, drunk, and vulnerable. All I'm saying is let's at least make sure she finds her friend or gets out of here safe before dismissing her completely," Chris said.

"Look, I don't know her and you don't know her! So don't give me some looking out for her crap! If you want to hook up with her, go right ahead, but don't expect me to hang around for it!" Jasmine replied.

Any form of romance with Kate was the furthest thing from his mind, but in that moment he realized that she wasn't going to see that. He wasn't even sure himself why he cared for strangers, but in a world of uncertainty and confusion there was one thing that was crystal clear: he was going to have to let Jasmine go. Chris stood up and forced a smile as he started a speech of having had a great time. He thanked her for the invite to Envy, but he was immediately stopped with a loud "Uuuugh!"

"Whatever! Erase my number!" Jasmine exclaimed before she disappeared into a sea of people.

Chris briefly stood all alone, as he figured out his next move.

"Great. Here we go again," he muttered under his breath as he began to look for Kate.

He first looked on the adjacent dance floor, but neither she nor the four guys that followed her were anywhere to be found. As Chris climbed the stairs, the tempo of music drastically changed as the BPM ramped up and the internal thud of the pounding bass went into overdrive.

The layout and size of the floor virtually mirrored the previous one, which made it relatively easy for Chris to maneuver through the crowd. Only a few minutes had passed since he had last seen her, so he figured that she couldn't have been more than a floor away, if she hadn't already left.

His assumptions proved to be right as he spotted Kate in the middle of the dance floor, only this time she wasn't dancing and carefree. She stood alone with her face frowned and arms crossed, and Chris figured that she had no such luck locating her friend or finding a way home.

She appeared to be a couple of steps away from crying on the floor as her eyes continued to look around the room. Chris went the bar, flagged down a bartender and explained how his stranded friend needed a phone to get home. He pointed towards Kate, and didn't even have to ask the question, before the bartender, and one nearby offered their phones simultaneously.

He turned around and walked towards Kate to give her the good news and possible lifeline out of there. As he closed in, he noticed that he wasn't the only one moving in on her. One of the three men that had watched their friend slap her ass earlier walked up towards her from the opposite direction with a goofy smirk plastered on his face.

The man made it to her first, and Chris switched roles to observe the two as he stood close in proximity. The man had a similar average, build, and stood at six feet. He was casually dressed with a worn out college baseball cap securely placed on his head, red t-shirt that looked a size too small, and blue jeans. He held a beer in his right hand, which he nonchalantly took a sip of right before he addressed Kate.

In a normal setting, Chris was close enough to hear every word, but the lively and jam-packed setting made it impossible. Instead, he relied on their body language to tell the story of the friendly stranger and his attempt to mend a fence previously bulldozed by his good buddy. Apprehensive at first, Kate eventually relaxed enough to crack a smile and soon after, he motioned for his three friends to join.

The trio included the guy that had blatantly disrespected her earlier, but Mr. Touchy Feely had no intention apologizing or justifying.

He enthusiastically took over the conversation as he gently swayed back and forth with the stringent smell of bourbon on his breath. He stood a half a foot shorter than his baseball capped friend and wore a blue and white striped shirt and dark blue jeans. With the top three buttons of his shirt undone, most of his scrawny chest was exposed as well as the flimsy gold chain around his neck. The other two guys were a direct contradiction of Baseball Cap and Feely.

Unlike being in their early 20's and immature, their friends looked to be about five years older and much more mature and reserved. Both men shared a mutual fashion sense of khaki pants and dress shirts. Both men were built like linebackers and remained quiet and observant as their huge biceps crossed over their chests. The only distinct difference between the two was that one wore a short-sleeved white shirt, while the other wore a snug long-sleeved black shirt that clung to his massively chiseled body.

Both men stood over a foot taller than Chris, with Black Shirt a couple of inches shorter than White Shirt. While Baseball Cap and Feely continued attempts to make nice and flirt with the girl, the antisocial duo's expressions alternated back and forth between stern and impressed as an occasional female would walk by and strike up a conversation.

"Damn, you're sexy as hell, girl! Why are you here all alone, looking all sad?" Touchy asked with a sly grin on his face.

Kate looked up at him with tired eyes. "My friend has my phone in her purse and ditched me! Do either of you have one I could borrow?"

Both men briefly glanced at one another and simultaneously shook their heads.

Baseball Cap took one final swig of his beer and said, "Don't worry about it, we'll take good care of you. Our friend is driving, so we can take you home. We only have one rule though: we only roll out with cool people that know how to have a good time. So you can't be all worried and sad and stuff now that you're with us. I'm Jimmy and this is my buddy Butch."

They took turns to shake her hand with sly grins affixed to ⏷ their faces. As the formally known Feely introduced the others as Steve and Nolan, they reciprocated with a quick head nod.

"Time for a refill!" Jimmy exclaimed as he glanced at his empty beer bottle.

Before he headed to the bar, he commanded the attention from the "muscle" of the group by hoisting the bottle in the air, and tilting it left and right. Both men nonchalantly shook their heads and returned their attention back to the dance floor while discussing the newest piece of eye candy. He looked at Butch and Kate, repeating his actions.

"Hell yeah, man, I'll have one," said Butch.

Kate shook her head and in a quiet, almost timid voice replied, "No thanks, I'm done for the night."

Both Jimmy and Butch looked at each other with disappointment etched on their faces.

"C'mon, you have to drink something so you can relax. You still look all stressed out and shit," Butch said.

Jimmy nodded his head in agreement.

"I mean, it's not like we're not going to leave you hanging. We'll take care of you."

Kate forced a weary smile before saying, "No, I think I just had enough to drink for one night."

The wild and crazy party girl was officially dead, and was ▣ replaced with a humble, rational, and exhausted woman that just wanted to get home and sleep. However, neither Jimmy nor Butch were too impressed with her newfound sense of morality and self-worth. After a few moments of silence, Jimmy spoke up and said, "Okay, well let me at least get you a Coke, then."

As Kate slowly nodded her head in agreement, Jimmy flashed a wide grin.

"Cool. We'll be right back. Butch, you wanna help me out?"

Butch nodded his head and followed Jimmy to the bar, while adding an extra strut in his step. At the bar, he occasionally glanced towards Kate while looking her up and down as Jimmy placed the order.

As the songs being played felt more and more redundant, Chris glanced at the nearby wall clock with huge, bright neon digits. There was a chance that Jasmine was lurking on the first floor still, wallowing in a fit of anger, jealousy, and revenge, which meant there were still two floors left for him to explore if she hadn't migrated already. If Kate was in good hands, there was no point in him sticking around.

They were definitely annoying and arrogant, but she made the conscious decision to stick around them, even after the mistreatment, so who was he to stop it?

He decided to take one last look around before taking off. Steve and Nolan were entertaining an inebriated female that shrieked with laughter at just about everything, when she almost slipped and fell. She was a second away from a wardrobe malfunction and their interest was piqued. Kate still appeared exhausted and defeated, as her attention was focused on happy dancers and couples in the crowd.

Jimmy was in the process of gathering drinks while Mitch paid the bartender. Jimmy handed Mitch a beer, and picked up a second, along with Kate's glass of Coke. Both men walked towards Kate, but suddenly stopped a few paces away from her backside. Chris found this bizarre to say the least, and he watched carefully to see what they were planning.

Both men turned to face each other, and Jimmy scanned the room as he held Kate's glass in front of him. Mitch quickly scanned as well as he slowly pulled out a small plastic bag from his front pocket. He expertly kept the substance covered with his hand, and Chris barely caught a glimpse as a tan oval pill entered Kate's glass and dissolved. Jimmy's head shot up towards Chris's direction and Chris's head instinctively shifted towards the dance floor. By the time he reset, Mitch has just finished using his finger to stir the newly modified drink.

Both men exchanged a sadistic grin and nod as they continued their walk towards Kate.

"Crap," was all Chris had time to say before he started moving in their direction. It was evident that he was the only witness, and there was no time to get help or explain the story to her. He was a stranger to her just like the rest of them, which meant their creditability was on an equal playing field. Not to mention there was four of them while he stood alone. He couldn't be sure on what they put in the drink, but common sense was enough to know he had to stop them.

The DJ was in the middle of playing yet another redundantly overplayed song, which Chris had never liked since the radio premiere. However, with months of exposure, he had grown to detest the noisy piece of garbage. On this special night, things were different; not only did he instantaneously enjoy the song, but it suddenly morphed into one of the best of all time.

He began to mimic several people around him, and enthusiastically gyrated to the music. With every move, Chris positioned himself closer to Steve and Nolan and within seconds he was directly beside them.

As Mitch extended his arm to hand Kate her drink and she lifted her arm to receive the glass, Chris carefully positioned his backside towards him and turned it up a notch. He danced even more exuberant and flamboyant than ever before, casting his pride aside. He consistently backed up while he carelessly flailed his arms to the rhythm, all the while waiting to hear a different sound.

SPLASH!!!

The glass flew from Mitch's hand and straight to the floor. Some of the liquid splashed Chris and Mitch but the majority found its way to the ground immediately forming a small puddle. Shards of the rim scattered, while the splintered base remained intact. A nearby bar-back scurried to clean up the mess as Chris stood face to face with the two men as they all shared looks of surprise.

Surrounding clubbers cleared space for them, while others jeered "ooh!" and "party foul!" in anticipation of a potential altercation. Jimmy and Mitch stared at Chris as their looks upgraded into menacing and volatile. Mitch glanced at his soiled pants and sneered back at Chris.

"Yo! What the fu--"

"Sorry, I'm really sorry, man! It looks like I owe you both a drink," Chris interrupted.

More people joined the sidelines to witness the action. Most clubbers occasionally experienced their shoes being stepped on or some form of drink spillage, and instead of a simple apology, the offender would try to deflect or walk away completely. People wanted the situation to escalate for entertainment and Mitch wanted it to escalate for retribution. Chris had not only owned up to the mistake, but had also apologized and offered to replace the drink. Inbound bouncers returned to their posts and meddling partiers went back to their business.

Mitch rolled his eyes and sucked his teeth, but in the end the only thing that he could say was, "Don't worry about it!"

"No, seriously. I should at least replace that drink. Who's was it and what was in it?"

"Mine. It was a Coke, but don't worry about it. I didn't really want it anyway," Kate responded.

Chris turned to face her and gave off another surprised look as if he hadn't seen her standing there the whole time.

"Oh, hey! I remember you!"

As she focused her eyes on him, Kate flashed a faint smile in the process, giving off a quizzical yet content expression.

"We met a little while ago downstairs. Still no friend, huh?" Chris frowned.

Kate shook her head.

"Yeah, that sucks. I meant to apologize for that girl I was with, but you disappeared on me. She was pretty rude with you when she didn't need to be. My phone is dead, but I'm sure I can help you find one so you can get the heck out of here. I know you're probably tired by now, right?"

Kate was renewed with energy and her smile widened. Chris glanced at the two bartenders from earlier, hard at work serving drinks to the crowd of people in front of them. Getting to borrow anything from them was going to be complicated, let alone trying to talk on the phone in such a loud place.

"In fact, I need some air anyway, so why don't we ask the girl at the entrance. I'm pretty sure that I saw a phone on her."

"Thank you! Thank you so much!" Kate screamed.

As Kate rushed him with an unexpected hug, Chris noticed the pissed off expressions of the two men next to him. Jimmy and Mitch had spent time and money on their prey, and after precise timing, plans were diverted from some clumsy dancing moron.

Chris flashed her a warm smile and responded, "No problem, are you ready to go?"

Kate nodded her head and turned to Jimmy and Mitch to wave goodbye. She thanked them for their kindness and ride offer, and waved goodbye to Steve and Nolan. As they made it to the stairwell, Chris glanced back at Jimmy and Mitch. They carried on a conversation while glaring at Chris with folded arms and balled fists. Chris and Kate headed downstairs and made it to the entrance of the club. As expected, the cashier had no problem lending her phone, as long as one would leave behind an ID and make the call in front of a bouncer.

Within a few minutes, Kate got in touch with her friend and confirmed that she was at Kate's apartment waiting for her. They began to argue, and as Kate yelled she had no money for a taxi, Chris quickly offered to spot her. Her mouth flew open as she was momentarily speechless, but nodded her head and quickly ended the conversation.

The front of the club happened to be on one of the more famous and populated strips for downtown nightlife. The strip contained a slew of clubs, bars, street vendors, and customers of all walks of life roaming the streets, which meant it was relatively easy to find bicycle cops, taxis, and other forms of

public transportation. Chris and Kate sought out the nearest
taxi and within a few minutes, Kate entered the hailed vehicle and redundantly thanked Chris as he paid the cabbie in
advance.

"Thank you so much. I promise I will pay you back the next
time I see you."

Chris shrugged his shoulders. "Eh, I'm not too worried
about it. Just don't forget to extend the kindness if I get
ditched by my friends. Deal?"

Kate smiled back. "Deal."

Chris shut the door and watched the yellow taxi roll down
the street, turn the corner, and disappear into the night. The
final bus home was at midnight, and being ten minutes til,
he headed towards the nearby stop. If he missed this one, he
would either have to pay for a second cab or walk for forty-five
minutes. He covered his mouth to block a yawn and reached in
his pocket to pull out his wallet.

A solitary Abraham Lincoln stared back at him which let
him know that his options were more limited than perceived.
He walked the opposite direction of Club Envy, but continuously glanced back. The line to get in was empty and two
bouncers remained outside. The further away he walked from
the building, the more he contemplated his next move, as he
initiated an internal debate.

He had already interfered with potential predators in order
to protect Kate, but what are they doing now? Did they call
it a night, or simply nominate another potential victim to get
drugged? Even if they called it a night, how many times have
they gotten away with it already? And how many more times
were they planning on doing it again?

Standing fifteen feet away from the bus stop, Chris halted
and turned his body around to face Club Envy once more.
He shook his head and exhaled a heavy breath as he ignored
the signs from his weighed-down body and droopy eyes that
pleaded for him to call it a night. He defiantly made his way
back to the building, wishing that he could be like the majority
of people able to stay in their own lane.

Most people had the luxury of staying in their own bubble
and as long as that wasn't violated, they were fine with minding their own business. At a young age, Chris knew that ignor-
ing potentially solvable problems would only haunt and bug
him until he changed his mind. There was no point in fighting
who he was and how he was hardwired.

Halfway back to Envy, Chris paused as he could hear the motor of the approaching bus nearing its stop. He looked down the path he had just walked, knowing he could still make it if he walked briskly. Last he checked, there were at least ten travelers ahead of him ready to hop on, not to mention the riders that would need to exit the bus first. Between the two natural delays, there was still time left to change his mind.

Chris suddenly cracked a smile and let out a soft chuckle as he continued his way to Envy. Who was he trying to kid? If he really felt that he was going to it let go, then he wouldn't have left the stop in the first place. There was no point in avoiding it; his mind was already made up the moment help was needed and now he was going to finish it.

Chris walked past Envy and combed the occupied streets. After a few minutes of searching, he flagged down a nearby patrolman positioned on his bike. The man appeared to be in his mid-30's, and maintained a stern look on his face as he positioned his bike to the side and lowered the kickstand.

He walked up to Chris, and straightened the blue mesh t-shirt which helped the embroidered "POLICE" across the chest fully show and reflect off the surrounding lights. He stood in front of Chris and immediately crossed his arms and said, "What?"

Chris took a pause to make sure he didn't reciprocate the rude greeting. He was certain that the officer's nights on ⏀ the strip were full of drunken idiots, vicious fights, and public urinations. One outburst to an on edge individual with power couldn't be good for anyone. Chris explained the events that led up to Kate's near drugging and as the cop's reaction showed that similar to a cat being stuck in a tree, Chris stuffed in hands in his jean pockets to suppress his annoyance.

"So, what do you think about that?"

"I guess it's a good thing you were there," the officer ⏀ shrugged.

Chris slowly nodded his head, waiting for some type of follow up that never came.

"So, I helped her out of there and hailed a taxi," Chris said to break the silence.

The officer nodded his head.

"Where are the four men now?"

"Still in the club, I'm sure, and I'm scared that they are just going to pick another victim."

"Well, people have to be careful.

No one should accept a drink from a stranger, especially if it was out of their line of sight."

The complacent notions irritated Chris by the second, and as he was reminded of a cheesy afterschool special. He kept his hands in his pockets and took a breath, making sure he had direct eye contact when he said:

"So what are we going to do about these guys?"

As the cop flashed a look as if Mandarin Chinese was spoken, Chris continued,

"I know you can't do much, but they have drugs in their possession. So can't you...."

"Not if they're in the club still! I'm not going to storm a club full of people and look for four men that might have...."

"Ok, so what if they weren't? What if they were standing right here, and I pointed them out to you? Would you do your job then?"

The cop squinted and his eyes once again locked with Chris's.

"I would search them and book them if it's justified!"

Chris nodded his head with satisfaction. "Then I ask one favor of you. I know that you are busy, but please wait here for like five or ten minutes."

He instantly saw the skepticism in his face and continued. "I'm not going to do anything wrong or break any laws, but I can get them to head out of those front doors. I'll point them out and you can talk to them."

The cop began to shake his head "I'm not go--"

"Please, sir," Chris pleaded. "You are the only one right now that has the power to force them to account for their actions. Even if it's a scare tactic, or a slap on the wrist, it's better than nothing at all. Please, just give me ten minutes and if we're not out by then, then I won't bother you anymore."

The cop stood in silence and his expression softened. Just as Chris opened his mouth to do more convincing, he responded, "You have fifteen minutes, kid. I'll be standing near the front doors. Fifteen minutes."

Chris nodded his head in agreement and turned around and walked the two hundred feet to reenter Envy. With no one in line, he entered the building and flashed the stamp on his hand to bypass the cashier. It didn't take long for Chris to find the same group of friends he was looking for. They were on a different floor and their group had increased by two, but everything else was right about where he left off.

Steve and Nolan were busy entertaining a slightly over-weight brunette with black stretch pants and a loosely fit-ted shirt which exposed part of a black bra strap. She may not have been their first choice, but they appeared relatively content. Meanwhile, her much heavier and unattractive friend stood about twenty feet away in a dark corner of the room with Jimmy and Mitch.

As Chris walked closer towards Jimmy and Mitch, he im-mediately cringed at the sight of the two taking turns grop-ing and making out with the brunette as if they weren't in a room full of people. He took a closer look, and observed how she could barely stand. Instead of helping her, the two found a work around by grabbing hold of her waist or shoulders at all times. The two shared grins as she clung on to their necks, or leaned in to talk, which they also saw as an invitation for more playtime.

Chris turned back to Steve and Nolan and noticed the girl with them wasn't nearly in as bad of shape as her friend. As both men sandwiched her as they danced on the floor, Chris felt thankful that she was at least able to stand on her own free will, and not fall all over the place. He walked directly towards the trio and immediately tapped the girl on the shoulder while mid-dance.

She stopped and leaned in, which naturally forced Steve and Nolan to stop. They both seemed to recognize him right away and established scowls while looking him up and down with disapproval. Chris ignored the unwelcoming gestures and cupped his hand over the girl's ear.

"I think you may want to take care of your friend. She doesn't look like she's in good shape right now."

Her smile faded and eyes widened as she spotted her recent-ly ignored friend.

"Oh my God! I knew she was a little drunk, but I swear she wasn't that bad a minute ago. She's going to kill me tomorrow; I'm supposed to be the responsible one!"

She quickly stormed off to her aid, and within seconds she was dragging the brunette towards the stairwell. As both ladies descended the stairs and disappeared into the night, all four men turned towards the one single-handedly respon-sible. As they stared him down, Chris quickly dipped his head towards each individual with a satisfied smirk on his face.

Mitch meandered towards Chris's direction, and Chris walked a different path, towards a nearby bouncer.

Each floor had bouncers spread out all over, and this one was no different. As Chris approached, the man dressed in all black leaned against the wall with his arms crossed. As the man checked his wrist watch, curiosity crossed his mind on how similar bouncers duties were to a cop duties. He could only imagine how boring and annoying both jobs could be at times. The only difference was that bouncers could work to a soundtrack. Chris stood beside him, and immediately greeted him.

"Hey, what's up, man?"

The bouncer remained silent, but nodded his head.

"So how many drunken morons have you dealt with so far?"

"Too many!" The bouncer smiled and rested his hands by his side.

"Probably same old stuff, right?"

"You know it."

"Well, at least there's a lot of potential here tonight, and you have the privilege of watching these fine girls without feeling creepy about it."

The bouncer's smile widened. "They are all over the place, man. In fact, why the hell aren't you hitting on any of them? You know I'm stuck here working, but if I wasn't...."

Chris matched his smile as he nodded his head in agreement.

"Yeah, it's about time for me to go on the hunt and find the baddest one here tonight. Where's she at, man?"

The bouncer chuckled. "I don't know, man, but there are defiantly some solid contenders."

"Well, I'm going to look for her, and I'll even get a phone number in your honor."

The bouncer gave a hearty laugh. "Alright, man, I'll be looking. Don't disappoint me."

With the affirmation needed, Chris headed straight for ⏴ Mitch. Talking to his friends immediately took a backseat as his eyes connected with Chris. Besides his friends, there was no else around Mitch and with both the bar and restroom in different directions, there was no mistake where Chris was headed. Mitch stared him down with anticipation, and Chris walked with speed and determination, while maintaining a cool and calm demeanor. He didn't have much time to waste, and needed him out, all of them out, as quickly as possible.

Chris lifted up his hand to shake as if they were long standing friends, and Mitch immediately crossed his arms while

Jimmy joined his side. The tension could've been hacked with a katana sword, as all three remained silent. Chris knew that simply asking the men to step outside would never pass, and that he would have to do something drastic. Chris lowered his hand but widened his smile and increased his enthusiasm as if he had just heard something comical amongst friends.

"Hey! What's up, man!" Chris exclaimed.

"What?" Mitch asked.

"Aye, man, I just wanted to tell you something: you are such a little bitch!"

In an instant, both Mitch and Jimmy were enraged, but Chris continued as if he were in the middle of telling a funny story.

"What the hell did you just say to me!?"

"Okay, man, calm down. I'm just saying, not only did I take one girl away from you tonight, but two! You even had your bag of "special candy" for them, and you still couldn't get the job done, you damn genius! At first I figured it was just because your dumb ass was scared of me, but now I'm starting to think there's a bigger reason. I figured out your little secret and who you really want to go home with."

He grinned while briefly alternating looks to Jimmy and Mitch.

"But hey, man, it's cool. It's the twenty-first century, so if a man wants to love on another man, it's your God-given right if you ask me."

Chris was halted by an abrupt shove that sent him flying backwards. Mitch was officially at his boiling point and had ▢ heard enough. Although the shove was forceful, it was far from intimidating, as he could easily overpower Mitch. He could've effortlessly countered the predictable attack, but instead decided to over dramatize the effect of the shove.

Chris flew backwards and crashed into a nearby woman who began to topple over, as Mitch prepared his follow up attack by clenching his fists. The woman screamed from the uncontrolled thrust and needed her boyfriend to stop her momentum before she fell to the floor. Chris flashed the couple a look of shock and embarrassment and quickly turned his attention back to Mitch.

"What the hell is your problem, man!? Look at what you caused, you jerk!"

Clubbers backed up and cleared the space and allowed two inbound bouncers jump in and target the attacker.

Chris continued to stare at Mitch like a monster, and the couple followed suit which enraged him even more. The two bouncers quickly grabbed hold of Mitch, and when Jimmy protested on his behalf, no one listened. Not only were there eye witnesses that have seen the out-of-control Mitch in action, but his new bouncer friend immediately vouched for Chris. As Mitch was escorted out, Jimmy stormed towards Chris, but a third bouncer blocked his way before he could get close.

"You gotta go, man."

"No, you don't understand! This dude was talking a lot of sh--"

"I don't care! You and your friend did enough tonight! Time to go!"

For a split second it seemed as if Jimmy was about to stand his ground, but with a fourth bouncer inbound, he began to back up. With balled fists he took one last glance at Chris and followed his friend towards the stairwell. Steve and Nolan walked up to the dispersing crowd and were left with two options: leave with their friends or finish the night without them.

They calmly walked up to Chris and with malicious grins plastered, they said, "We'll see you later. This isn't over." Both maintained grins and at the stairwell, nodded their heads with anticipation before walking down the stairs.

The moment he re-entered the building, he was well aware there could be a confrontation, which was often the price for not minding his own business. He rarely found a need to fight and could come up with a better solution.

Most fights to him were a waste of time and typically solved nothing, as they originated from miscommunication and misplaced pride. He never cared about being called names and thought it was comical when people thought they could get under his skin that way. Opposite of the intent, his lack of reaction in turn made them upset, which only increased Chris's entertainment.

He feared no man, not even the behemoth sizes of Steve and Nolan that were supposedly waiting for him. He was hardly the biggest, strongest, or smartest, but he was confident he could handle himself, which was enough for him. Besides the man still calming down his distraught girlfriend, everything was back to normal. Bouncers scattered to their posts, and clubbers went back to dancing, talking, and drinking like there was never a disturbance in the first place.

Chris looked around at the unoccupied seats and thought how easy it would be to sit down and relax. Unlike before, the music was pleasant, and he had already done plenty by protecting others for the night. So why not relax for a minute, listening to music while sipping on some tamper-free Coke. He glanced back at the stairwell and with one long exhale, his body answered for him as it instinctively headed down the stairs and towards the exit.

As he exited, the cashier took advantage of the empty line and played on her phone. Two bouncers remained outside and debated about great athletes. Chris walked past the two and looked at the spot where he talked to the cop, which was completely empty. He scanned the surrounding area but there was no sign of him or any of his friends.

His heartbeat pulsed faster and looked around a couple of more times before accepting that he was gone. Chris was agitated; there was no way that the time elapsed past ten minutes, let alone fifteen! As his eyes scanned the area one last time, his heart jumped as his eyes locked onto the familiar sight. However, it wasn't a police uniform nor a bike. His heart thumped faster as he recognized the baseball cap atop the head of the man that owned it.

Jimmy stood across the street and positioned himself directly in front of the entrance. His hands were shoved his front pockets as his eyes searched through the crowds of people with determination. Every few seconds, he looked at the entrance, which convinced Chris that he must have been missed by a second or two.

As he moved a little further away, Chris quickly spotted Nolan standing off to the side, about fifty feet away. He stood at a different angle, but shared Jimmy's look of anger and determination as his eyes looked through the busy street.

"Great," Chris muttered to himself as he made his way back inside.

Chris was certain the remaining two were lurking around somewhere, to cover all of their bases. He had provoked them, embarrassed them, and even falsely accused them to get his way. They weren't going to stop until they found him, and God only knew what would happen then. Back inside Envy for a third time, Chris stayed on the first floor and immediately made his way to the rear of the club. In no time, he spotted the "E-X-I-T" sign suspended in the air with big red letters and the door under it.

He quickly went through and didn't bother to look around or wait to be told to go around front.

The rear exit of Envy was very popular with the bouncers on staff. Being under much scrutiny, the last thing they wanted to do was eject people that were deemed too rowdy or drunk for their establishment. Unlike the rear, the front was full of potential witnesses and police on a daily basis. Not only could Envy gain a negative reputation, but certain truths could be twisted and turned to the staff's disadvantage.Aware that one slip and fall by a clumsy drunk could easily transform into a lawsuit against him, the owner established a policy for staff to use the back door whenever deemed necessary.

Chris was unaware of the house rules, but a secondary exit only felt right in such a massive building. As he shut the door behind him, Chris immediately picked up the vast differences between the two exits. The exit was relatively silent as the dark alleyway was free of the countless pedestrians, cops, taxis, and promoters that bombarded the strip out front. He quickly picked up on the line of plastic garbage containers, cigarette butts, and shards of glass, as the pungent smell of spilled beer and piss invaded his nostrils, the dim lighting silhouetted figures a little further out.

The mutually eerie and nauseating impression encouraged Chris to leave the area as quickly as possible. There was no handle on his end of the door, which meant there was no turning back and his only way was forward. The alleyway sat in between the backs of two huge buildings, which both consisted of a few barred windows and a few doors, also without handles. The brightly illuminated nearby street was straight ahead at the end of the alleyway, which gave off a proverbial light at the end of the tunnel feel to him.

The cross street was filled with streetlights and occasional cars that zipped by in both directions. Chris moved with urgency, like an athletic speed walker, while remaining very cognizant of his surroundings. He took an extra couple of seconds to investigate every dark corner that he couldn't quite make out from a distance. Each time felt sillier, as they all proved to be harmless items that his mind and imagination blew out of proportion.

By the time he reached the halfway point of the quarter mile stretch, he slowed down to a stroll as he felt a bit more relaxed.

He had discovered nothing more than alleyway clutter at all of his danger crossings, and the lights of the cross section shone brighter on his face. He laughed at himself as he allowed for a threat to make him paranoid, like he was in a warzone. They would probably wait hours for him to step out, when in reality he was seconds away from making his escape on the opposite side of the building. Chris pulled out his iPod and began to unravel his earphones when he suddenly heard a familiar voice address him.

"Yo! Where the hell you think you going? We have some business to finish!" Mitch cried out.

He was joined with Steve and both entered the alleyway from the cross street. Chris stopped and looked around for options as his heart rate increased. There was no point to try to make a break for it, since he was boxed in. More importantly, he didn't want to. He remained still and awaited their approach.

"So your punk ass thought you were slick enough to get out by using the back door, huh? You're not getting out of this that easy."

As Mitch antagonized, Steve yanked out his phone, pushed a few buttons, and held it close to his ear.

"Yeah, he's back here. Head this way," Steve said and hung up.

Certain that he had just rounded the crew, Chris concluded that he was minutes away from receiving the most vicious beating in his entire life. Observing the emptiness around him, he began to regret his decision to use the back door. At least the front area provided more witnesses and maybe he could even find another cop that was actually willing to do their job. The odds of a police officer or good Samaritan interfering at ⍰ this point were nonexistent; he was all alone in this fight.

As Mitch stopped in front of him, Chris took a step closer and kept his hands to his side. He spoke in a low, calm voice and maintained eye contact with Mitch.

"Look, I'm really sorry for talking trash earlier, but I was just trying to prove a point. You guys tried to drug an innocent girl that was just trying to make it home. Please don't deny it, because I saw you guys do it, which just isn't cool. There are many ways to talk to someone and drugs shouldn't be a factor. I hope I don't have to see that again."

Chris also hoped for a reaction from Steve as he glanced his direction.

Maybe Steve didn't even know about their actions, which led to the big fiasco in the first place. However, Steve remained focused on Chris as he crossed his arms and stared intensely. If anything, Chris had only managed to make him angrier.

"How the hell is that any of your business?" Steve asked with his feet shoulder length apart and knees slightly bent, fully positioned for confrontation.

"It's my business because I don't think that anyone should be taken advantage of like that, especially someone that was stranded and looking for a little bit of help. What the hell gives you douches the right to treat anyone that way?"

Chris had no intention of raising his voice or escalating the confrontation, but he refused to perpetuate an image of acceptance just to get along with them. Steve moved in closer towards Chris until they almost stood nose to nose. Mitch stood off to the side and smirked like a fight promoter with one hundred bucks on the reigning undefeated champ. He alternated his looks between Steve with admiration and approval, to Chris with taunting hilarity.

"Where I come from, people tend to mind their own damn business or get their asses kicked!" Steve declared.

Chris was close enough to him to smell the musty cologne on his neck and see hair stubbles on his chin. He listened to the two footsteps meandering from behind, closing in on their location. Chris pretended not to notice as he remained focused on the man in front of him.

"Well, where I--"

"Shut the hell up!" Mitch interrupted with a glancing blow to Chris's jaw.

He instantly covered his face as he reeled in pain from the unexpected punch, and Mitch immediately squared his body on him and raised his hands to prepare for retaliation. Chris, however, accomplished the opposite as he took a few steps back. His left hand clung onto his jaw as his eyes grew three times in size. His entire body trembled and remained focused on the confident Mitch. Steve immediately switched roles from aggressor to proud observer with a satisfied smirk on his face.

"Why...why...why did you do that!? I don't...I don't want any trouble. Just go away. Please!"

Chris's eyes were full of sorrow and sympathy as he continued to tremble. Mitch and Steve looked at each other for a second before roaring with laughter.

"Stop laughing at me! Stop it!"

The laughter increased as they mocked him and alternated responses in high pitched voices.

Chris turned his attention to Steve, and moved in closer to about the same distance as before, but without the confidence. He lowered his voice and defensively opened his hands in front of his chest.

"Please, just let me go. I don't want any trouble, and you made your--"

Chris was cut short as Steve grabbed hold of his shirt and yanked him forward with a cruel smile.

"Let you go!? We didn't even start yet, you little bit--"

Steve was interrupted and the impending slap towards Chris's face was halted. Blood tricked down Steve's face and as he went to his knees, screaming in agony on the way down. Chris hovered over his injured body, with the right palm he used to strike Steve's nose still positioned. Within a split second, Chris's confidence and determination were completely restored while Steve's was obliterated.

Irate and embarrassed, Steve attempted a punch with his right hand while is left covered his nose. The punch was easily deflected, and the downward motion allowed Chris to side-step and use his foot to introduce Steve's face to the hard cement. Steve was still conscious, but refused to get up as he kept his eyes closed and winced in pain.

The two pairs of footsteps behind him quickly turned into sprints, and Chris knew he didn't have much time before his one-on-one fight would turn into three-on-one. He needed Mitch out of commission, and he needed him out now! He looked at Mitch and he decided to stand his ground. His ego was big enough without Chris exaggerating his injury sustained from the sucker punch. In truth, the hit was hardly a knockout blow, and Chris recovered almost as quickly as it was thrown.

Instead of Mitch waiting for his friends, he let out a loud war cry and charged Chris head on. This was the ideal situation for Chris and he smirked at the opportunity. He patiently waited for Mitch to put all his energy in to his "one hitter quitter" punch. When the time was right, he easily ducked and blocked follow-up swings until Chris connected Mitch's face with a right elbow of his own. As Mitch fell back, Chris followed up by grabbing his torso and body slamming his back, hitting the ground.

He straddled atop his chest and landed four solid punches on his face before Jimmy kicked him off. The shoe hit the back of his head, but he didn't have time to wallow in his pain if he wanted to make it out of the alleyway. Chris immediately rolled off and when in a safe enough distance, he stood to his feet.

He glanced down and Mitch as he stared at Chris in bewilderment, with one of his eyes starting to close. Chris definitely was not the man he pegged him to be a minute ago. Jimmy looked at his friend who refused to get to his feet, and his eyes filled with rage.

"Get up! Get up! You're going to let this jackass embarrass you like this!?"

Chris saw this as a great opportunity and instantly chimed in.

"He's right, man. You should just stay down and let your friend teach me a lesson instead. I mean, he obviously can do so much better than you."

There was no point in pretending anymore: he wasn't afraid of these guys, nor had he ever been. Just as much as they were angry with him for ruining their plans, his rage was at least doubled for them attempting to snuff out free will. As Chris continued to taunt, Jimmy inched closer in response and Nolan carefully trailed behind.

Although Jimmy looked ready to fight, Nolan looked anxious. He removed his shirt, with pecks looking like something from a Men's Health Magazine cover. Stuffing part of the shirt ▯ in his back pocket, Nolan's gaze remained fixated on Chris and he rotated his arms clockwise a couple of times, clenching and unclenching his hands and wiggling his fingers. Established as the far greater threat between the two, Chris kept an eye on him, even when he addressed Jimmy.

"Look, it's not too late. Just run away. You can tell the tale of how you went against twelve dudes packed with mace and rocks or something. I can tell you really don't want to do this and end up like your..."special little friend" over there." Chris said, making sure to pause and air quote at the most inappropriate moments.

Jimmy spun his head around and made eye contact with Nolan, shook his head, and snickered in disbelief. As he turned back around, the snicker and talking were over as he ran towards Chris. He charged with his fist cocked, ready to finish what the other two had started. Nolan trailed behind, and made sure to keep his distance close and angled from Jimmy.

Chris playfully trotted towards Jimmy with his hands in his pockets and smirk on his face as Jimmy clenched his teeth and pursed his lips. Nolan grinned as the speeding punch soared towards Chris's face, and his heart skipped a beat as Chris easily ducked it, and kept running. What first looked like an escape attempt shocked both men as Chris ran full speed towards Nolan. He was no longer full of smiles and playful trots, but of rage and determination.

Stuck in the momentum he used to trail his friend, Nolan was helpless to stop Chris as he jumped high in the air towards his massive body. As he went downward, Chris angled his foot to strike his exposed right tree trunk of a leg. Chris felt his shoe dig deep into the side of his leg, followed by Nolan's screams of agony as he hit the ground. Chris had no clue if the leg was broken or injured and frankly, he didn't care. The biggest threat wasn't an issue and only one man remained.

Chris snapped his head towards Jimmy, who had just come to grips that he had been baited and remained as the last man standing. His eyes were wild as he looked around the dark alleyway, and only saw his comrade's littered bodies. The last of the muscle was rendered helpless, which drained his willingness to fight. Chris stormed up to him and quickly swept the feet from under him like a freestanding broom.

As Jimmy's back hit the ground, Chris firmly pressed his knee firmly on his chest and Jimmy immediately pledged his surrender. The barely coherent nervous chatter annoyed Chris and he tapped his face a couple of times to shut him up so he could focus.

"Hey! Listen up. I'm not going to hurt you. Pick up your douche bag friends and head home. Have a good night's rest and think long and hard on what happened here tonight. Never again will you take advantage of anyone the way you tried to tonight. Whatever crap you tried to feed Kate, you will flush down the toilet. If I ever EVER see any of you do some crap like that again, next time I'll kill you! Now get the hell of out here!"

Chris moved off his chest and allowed him to pick up his buddies. He tried hard not to smile at such a job well done. He was surprised at the seriousness of his own voice and thankful that nothing he said was challenged. He was certain that he didn't have it in him to torture a man, let alone kill him, but it seemed that Jimmy believed him, which was all that mattered.

Five minutes ago he wasn't even sure if he would be able to live to fight another day, and he managed to gain the upper hand with the odds stacked against him.

He waited for the four men to pick themselves up and hobble out of the alleyway before he chuckled to himself about the whole ordeal. The scene looked like something from an old war movie where the young soldiers had just gone through hell and barely made it out alive. However, it would seem in this story, the holder to the keys of hell's gate didn't belong to Nazis, Charlie in Vietnam, or even El Diablo himself.

They belonged to an untested Chris Andrews, who if backed into a corner can do the impossible. With that fleeing thought, Chris started his long walk home to enjoy some much deserved rest.

# CHAPTER 5

Chris awoke from his sleep in a good mood. He always loved when he didn't need the annoying buzz of his phone's alarm to get him up. He found out the hard way that music made him feel like he had permission to lounge, and his half asleep zombie mode would turn it off if it was in reaching distance. Therefore, he set the alarm to the most annoying sound, at the loudest volume, and left his phone on the dresser.

His day would typically start with him jumping up to save his sanity by turning off the alarm as quickly as possible, so it was always a good start when he could beat the clock. He arose from his bed and his feet landed on the carpet, he felt soreness in both legs as if he just ran a 5K. He hobbled over to his dresser, and with one glance at his phone, it all came back to him.

As memories of the night before flooded into his brain, a smile emerged on his face. He hadn't been in a fight since grade school, and yet he kicked ass when he was sorely outnumbered. Also, he stood up for what he believed in, which meant his day wasn't going to be filled with mental play-by-plays of all the things he could've and should've done differently. His conscious was clear and he was content.

He picked up his phone to turn off the alarm that was set for noon, and checked the time, which showed ten minutes til. There was no missed call or text from Jasmine, and he expected there never would be. She didn't exactly seem like the second chances types, nor would he want one in the first place. He put down the phone and headed to the bathroom to get ready for work, which started in a couple of hours. Today he was scheduled to work with Evan, which was always a good thing for him.

Evan wasn't the ideal employee for a manager; in fact, he was quite the opposite. He accomplished every task with the minimum amount of effort necessary, instructions constantly needed to be repeated, and tasks were often corrected.

However, he had one unique personality, which often made the time fly. Evan seemed to gain a new "calling" every few weeks from the sporadic community college courses that he attended on his parent's dime. At the current rate, the man in his mid-20's and was well on his way to receiving the first honorary PhD from a community college.

His newest "calling" was dream interpretation, and he recently surveyed staff and classmates on their recent dream experiences. For Chris, dreams were a rarity. He knew the one he had the night before would put Evan in a frenzy of analysis, which meant hours of entertainment for Chris. Evan often reminded him of a stoner beach bum trying to make it in the real world. Chris was certain that either a random drug test or Evan's incompetence would eventually terminate his employment, but until then, he savored the good moments.

Since the movie rental store wasn't a chain, the owner didn't have to worry about what actions were needed to appease the masses, but only focused on his shop and ran it how he saw fit. After Chris had proven to be a self-sufficient leader with min-imal supervision, the owner mainly contacted Chris via email for updates and changes. Mr. Omana rarely called or popped in for a visit, which was fine by Chris.

After lunch and showering, Chris peeked outside to determine what to wear for the day. The sun was shining with no dark clouds in sight and birds chirped in a nearby tree. He saw an older man with pants and short sleeves walking his dog and decided to follow his lead. Chris put on his white short-sleeved, collared shirt and loose fitting blue jeans and left the house when he finished getting ready.

Before leaving the apartment, he made sure to grab his keys, wallet, and cell phone. He locked the front door behind him and walked five minutes to the nearest bus stop. His commute consisted of using the Septa bus to get downtown and transferring busses to a direct route to work. Although a bit time consuming, the transportation was convenient and cost efficient.

He never bothered to look at a schedule, since a bus he needed stopped by every fifteen minutes or so. He waited about ten minutes before the bus arrived and within twenty minutes he had arrived at his downtown bus stop. The stop was one of the central hubs, which made the area larger than most. Some buses remained still while others were on the move, and the connected building gave riders the option to sit inside or outside while waiting for their bus to show. The warm weather made Chris's choice extremely simple, and he immediately searched for the outside bench that correlated with his bus stop.

As usual, the station was almost empty as Chris missed the majority of rush hour commuters. Working swing shifts gave Chris the luxury of avoiding the rushes of the day and allowed him to always find the best available seat on a bench and bus. As he sat down on an empty bench, he pulled out his iPod and began looking for the right artist within his massive library, when all the sudden his cellphone rang. Surprised to see Mr. Omana's name on the caller ID, he put down the iPod and answered immediately.

"Hey, Mr. Omana. What's going on?" Chris asked.

Rare phone conversations made Chris almost forget how difficult it was to sometimes understand that native Filipino. He put the phone closer to his ear and focused on his words.

"Helloooo, Kreeese! How are you?"

"Not too bad, sir. Yourself?"

"Oh good, Kreese! Good! Where are you?"

Chris flashed a baffled look and quickly checked the time before he answered the question. He still had about an hour to get to work, and by his calculations he would arrive thirty minutes early.

"At the bus stop. Is everything okay?"

"Yes, good. Good, but you don't have to come to work today, okay?"

"Excuse me, sir? Did something happen?"

"Yes, everything good. You are good worker, a good man. Good man. But don't come in today. I will explain later. Okay?"

Chris gave the phone a puzzled look, and eventually mustered, "Okay."

"Okay, Chris. Bye!" Mr. Omana said in the same cheerful voice he had at the start.

"Bye."

Chris hung up and put the phone away, but remained seated.

In an instant, his busy day had just been freed, and he had no idea why. If it weren't for the cheerful attitude and the "good worker" talk, he would assume he was fired; instead he was simply confused. With a completely open schedule, he decided to enjoy some good music in the beautiful weather until he figured his next move. He pulled out his iPod and searched through artists, only to be interrupted again.

Only this time, by one of the most gorgeous women he'd ever seen.

She seemed to have come out of nowhere, as she walked up to the opposite end of the bench where Chris sat. She had a slender build, yet she seemed athletic and toned. Her white sneakers, ankle socks, black shorts, and lavender blouse showed off her proportionate body and well-defined arms and legs. Her curvy body and washboard stomach were enough to take notice, but her beautiful face captivated him. As she sat down, she caught Chris's glance and greeted him with a warm smile. Her straight white teeth and lightly applied lip gloss momentarily glistened from the bright sun and accentuated her beauty.

"Good afternoon," she said in a sweet soft voice as her big and round hazel eyes locked on his. She sat down and pushed back her long, flowing auburn hair as Chris repeated the words. She crossed her legs and pulled out a book as Chris sat in silence. He got annoyed by the second as he continuously snuck glances without saying a word, like some nerdy high schooler bumping into the head cheerleader.

By no stretch would he classify himself as a timid or fearful person. If he was interested in a person, he would strike up a conversation, and whatever happened, good or bad, he would have closure. He had done this many times before, and yet there he sat, wasting away a rare opportunity. He had never seen her before, so it wasn't likely that she lived around him or that he would see her anytime in the near future.

However, it seemed like this random stranger had the power to nullify every bit of confidence he had mustered over the years, as if she was in a completely different league that he had never encountered or prepared for. The clock was ticking for him; she sat at a bus stop, which obviously meant her ride would come any minute and whisk her away.

He really didn't want her to turn into a future "what if" situation for him, and even if she turned out to be some annoyingly clingy and whiney chatterbox, at least he would be able to shove her off this inexplicable pedestal that he had placed her on. As she put away her book and began to play with her phone, he put away his iPod, forcing himself to take action before time was up. All he had to do was speak up, say anything to start a conversation like he had done a million times before.

"Hi, so how are you?" he thought to himself. No, we already established the greetings.

"So, where are you going?" he thought again. No, that sounds stalkerish!

"Do you live around here?" he thought. Dammit! Stalker again!

What seemed like a ridiculously simple task suddenly felt like a milestone for him as he continued to sit in silence.

"So how's your day going today?" she spoke up.

He was certain that she was talking on the phone, but as he looked her direction their eyes met for a second time. Her skin glowed radiantly in the sun and if she was wearing makeup, Chris couldn't tell.

"I'm pretty good. I kind of wasted my time coming here though. My boss just told me not to come in today."

She smirked and said, "Oh, that was nice of him."

"Yeah, tell me about it. So now I'll just head back home."

"Well, that's cool. At least you'll have more time to recuperate. You know, from starting fights at Envy."

Chris's heart jumped. He wasn't sure how to respond or how much she knew. He kept his mouth open, but nothing came out and she began to chuckle softly.

"Don't worry, I'm on your side. You're an unsung hero who helped protect that girl."

Chris closed his mouth and slowly nodded his head, but remained silent. He was certain that no one noticed him and yet it appeared that she knew all about what he did. He knew that they never met before, because he would've surely remembered. Yet she acted like she was right there next to him. He was seconds away from asking her how she knew so much when she said, "Actually, I have an interesting question for you."

Their eyes locked and Chris remained silent.

"If you could do more in life to stop bad things from happening all the time, would you take it?"

Chris gave her a confused look, and she flashed him a smile as she refined her question.

"Let's say Superman or Captain America. If you were handpicked to be a superhero today, would you even want to take on the burden of all the crap they would have to go through? Would you go through all of the struggles and sacrifices just to make the world a little better?"

"Wow, that's random," Chris chuckled, but the woman looked serious and focused.

She remained silent and continued to look at Chris, awaiting his answer. His smile quickly faded as he was forced to think out the hypothetical scenario.

"Okay, if you're serious, then I guess I would ask myself if there was a demand for my powers. If they were needed, then I would feel almost obligated to make the world a better place. Right?"

She flashed a sincere smile and quietly said, "Right."

She stood up and stretched out her arms.

"Yeah, I figured as much."

"Okay, what kind of que--" Chris started, when he suddenly felt a sharp sting on the back of his neck. He jumped up and reached for the point of pain, but his hand returned empty He looked at the woman with an embarrassed expression.

"Sorry, I think a bee just stung me."

She smiled and nodded her head.

"I think it's time for me to go. Nice to meet you, Chris."

She walked down the sidewalk and disappeared around the corner. Although he didn't think to question her on the spot as she left, questions began to build up as he waited for his bus. Who was she and where did she come from? How did she know so much about him and what he did the night before? As he boarded the bus that was homeward bound, two questions haunted him and the more he thought about it, nothing made logical sense to him. Why did she sit at a bus stop when she had no intention on boarding?

The question that scared him the most: How the hell did she know his name? He played the conversation back in his head and at no point did they share names, and yet she knew it. If she turned out to be friends with Kate, then he was in good standing. He helped her out in a time of need, but what if she was friends with the four douches or Jasmine? He was certain that both parties equally hated his guts and she could some-how be the key to setting him up in a bad way.

As Chris tried to piece together the enigma, he suddenly felt sick to his stomach. He tried to ignore it by focusing on other things, but the more he did the stronger the pain increased. As the bus stopped near his house, it took everything in Chris to stand up and hobble off the bus. The pain felt five times stronger than any cramp or indigestion issues of the past and it still felt like the pain was increasing.

He ascended the stairs to get to his second floor apartment and immediately felt dizzy and winded.

He was forced to sit down twice before completing the small flight of stairs. Hoping that water would solve his problem, Chris eventually made it to his apartment and went straight to the kitchen faucet. He poured himself a large glass of water and without hesitation, downed it without taking a breath. He placed the glass in the sink, sat down on his living room couch, and turned on the TV.

Chris was in the process of flipping channels when the dizziness set in again. Hitting him all at once like a powerful tidal wave, Chris uncontrollably dropped the remote to the floor and the two batteries ejected on impact.

This time the dizzy spell came equipped with stabbing pains in his feet and hands, as Chris knew he was in the worst pain of his life. It felt like little pixies had invaded his body with one goal in life: inflict as much pain as possible. The one in his head handled a sledgehammer and was hell-bent on reaching the gooey center, while the muscle bound one in his stomach ran out of punching bags that were settled for Chris's stomach.

Chris no longer had a desire to watch TV or do anything else for that matter, and wondered if the bee had some string of virus that needed an immediate vaccination, or if it was even a bee at all. He glanced towards his bedroom, and he immediately yearned the comfort of his soft mattress and warm blanket. Whatever bug he caught, he was convinced that a little rest would heal it all. Besides, he barely had enough energy to stay awake, let alone plea for help.

The back of his neck began to throb as his extensive list of physical issues continued to increase. His heart jumped as his hand felt the back of his neck puff up to at least two inches in diameter. He stood to his feet, but immediately toppled over on the floor. He slowly crawled his body to the bedroom, and mustered as much energy he had left to pull his body up on the dresser.

As his eyes focused on the mirror's reflection, Chris became increasingly terrified. The man that looked back at him was not the same man that woke up that morning in his bed. A sickly worn down man looked back at him, with bloodshot eyes. As he tilted his head, he could only see a small portion of the reddened and swollen circle that surrounded the point of the sting. Being able to stand at all took a tremendous amount of willpower.

As he looked for other abnormalities, Chris uncontrollably leaned forward and rested his forehead on the mirror. As his eyes tried again to focus, his heart skipped several beats while he looked at a foreign object flushed against his neck. From a distance, one could mistake the jet-black two inch diameter as an ink spot or oversized birthmark, but up close Chris gazed at what appeared to be some piece of fabric.

It looked premium and unique, but fabric on his skin nonetheless. He made a couple of attempts to yank it off, which felt like an eternity as he struggled to muster the strength to lift and maneuver his hands the way he intended. After his third attempt, which subsequently pulled at his skin, his eyes began to blur as he drifted in and out of consciousness.

Through the mirror, he looked at the comfy bed directly behind him and used his arms to push himself off the dresser and stumble backwards onto his bed. As he plopped down, he yearned to be surrounded by his comforting, cotton blanket, and slowly stripped down to his underwear. As he grabbed the top cover, his eyes widened and he began to pant.

The black spot wasn't only on his neck, but on his chest, torso, and thigh. They varied in size but matched in the same jetblack color and look of premium fabric. He tried one last time to remove a section and grabbed a piece without pinching his skin. He started off gently, but after learning his skin wasn't remotely affected, he tugged vigorously. The last spurt of energy was all Chris had left as he blacked out and drifted off to a deep sleep.

Chris awoke in a world completely unfamiliar to him. He was no longer in his bedroom, or in his apartment for that matter. As he rose from the pavement in the middle of a dilapidated highway, he noticed the black t-shirt, checkered pajama pants, and black slippers, but he didn't recall putting them on. The sky contained an eerie, dark grayish tint, which gave him the feel of a pending tornado, hurricane, or some other destructive force.

Neither cloud nor sun protruded the sky, and the further he looked, the more things appeared the same. As he scanned for anything familiar, his eyes grew in bewilderment, as everything around him was brand new.

He opened his mouth to cry out for assistance, but realized he wouldn't even know which direction to turn. Not only couldn't he spot another human being, all signs of human life were absent as well. There were no automobiles to drive, machines to operate, stores to shop in, or homes to dwell in. Even trees, plants, animals, and insects were all absent in this desolate new world. Chris stood still in the silence and he tried to make sense of any of it.

It was like someone snuck into his place, dressed him up, and then shipped him to some far off desert. No matter how inconceivable, he was standing on a strip of pavement within a sea of sand and nothingness. There wasn't a hint of greenery or life, as if some corrupt world leader had finally went one step too far and had ended all life, even down to the resilient cockroach. As he took another look onward, he began to spot scattered pieces of rubble in the distance.

Chris strained his eyes to identify what could only be old buildings and monuments that appeared to be evacuated and demolished long ago. Chris looked puzzled; he appeared to be in the middle of nowhere and yet someone thought it wise to build infrastructure. Chris muttered, "Where the hell am I," and turned around to face the opposite direction.

He momentarily stood in awe at the colossal ruin that stood straight ahead and slightly towards the left. The pyramid shaped stone structure was at least a hundred feet tall and on the center of each side there was a series of steps that led to the very top. The singular focal point contained a rectangular eight foot tall archway and a white light shone brightly inside the archway. To Chris, the light felt more like a beckoning lighthouse that would provide guidance to his sea of confusion. He had no idea where he was or how he got there, but he now had a destination.

Although it appeared really close, morning runs during his Myrtle Beach visits taught him not to assume the distance of large structures. Chris started his journey to the ruin and kept checking to make sure the path was headed in the right direction. Twenty minutes passed and as Chris had feared, the structure wasn't getting any closer to him.

The pyramid looked oddly familiar, but he had no idea why. The site looked like it belonged on the History Channel, with all of the other priceless artifacts that were hundreds of years old. Maybe he skimmed past an image off TV or a magazine, but didn't recall.

As he continued to walk, the ruin appeared to get closer bit by bit, and Chris gradually increased his stride until he heard a voice that emitted directly behind him. The sudden break in silence made him jump, since he hadn't seen or heard anything besides his own voice and footsteps since he arrived. Chris spun around and in that moment, he confirmed what he assumed for a while now: he was dreaming.

That was the only logical way he could've been whisked away to this peculiar land and the way he was witnessing what was before him now. Usually acknowledgment of a dream would wake him up, but he figured at this point, he was either a raging lunatic or still sound asleep, so he chose to put faith in the latter.

A man, or at least he thought could be, stood no more than fifty feet away from him. He had a similar height and build and wore a black robe, which draped down to both feet. A hood hung over his head and completely darkened his face, leaving all too much for the imagination. As Chris eyed the newcomer, he quickly recognized that none of his skin was exposed. Besides the robe, the man also wore white arm sleeves with white gloves.

"Hello, Chris," the robed man said in a cold and sinister voice, like an actor promoting a bone chilling movie trailer. At this point, Chris was confident he was dreaming, but the dream felt more realistic than ever before. He could feel the cool wind and grains of sand brush against his face, he heard and felt the clacking of every step he took. There had to be some reason he was going through this; some reason why he was rational and coherent, and he intended to find out.

"Hello. Who are you?" Chris responded.

The robed man held out his hand, and Chris instinctively moved in to shake it. Inches away from their hands meeting, Chris once again tried to look at his face, but was only met with a black hole where the face should've been. Lost in the nothingness of space, Chris kept his hand suspended as the man let out a deep and hearty laugh.

"What? You're too afraid to shake my hand, kid?"

The man spoke in a voice that could possibly petrify the likes of Darth Vader, but knowing it had to be a dream gave Chris unhesitant bravery. Chris smirked and immediately shook his hand, matching the firmness of the robed man's grip. Chris felt the grip tighten as the robed man moved in closer, as if an opponent was sizing him up.

Suddenly Chris felt something he thought he never would in this strange land: pain. Excruciating pain as he struggled to pull his hand free.

"Welcome, Chris. You and I are soon going to be good friends."

The man let out a loud menacing laugh and Chris's eyes widened as he continued to pull himself free.

"Where the hell are you trying to go? We just met!" the man said as he moved in closer and continued to laugh.

Suddenly loud music blared in Chris's ears, which sounded like pots and pans to a rhythmic beat. He opened his eyes, relieved to find himself in his own bed. The sound could only mean that he was getting a call on his cell phone, which simultaneously confirmed that he in fact wasn't going crazy.

He allowed the call go to voicemail as remained perfectly content in his bed. However, the persistent caller dialed right back, which went to voicemail again. During the third consecutive call, Chris finally gave up on his moment of tranquility and jumped up to answer the phone.

As he stood to his feet, he smiled. All of his ailments had disappeared. Not only had his pain gone, but he felt better than he could ever remember. As he walked to pick up the phone, he felt the back of his neck and looked over his body, but there was nothing abnormal.

There were no black marks or sores. Whatever that was going on with him had passed, and he no longer cared about one weird dream, knowing he would live to have many more. As he checked, Chris saw that the phone had an unlisted number, but he didn't care. He was content, and it would be hard for even a telemarketer to bring him down.

Chris held back an impulsive laughter as he exuberantly answered the phone.

"Hello?"

The man on the other end, however, was furious and the more he talked, the faster Chris' smile faded. Within five minutes, Chris had rushed to put on his clothes, grab his belongings, and bolted out the house. As he desperately scoured the streets for an available taxi, his short-lived celebration was replaced with thoughts of possibly sharing a jail cell.

# CHAPTER 6

Chris impatiently tapped his feet and drummed his fingers as the taxi maneuvered through the downtown traffic. He had already pleaded with the cabbie to hurry twice and he was working hard to oblige, knowing he would surely be rewarded for his efforts. The twenty minute ride flew by as Chris mentally prepared himself to counter every question and accusation that came his way.

The shop owner had already confronted him on the phone, giving him no more than an hour to meet face-to-face before going to the police. Initially, Chris was willing to meet at the police station anyway. He had nothing to hide, and the moment he disproved the owner, he would accuse him of slander and begin the administrative process.

Mr. Masterson claimed to be a silent partner, and as the majority shareholder, he was in charge of all of the finances and major operations. The more he tossed around words like infringement, copyright violation, and embezzlement, Chris became more and more nervous. As he boasted how his private investigator had undeniable proof of wrongdoing on both himself and Mr. Omana, it occurred to Chris that he may not be in the clear.

He doubted that Mr. Omana was the type to throw him under the bus or knowingly involve himself with shady business practices, but Chris had learned long ago that people were full of surprises. The more possibilities of the unknown stacked up in his brain, the more determined he became to find out what he knew.

The taxi pulled up with twenty minutes to spare and before exiting, he double checked the address that he had written down before leaving the apartment. Chris handed the cabbie a large bill, which covered nearly double the fair and he watched Chris in silence as he exited.

"Did that cover it?" Chris asked with a perplexed expression.

"Oh, we're good!"

As the cab drove away, Chris turned around to face the beautifully constructed glass building that towered at twenty-nine stories tall. "Philadelphia Bank & Trust" was scattered on various places on the building and although it stood alongside some of the largest and most powerful financial institutions in the city, it appeared more grand and sophisticated. Chris was in awe of the elegant and contemporary design as he walked towards the glass entrance doors.

Being after office hours, he tugged the chrome door handle ▢ expecting resistance, but instead the door pulled wide open and he walked in. Being surrounded by an attractive and spotless décor did nothing but accentuate the already pristine marble floors, columns, and ceilings. A fountain was placed in the middle of the lobby with plush leather furniture surrounding it.

The area next to the closed café gave off an upscale coffee shop feel. A series of teller stations stood about one hundred feet to the left, each with its own individual sign stating that they were closed until the next duty day. Although the café and teller areas were dark, the rest of the lobby was well lit and inviting.

Chris was running out of time to meet his accuser, who agreed to meet him in the lobby. He pulled out his phone to give him a call, but his eyes shot up as he heard footsteps approaching him. Within a few seconds, a man stood before him wearing a white button up shirt, black slacks, and a badge. The lack of firearm and physical condition were immediate giveaways that he was dealing with a security guard.

"Good evening, sir. We're closed. Were you expecting someone?" the stocky man asked in a pleasant, yet assertive tone.

As Chris turned to face him, he noticed the administrative desk a few feet away from the entrance door that was clearly overlooked. His partner remained seated at the desk, but fully attentive to the conversation.

"Yes, I received a call from Mr. Masterson. He told me to meet him here."

"Yes, sir, follow me, please."

Chris followed the man back to his desk and watched as he picked up the phone and dialed.

"Sir, this is Kelly at the front desk. I have a gentleman here to see Mr. Masterson. His name is...."

"Chris Andrews."

"Chris Andrews, sir."

There was a momentary pause and he followed up with a final, "Yes, sir, will do," before hanging up the phone.

"He will be with you shortly. You can have a seat if you'd like."

Chris remained standing.

A few minutes later, Chris listened as the empty room echoed a soft chime followed by footsteps that started off distant and grew louder by the second. As his eyes pinpointed the sound, Chris watched as a man turned a corner from behind the teller station and headed in his direction. The man stood in front of him and extended his hand with a warm greeting as he introduced himself as the man that had called.

Chris tried to conceal his shock. Mr. Masterson was not at all what Chris had expected. He visualized some middle aged CEO type that was either balding or had a head full of grey hair. Instead, he was introduced to a man that couldn't be any older thirty-five. His black blazer, slacks, tie, and white button up shirt made him appear official, but his worn out Nike ⍰ sneakers told a different story.

Mr. Masterson seemed to be in a really good mood, which made Chris both pleased and confused. Ever since he hopped in the cab, his mind raced with every decision he had ever made at the shop and what actions he could possibly be blamed for. Drawing a blank only increased his fear, for if he knew of a particular incident, he could build defenses. However, when he walked into the building, he was just as confused as when he received the phone call.

As Masterson talked to him in person, Chris could tell he matched the voice on the phone, yet that guy seemed angry, vengeful, and impatient. The man before him, however, seemed calm and relaxed

After they shook hands, Masterson immediately placed his in his pockets and said, "Follow me, Chris."

Both guards returned to their desks as Chris trailed Mr. Masterson to the nearby elevators behind the teller station.

"This is Philadelphia Bank & Trust. The bank was established sometime in the fifties and has been going strong ever since." Masterson said with tour guide qualities as he pushed the round button for the elevator door and watched it open. As they entered the elevator, he pulled out a black keycard made of metal and inserted it in a key slot directly under the numbers that led to the twenty-eighth floor.

He pushed for the fifteenth floor and as the doors closed and elevator moved, the card spit out like an ATM. Masterson immediately pulled it out waved the card in front of Chris.

"Everyone needs a keycard to go on any floor of the building, but my company owns floors fourteen and fifteen, so we have a specialized key just for those two floors. This actually isn't our building and we don't give a crap about the success or failure of Philadelphia Bank & Trust. All that we care about is operating in public, yet under the radar. To anyone else, this is just another bank working in the Financial District.

Masterson continued to speak casually as if everything was just small talk amongst new acquaintances, and it began to annoy Chris. He was threatened with jail time and given a miniscule window of time to clear his name before authorities were involved. He rushed over and held his end of the bargain, only to get some lecture about a company. He wanted to let him talk and make sure he didn't get on his bad side, but the more the man talked, the more confused Chris became on why the hell he was there.

"Excuse me, sir, I don't mean to be rude, but you threated to call the cops, and I came here to...."

"Yes, yes. Don't worry about that for now. We're almost there."

"Almost where?"

The chime of the elevator answered his question as it stopped and the doors opened.

"After you," Masterson said as he tilted his head towards the open door.

Chris always hated extended courtesies of being first when he had no idea where he was going. Chris stepped out and, as expected, he was forced to turn around and wait for direction from his host. Right before Chris turned left to follow Masterson, he saw that the path to the right was blocked by a wall, anyway.

As Chris trailed behind, he looked for some sign or indicator to hint where he was going, but the harder he looked, the more he saw of the same redundant pattern. On the long stretch of hallway there were no doors, pictures, or restrooms. There was nothing but plush carpet and two walls on both sides with the same neutral color of wallpaper. There were only two directions to go and he already knew where one way led. Chris frowned behind him as he walked in silence to his undisclosed destination.

Chris had already tried once to clear up the accusations, only to be silenced. If he became too persistent, there was a good chance that his good intentions would backfire, so he decided to play along with the man's impromptu facility tour.

The two men stopped at two massive oak doors. Once again there were only two options: go through or turn around. Much like on the lobby floor, there was a man dressed in a black suit and white button up shirt sitting in front and to the side of the door. However, with his clean cut face, expensive looking suit, athletic build, and confident demeanor, it was evident that we was leagues above the local "rent-a-cops" on the main floor.

He had a small Bluetooth attached to his ear and sat at an executive looking desk and chair, typing on his laptop. With one glance of the approaching two, the man stopped typing and stood up. He retrieved a black metal card and inserted it in a key slot next to the door frame, positioned at his eye level.

With a closer look, Chris realized the door had no door handle. His eyes curiously looked around the obvious doorway until he saw the man's hand hovering over a flat Chrome square that sat directly above the key slot. Masterson walked towards the threshold as the man pushed the button and the doors flew open. The man acknowledged him as he walked past by dipping his head and saying, "Masterson." Masterson dipped his head in response and continued on. Chris followed behind him and the man continued the same gesture.

"Andrews," the man greeted as Chris flashed a puzzled look, unsure on how to respond.

After walking inside, the door slowly closed behind them. Chris's eyes immediately wandered in amazement, as if he was a kid stumbling across Santa's workshop in the middle of a mall for the first time. He felt like he was tossed in some cool futuristic wonderland with vivid colors and technology too complex to understand, but cool to look at. The deeply expanded one leveled room had to be at least seven thousand square feet and the entire floor space was illuminated with a soft white light.

The room was bright, yet and there was no sign of a lamp or overhead lightbulb. Drawn to the floor tiles like a human moth, Chris was impressed that he didn't have to squint or look away from the intensity. Chris looked up and shifted his gaze to the next piece of attention grabbing eye candy. At the end of the room stood four enclosed glass structures that stretched from floor to the thousand foot tall ceiling.

Each facility was a different color and the material made it impossible to peek inside. They stood in line ten feet away from one another, with a massive electronic sliding door at the front. As Chris's eyes scanned the beautifully designed set, he stood in awe from the contemporary design and four distinct colors of black, blue, purple, and red glass. The group of structures took up a little less than one-third of the room.

Besides a mini-gym that contained free weights, pull-up bars, and other traditional workout equipment, everything in between Chris and the structures was either some type of expensive and awe inspiring electronic device or in support of one. Two high powered contraptions that appeared to be a cross between treadmill and conveyer belt stood alongside the matted floors of the gym equipment.

The one on the left faced a standing foam board that looked like a giant bullseye target. Shurikens were housed in a compartment near the center control panel and the side arm rests also stored wooden pointed spears. The right contraption was accompanied with a seven foot tall iron structure overhead. The design looked like three monkey bars front and back, and three side to side.

The plush black leather sectional and love seat faced the most highly defined and largest TV that he had ever seen. Two slightly smaller ones sat on the left and right of the behemoth. The artfully positioned lounge area sat in the middle of the room, along with a high-tech looking workstation.

Four touch screen all-in-one computers lined up in cubicles, while a fifth computer sat twenty feet away atop an executive looking desk. Next to both the cubicle and desk stood what one could only guess as an oversized tablet, fit for the likes of an ogre. Like the computers, chairs sat in front of two enormous freestanding screens.

Chris stood utterly speechless, as Masterson watched him with a pleased look on his face.

"Here, this is for you." Masterson said breaking the silence and handed him a card that looked identical to what both Masterson and the man at the door had just used. Chris grabbed hold of the card and stared with a baffled look, as if it would provide answers to the questions that were lining up in his head.

Masterson checked his watch.

"Alright, looks like I have time to show you one more thing, and I promise to explain everything to you."

Chris was tired of being yanked around without having a clue of what was going on, but he couldn't possibly argue the displays of awesomeness that he imagined only a handful had witnessed. Masterson led Chris past the lounge and directly behind and to the right of the workstation. A singular elevator stood against the wall and doors immediately opened after he pushed the button. Both walked inside and Masterson pressed the only button available, which led them one floor up.

As doors opened and Chris stepped out, he regained his level of amazement. The place felt like a top tier timeshare penthouse unit with all the comforts of home, if Bill Gates or Oprah Winfrey owned the home. The size, for starters, had to be at least quadruple the size of his moderately sized apartment, and once again the luxuries were on point.

This time Mr. Masterson gave him a tour and boasted about all of the amenities as if he was a high-class relator trying to make a sell to Bruce Wayne. Masterson was about to transition from showing off the Jacuzzi room with room for eight people to the theater room with Bose surround sound and leather recliners, when Chris spoke up.

"Mr. Masterson...."

"Call me Ken."

"Ken, you have a nice place and I don't mean to be rude but...."

Ken dismissively waved his hand in the air at him, "This isn't only my place. That key gets you in like it does me and you have just as much ownership. Let's call it...the perks of your new job. Chris, everything about your life is about to change, and I'm not talking about jail."

Ken checked his watch again and sighed.

"I guess it is about time to talk business and give you the speech."

Ken took one glance at Chris's stone-cold face and chuckled.

"Don't worry, kid, it's not a bad thing, I promise. If anything, you're being rewarded and given a gift. Let's go back downstairs and talk on the couch. I can only explain things to a certain degree, but you'll never believe me. But you'll see soon."

Both made their way to the lounge area downstairs, and Chris prepared himself as his skin touched luxurious couch cushions, which helped him relax.

"I'm not calling any cop, and I don't think you're a criminal. In fact you're a hero, or at least you will be.

My name really is Ken, but I work for the CIA. Back in the seventies they created a secret branch called Project G4, which is in direct support of the Guardian Program. Guardians are protectors of certain regions in the United States. They prevent evil from spreading and good people from suffering. The reason why you're here and being shown all of this is because, well, you're our newest Guardian, Chris."

Chris sat in silence and waited for him to laugh or crack a smile, but his was serious and focused.

"Well, that's it. I'm not going to give you some long winded speech just so you can think I'm making it all up or that I'm cuckoo for Cocoa Puffs, so I'll have you ask the questions. So, any questions?"

Chris's eye's narrowed as he crossed his arms. He had rushed halfway across the city, the whole time trying to think of ways to plea his innocence to some stranger, only to play twenty-one questions! Chris's eyes met Ken's, who was looking at him with watched anticipation. Chris rolled his eyes and shook his head.

"So, I'm a Guardian. That's some type of superhero, I suppose?"

Ken smiled and quickly stood to his feet.

"Yeah, I suppose you can call it that. You can wear a suit that amplifies your strength and speed. The amount depends on the Guardian, but typically, anything you can do is amplified by five to ten percent. If you never performed gymnastics or track, it can't make you do the impossible; it just enhances your natural talents. If you can punch, you can punch harder and faster. If you can withstand pain, you can withstand more."

Ken's eyes met Chris's skeptical gaze and he walked to the executive desk and pulled out a drawer as Chris asked his next question in a monotone voice.

"So why do we exist? Isn't the whole theme of the police to protect and serve? Same thing with government agencies? Don't they already work together to stop evil? Or whatever you said?"

Ken continued to search through his drawers while responding.

"You're right. Police and government agencies are there to protect the public, and they do what they can. The truth is, our nation isn't nearly as safe as people make it seem. You hear stories of murder, crime, and evil all of the time from media outlets, and like most Americans, you accept that as reality.

I'm sorry to break this to you, but the world is a much much darker place than how it's portrayed. I mean think about it, we have over three hundred million people that live in the United States from all different types of backgrounds and walks of life. Do you honestly think there were only a handful of people with the knowledge and willingness to successfully inflict mass casualties on our soil?

You may think there were only a handful of people like the Timothy McVeighs, Charles Mansons, Jeffery Dahmers, or religious extremists, but the G4, we call that a monthly quota. The reason why you haven't heard of the majority of the truly sick and deranged individuals is because of the Guardians. People in society love the real life stories of violence, murder, and mayhem, but the trick is they only like it in small doses.

They want to hear the ending with the person being captured, jailed, or executed. Knowing the actual number of unsolved big cases could easily cause mass hysteria."

Ken's eyes widened and he smirked as he retrieved and item from the drawer and quickly place it behind his back. As he returned to his seat, Chris raised his eyebrows from the suspicious behavior. Chris watched carefully as Ken sat down, and his heart sped up as Ken placed a 9mm pistol on his lap.

Suddenly, everything Ken needed to say had more merit as Chris remained focused on the gun less than twenty feet away from him. Ken pushed the magazine release and gently slid out the magazine from inside the pistol. He removed three bullets and stood up to place them in Chris's hand.

"Did you ever shoot a pistol before?"

Chris slowly nodded his head. "Twice. Why? What are you doing?"

"Just humor me; do you know how to tell if these are real bullets?"

Chris grabbed hold of the bullets and individually observed each one by rotating the bullet and looking at the primer.

"Yes, they're real. Now why do I...."

Ken smiled, nodded and held out his hand.

"Don't worry, you have nothing to worry about."

Chris slowly placed the ammo in his hand and Ken walked a few feet back as he placed them back in the magazine and re-inserted it into the pistol.

Chris instinctively stood to his feet.

"I'm lost. Why do you—"

Chris was immediately silenced as Ken raised the pistol and pointed the barrel towards Chris's chest.

"Hey...hey man...what the hell you are doing!?"

Chris had little time to react as Ken pulled the trigger and fired four times in rapid succession. Chris barely had time at all and managed to extend his arms as if attempting to stop the bullets with his bare hands while he stammered a singular word: wait. He heard the deafening booms of the gun and witnessed the gun jerking up in reaction to the bullet exiting towards his body.

A range of emotions swept through Chris within a short span. First, he was shocked that Ken to turn on him without any warning or build up. As the shock subsided, outrage ensued as he balled up his fists, preparing to rush the man that attempted to take his life. Soon after, reality sunk in as he was still standing.

Ken had already lowered the gun and gave off a satisfied look. He scanned his body, and there wasn't as much as a baby scratch on him, and yet three shell casings lay at Ken's feet. Bullet remains were on the floor next to Chris.

"What the hell was that?"

Ken let out a small chuckle.

"Pretty cool, right? That Guardian suit that amplifies your power is inside you and protects you from any weapon that has gunpowder residue. In other words: guns can't harm you, but conventional weapons like knives, swords, and bats can."

"But...how did...what the...."

Chris was at a loss for words now that Ken had just earned a great deal of merit. No matter how farfetched it sounded, he couldn't deny the fact that he didn't even have a flesh wound when he should be dead.

"Okay, tell me about this suit again."

"We injected you yesterday, so you probably felt the worse sickness you ever had, right? Like you were moments away from death?"

Chris nodded his head.

"You probably saw part of it then. Did you see black spots all over your skin?"

Chris stopped nodding and remained silent and Ken smiled and nodded in response.

"That is part of your suit. You can activate it and deactivate it with your mind, but the suit never goes away completely."

"But, why me? If you're some top secret organization, why did you randomly pick me as this Guardian person? Shouldn't there be some type of interview or application process?"

"Your interview was earlier today with Ava."

"That girl on the bench?"

"She's a Guardian. There are four total: Purple, Blue, Red, and Black, which is you. Every Black Guardian is the leader of the group, which means, congratulations! You're their new leader."

"Are you serious?"

"Do you think I would joke at a time like this? Don't worry, we'll set you up right."

"Okay, but how do you even know I'm qualified or that I'm not evil myself? Shouldn't there be an application process?"

Ken laughed hysterically.

"I'm sorry, I don't mean to laugh. Yes, you are right; you're not just some kid we picked up off the street. When you were a baby, like all other newborns in your hospital, we injected you with a serum that we nicknamed Genesis. It takes over twelve years to mature, so we've been monitoring you ever since then. In other words, your entire life was an application process for you.

Everything you ever did good or bad was monitored, and that's why you're here now. The reason why you're a Guardian isn't only because you'd do a good job, but because you would love to do it.

"It doesn't matter how long you decide to work with us, as long as you remember that everything shared is top secret information that shouldn't be shared with anyone. We take that rule extremely seriously and violation could easily land you in federal prison, alongside the people that you blabbed to, for a long time.

I'm trying to warn you now, because to my knowledge there were two past incidents where a newly appointed Guardian couldn't keep his mouth shut. On both accounts, it didn't end well for the Guardian or the person they confided in."

"Wow, I'm really glad I said yes now," Chris replied sarcastically.

Don't get me wrong; we're not exactly the mafia. You can quit whenever you feel like it, as long as you understand our confidentiality rules that are set in place. Plus, if you do ten years with us, you are automatically considered retired and we pay you your yearly salary for the rest of your life, inflation included. You will be paid well now, but we will have to with-hold the majority until you stop being a Guardian. Let's just say that riding around town in a Lamborghini, while living in a twenty bedroom mansion, is a great way to paint a bullseye on yourself for potential enemies. Trust me, you will already have plenty as is."

"So, how much money are we talking about?"

Ken pulled out his phone and pushed a few button before he handed it to Chris.

"This is your salary while a Guardian and if you make it to retirement."

Chris's mouth widened as he stared at the unbelievable figure.

"What's the catch!? This would easily make me a millionaire in no time, just for stopping some crimes from happening?"

"You say that now, kid. Tell me how easy it is a year from now."

"Really, Ken? Is it that serious?" emerged a gentle feminine voice towards the entrance. Chris turned his head and was im-mediately captivated as the same girl from the bus stop walked towards them. He tried to maintain some sort of poker face and fought every urge to grin. As she walked towards him with poise and confidence, she was just as, if not more, gorgeous than before.

"Hey, Chris," she greeted as she stopped in front of him.

"Sorry for all of the super-secret squirrel crap; we all have our rules to follow. But hey, at least you're a Guardian now. Or did you two get to that part yet?"

She turned her attention to Ken and he pointed his index finger to the floor. She looked down and smiled as she bent down to pick up one of the shell casings.

"God, I hated my first Guardian gun experience. How did he do?"

Ken immediately returned her smile and turned to Chris.

"I don't know, how do you think you reacted, Chris?"

The woman chuckled.

"I'm pretty sure like I did. Scared as hell and thought he would die. Sorry, there was probably a much easier way to show you're bulletproof, but we have our own ways. I'm Ava, by the way."

They shook hands as Chris barely stopped himself before replying with his name.

"So, are you officially one of us yet?"

Chris quickly glanced at Ken's phone and looked into Ava's beautiful hazel eyes and nodded his head.

"Looks that way. So I guess we make up three of the four Guardians?"

She smiled and shook her head. "No, not quite. I'm a Guardian, aka Purple, but he is the G4 Leader. There's G1, G2, G3, and G4. They are pretty much our support team and all play different roles to make sure we and this whole program succeeds. G4s are the ones that give us direct support.

They do everything from providing vehicles to covering our tracks. As the G4 leader, Ken is in charge of them in this city. He's the only one that works out of here and gives us missions. I think the other two Guardians are on their way, though."

Ava looked at him and laughed.

"I'm sorry, but I had the same look on my face about two years ago when Ken brought me in. It's just funny being on the other side of the process. I mean, I know how it sounds: superheroes, magical suits, and special powers. I thought ol' Ken was crazy as hell, too.

It really took me a second to wrap my head around the CIA injecting the many just to locate the select few but then I remembered it was the government and how they just may be both powerful and manipulative enough to pull it off." She flashed Ken an innocent smile as he frowned at her.

"Don't worry, Ken, I'm not jumping ship. I'm well aware that we're the good guys and make the world a better place."

"I'm still confused, though. Why me? I mean, how do you know you can even trust me not to go to CNN in an hour and tell the world about everything you're telling me?"

Ava shrugged her shoulders.

"I just met you today, so I don't know what you're capable of, but apparently they know enough about you to understand that you're not the type to do that. Just like me, these guys have been monitoring your whole life. From what I learned about my own situation, they are pretty tricky with it. They could've posed as school teachers, a mailmen, random strangers, or even friends to get information on what kind of person you are.

You know how I told you about our support team G1 to G4? Well, the sole purpose of the G2 is to watch us and analyze. Unless we disqualify ourselves, these guys stalk us well into adulthood. Imagine you're a kid on the playground and you witness some kid getting beat up by bullies.

It would be your choice to jump in, run away, or look for help. Whatever that decision is would either drive you towards or pull you further away from being a Guardian. I have no idea what they know about you, but I guarantee you that they know you better than you know yourself."

Chris nodded his head in understanding while looking simultaneously disturbed.

"What if a candidate lives a relatively stress-free life without conflict? How would the person become qualified or disqualified?"

Ava flashed another gracious smile.

"I thought you should know that answer best after last night."

Chris returned her smile with a baffled expression.

"Last night? What about last night?"

Ava turned her attention to Ken with a surprised expression.

"You didn't tell him yet!?"

"Well, I was about to, but I didn't get around to it," Ken replied.

"Tell me what?" Chris asked timidly.

Ava shook her head at Ken before she looked into Chris's eyes.

"I thought you already knew this part, but that incident last night where you came out as the hero was staged. Two of those guys were G2 and they hired the two other guys along with the damsel that was going to get drugged. The drink wasn't really contaminated nor was she in any danger."

"But why?"

"Apparently, you're really good at dodging fights," Ken chimed in.

"You had checked every box for being a potential Guardian, except one. We needed to see what happened if you were backed in a corner where you had to fight, so we created one for you. You did well. In fact, a little too well. I don't think anyone could've called you breaking Agent Snuff's leg like you did."

Chris apologized out of instinct and Ken immediately looked offended.

"Sorry for what!? All agents in the program are well trained in hand-to-hand, among other things. It was their job to test your resolve and skill, but he had left his guard wide open and you surprised him.

You're not only a Guardian, but you're the leader. You should be proud. You all need to video chat, so I guess now is as good a time as any."

Chris followed Ken to the oversized tablet screen and the screen lit up with vivid colors and options. After a few swipes and pushes, the screen dialed what sounded like a phone and a few seconds later, Chris was face to face with one the man he knew as "Nolan."

"Good evening, Agent Stoffer. As you can see I have Chris on the end. Where's Agent Snuff?"

"Sir, he's still recuperating but he sends—"

"In other words, he's still mad at Chris for his slip up."

The man on the screen was silent for a second. Then quietly replied, "Yes, I believe so, sir."

Ken exhaled a deep breath of annoyance, but quickly recovered.

"Well, as you can see, we have our newest Guardian here."

The man shifted his gaze and looked at Chris as he took a step closer.

"Good evening, Chris, and congratulations. I'm sure you still have a lot of questions that you're getting sorted out, but I just wanted to say that last night was nothing personal. It was just a test, which you obviously passed. You surprised all of us, which isn't easy to do. I'm sure you'll make a great asset to the team."

Filtering through the correct response, Chris settled for a head nod in which the man copied and bid his farewells.

Chris began to feel more like he belonged and felt more at ease. He turned his attention back to Ava.

"Okay, you've been doing this longer, so why am I the leader of our group again?"

"Like I said, we have many rules to follow and one is that in every city, the Black Guardian is always the leader."

"Fair enough. Calling you Ava is okay, right?"

"Yup. Well, for the most part. We never use real names when in uniform. That's very important; how we practice is how we perform, so whenever we see the uniform, we call each other by the color."

"So I would call you Purple, right?"

"Oh, that's right, you still haven't seen our uniforms, have you?"

Chris shook his head and Ava squared her body off of his.

Before his very eyes, Chris witnessed Ava transform into something unrecognizable. Her fuchsia and black puma sneakers turned into purple athletic pumps, blue jeans into purple leather pants, and her shirt was replaced with a black and purple leather top.

The form fitted uniform covered every part of her body, including the black arm sleeves that were attached to her purple center vest and gloves. The black mask sat perfectly on her face and connected the black leather material around her neck and the purple hoodie that sat atop her head. Everything on her body gave off both an elegant and dangerous appeal, and as Chris watched the transformation from head to toe, his eyes focused on the mask.

Besides the slots for eyes and poked holes through the mouth region, the upscale hockey-looking mask was one solid piece that covered her face. Although impressed with the entire ensemble, Chris was drawn in by the oval shaped jet-black mask that gave off a glossy and sleek appearance.

"This is what a Guardian looks like," Ken announced.

"Now that you see it, you should be able to imitate and activate yours. The only difference between the two will be the color change. I'm not going to stand here and explain all the capabilities, because truthfully, half the information would go over your head anyway. The best way to learn on how to be a Guardian is to learn from another one. The only thing that sucks for you is that you'll have to catch on pretty quickly. At the end of the day, you're still the leader and you'll soon have to make some tough decisions."

"But I don't even know if I can do it."

"Yes, you do, just like we do," Ken said as he turned to Purple Guardian.

"So I guess you can start him off and teach some of the basics."

"I will."

"Wait! Wait!" yelled a voice near the door.

All three turned and watched as two men in their early 20's, of greater athletic build, and similar height enter the doorway. One was slightly shorter than Chris and a bit more athletic. He trotted towards the group with urgency, while the second slightly taller muscle bound God of a man casually walked over.

"So this is our new fearless leader, huh?" the first man smirked while looking Chris up and down.

"Chris, this is Tyrell. The Red Guardian." Ken announced.

Chris instinctively extended his arm to shake his hand, but Tyrell flashed him a quick head nod and left the handshake unanswered. Chris enthusiastically responded by shaking his own hand and happily exclaimed "All right!" in the process. Both Ken and Purple chuckled amongst themselves, but Tyrell was not amused. "So this is the chosen one, huh?"

"Tyrell, don't start. He hasn't even started his first day yet!" Ken said.

"What! I didn't even say anything bad! In fact, how about you let me train him? I can show him the ropes and take him off your hands, Purple. Probably doesn't hurt to get tips from the strongest around here." He gave off a wide grin as Ava narrowed her eyes with suspicion.

"This is not the time for immature games. He's brand new and we have to train him correctly."

"Who's playing games? I'm serious, I can train him. I'll do a good job, I promise."

The big man had made his way over and extended his hand towards Chris.

"Well, while these two figure that out, I'm Max, Blue Guardian." Along with the bulging muscles fully exposed by his sleeveless t-shirt and workout shorts, there were two things that stood out to Chris. He had bleach blond crew-cut hair with matching eyebrows and wore a chain with two dog tags around his neck.

With one blue in color and one in black, both inscribed dog tags popped out in contrast to his white shirt. Headphones wrapped around his neck as the cable led to an mp3 player attached to his maroon workout shorts. As he shook hands with his right hand, Max clung onto a black gym bag with his left.

"Well, I'm going to workout for a bit, but I'll see you around."

The conversation lasted less than a minute, and yet he felt a significant difference in feeling at ease and welcomed.

As Max walked towards the workout equipment, Purple turned her attention back to Tyrell.

"Fine, but I swear, if there's some kind of accident on his first day...."

"What the hell are you talking about? He'll be fine. Anyway, he's the one in charge of us misfits, right? I'm sure he can handle anything."

Purple rolled her eyes and placed her hands on her hips.

"Fine. Whatever."

In an instant, Purple had transformed back to Ava. She had the same shirt, pants, and shoes she had come in with and not even a strand of hair was out of place. She seemed annoyed, but forced a smile as she turned her attention back to Chris.

"Chris, once again, welcome to the team. I'm sure we'll talk soon."

As Chris tried to reciprocate, Tyrell emitted a softly spoken "aww" as he placed his hands on his cheeks. Ava rolled her eyes in response.

"And you better not go all crazy and over work him on his first day!"

"What!? We're just going to bond and become besties! All I'm going to do is show him a few things."

Ava flashed a thumbs up, said bye to Chris, and walked towards the elevator.

Ken turned his attention to Tyrell.

"Alright, I guess you can teach him the staff and glider, but I already showed him the gun thing."

Tyrell frowned at the end of the sentence and took a deep sigh.

"Oh, well. Let's go, Chris."

Chris followed him towards the back of the room at the four enormous colored glass structures.

"These are our training rooms. I'm not going to have to explain which one is yours, will I?"

Chris frowned at Tyrell in silence, who chuckled and raised his hands defensively.

"Hey, man, I'm just asking."

Tyrell led him to the center of the black structure and when close enough, the automatic doors slid open to allow them both to enter. The entire exterior was mirrored, which made it impossible to peer inside. Once he did, Chris found himself yet again fascinated. The floor space was covered with a thick padded mat. However, unlike a gym, the mat seemed to be permanent and fitted perfectly for the room like carpet.

The room lit up brightly as light fixtures hung on the wall. Chris immediately took notice of the mannequin-like objects lined up against the left and right wall towards the back. Black in color, these non-gender specific dolls stood upright and free of all clothing. Each mannequin was positioned with its head down and balled fists to its side as if positioned in some sort of bizarre military formation.

"What the heck are those?"

"Wow, a little eager, aren't we? They're Trainers. There are some in each one of our rooms, but we're not there yet. I was going to start with the basics first, if that's okay with you, bossman. I've only been doing this a little longer than you."

"Yeah, I think it's weird that they made me leader. They should award the position based on tenure as a Guardian, not because of birth rights."

Tyrell's eyes narrowed as they looked into Chris's.

"And you felt so strongly about this that you accepted the job anyway, right? Anyway, our suits power mostly deals with the mind. They automatically nullify the damage of firearms and amplify our physical abilities. For you, that was what, cheerleading or band practice?"

Chris recognized the rhetorical question and remained silent as he waited for Tyrell to continue.

"The suit also comes with some other advantages, and some major disadvantages. Our suits are kind of interconnected and we can communicate through our minds when we wear them. These things are also low jacked with some kind of internal GPC system. Sucks for me, but it's good for you to know when you call for one of us to save your ass.

"Besides comm, we have something that we call gliders. Ever see Back to the Future 2, when Marty used that hover board?"

Chris nodded his head.

"Yeah, think of that, but only real. And cool."

He lifted his right leg one foot off the ground and said, "Now watch the birdie."

Chris witnessed a two foot long and six inch thick silver blade looking object materialize and attach to the bottom of Tyrell's suspended foot. Suddenly, Tyrell lifted his left leg and just like that, he was airborne. Atop the board, his body suspended in the enclosed room, began moving forward, and circled Chris at a crawling speed.

Chris was mutually surprised and impressed, but after witnessing everything else that led to that moment, he was finally able to bypass his skeptical and disbelief stages. After all, the government withholding secrets had been widely publicized truth for generations.

"When it comes to the glider, your feet can either latch on or stay disengaged. It's vital to know which function you're using at which time."

Tyrell demonstrated both functions. At first he jumped up and down on the board, which remained still.

The board dipped down as his weight crashed on it, but reset to the original height. He paused and closed his eyes. As they re-opened, he lifted his feet high in the air, and the whole board stuck with him, as if he had suddenly glued the board to his soles.

"Just remember, you can't recover from a hundred foot freefall, and if it was from you being an idiot and not paying attention to your glider, don't expect me to sugar coat it to people. I would tell everyone that I can that you died like a damn moron."

"Gee, thanks."

Tyrell shot up a glare in response and rapidly accelerated towards the back walls. Chris's eyes widened as Tyrell showed no signs of slowing down, and just as he expected Tyrell to splat against the wall like an old roadrunner cartoon, he scaled the wall with ease and used the sidewalls to turn around.

Being approached at breakneck speed, Chris's body was frozen stiff, unsure how to respond or where to go. Tyrell grinned as he zoomed past him, inches away from making contact. On the opposite end, Tyrell repeated his actions as he treated the room like a modified new age halfpipe. Chris looked him in the eyes as he once again picked up speed and headed directly for him.

As he closed in, Chris's heart raced but he refused to give Tyrell any satisfaction at the obvious showcase to prove a point. Neither broke eye contact, and the front of the glider tilted upward as Tyrell came to an abrupt halt mere inches away from Chris.

In an instant the glider vanished, and Tyrell immediately took a knee with his left knee bent, right foot on the floor, and right hand behind his back. He looked up to Chris with a malicious grin then suddenly jumped to his feet with a crimson four foot long staff in his hand. A little over three inches in diameter.

The staff appeared to be made of steel or some other sturdy metal, but Tyrell twirled it as effortlessly as a pool noodle. Tyrell inched closer and when in striking distance, he cocked back and vigorously swung towards Chris's sternum. Chris instinctively closed his eyes, put up his hands to block, and braced for impact. Chris felt nothing and he immediately opened his eyes to find an empty handed Tyrell snickering.

"Damn. You okay, man?"

The staff was nowhere to be found.

Chris narrowed his eyes and moved a step closer to him. "How did you do that?" Chris demanded.

"Use your brain, genius."

Tyrell stepped back a few feet and positioned his right arm in front his waist with his hand palm up. Much like the glider, something red began to materialize in his hand and within a couple of seconds, the beautifully crafted red staff had returned, only this time it was about the size of an ink pen. Tyrell gripped the staff and pointed it towards Chris like a sorcerer holding a magical wand.

Suddenly, the diameter doubled in size and Chris watched as the stick extend and crept closer and closer towards him until he felt a sharp poke on his left shoulder from what felt like strong and dense metal.

"Some say that the staff is an extension of yourself. If your mind is weak, then so is the staff, and vice versa. And as you can see...."

Tyrell poked a little harder and as Chris grimaced in pain, he quickly backhanded the distraction as it willingly invaded his personal space.

"I get it, it extends too. You could've just told me instead trying to turn me into the Pillsbury Doughboy," Chris smirked.

Chris hadn't noticed that the staff was back to the original size until Tyrell moved in closer and swung it around as if performing a martial arts demonstration. Tyrell began a flurry of whimsical moves and as his movements became increasingly complex, the streams of red that Chris saw were getting closer by the second.

Soon enough, Chris felt that his personal bubble was yet again on the precipice of being violated and took a couple of steps back. Tyrell took one look at him and let out a war cry as he cocked back and swung for Chris's face. Chris attempted to duck the hit, and once again Tyrell stood empty handed with a smirk on his face.

"You have to keep your eye on the prize in this job, dude. You know you can still back out, right?"

Chris glared at Tyrell as he shrugged his shoulders and blindly took a jump backwards, where his glider was waiting for him. Tyrell continued a couple of laps around the room while he continued to talk.

"No one is going to think any less of you if you decide this life isn't for you.

One injection gave you the power and one simple injection, more or less, can take it all away. It's better than getting killed out there for nothing!"

Positioned behind Chris, Tyrell moved in, hopped off the glider, and used his staff to continue faster and more aggressive movements inches away from Chris. As the wind of every close call brushed across his face, Chris crossed his arms and stood his ground.

Tyrell glanced at his face, which seemed to have a newfound calm. Tyrell grimaced and cocked back a third time and swung for his face harder and faster than ever before. However, Chris refused to budge. He remained still with his arms crossed and watched as Tyrell made the staff disappear within a split second of impact.

Tyrell's smirk quickly faded when he saw that it was returned.

"That's a pretty cool trick."

Both men stood in silence as Tyrell scrunched his nose, pursed his lips, and eyes burrowed with rage.

Within an instant, Tyrell changed his footing and let out a second war cry as he tightly gripped the staff and reversed his direction with full force. Chris's heart jumped as Tyrell's face showed no signs of stopping. Chris instinctively held out his arms and a second later, Tyrell's staff instantly clanked with Chris's.

Glossy and black in color, the metal looking staff appeared to be of similar size. Tyrell held on to his staff with his arms fully extended and body slightly bent forward, which made Chris think of a baseball game, in which the batter had just gone for a homerun.

Tyrell smirked as he let go of the staff, which disappeared into the air. He took a step back and without a word said, he transformed into Red Guardian. The suit was almost identical to Purple's, except for the obvious differences in gender tells and the change in color. The suit had the same leather material that covered him from top to bottom and was all crimson red. His red hoodie was placed on his head and securely attached to a mask that covered his entire face, other than his eyes.

As the door opened from behind them, Chris's staff vanished.

"So, how's everything going in here?" Ken asked as he walked towards them.

"Pretty good, just finishing up one last thing. So, Chris, like I was about to say, this is what my suit looks like. So when wearing this, you would address me as "Red Guardian" or "Red." That's all I have for you. Do you have any questions about anything?"

Chris chuckled softly.

"No, I think I'm good."

Ken interjected.

"Well, in the next couple of months you're going to get a lot of information and training, so you don't have to worry about trying to figure out everything on the spot. However, before we go over paperwork and make arrangements, we can answer any question that you might be really curious or confused about right now. Is there anything that comes to mind?"

Chris glanced at Tyrell as he listened intently to every word.

"No, I'm sure I'll figure it out soon enough. Are we doing paperwork now?"

"No, it's getting late, so we'll take care of it first thing Monday. That will give you a day to rest first. How about you come back here at 10am?"

Chris nodded his head in agreement, and turned to Tyrell.

"Thanks for the lesson."

"Anytime."

Ken led Chris back to the main entrance.

"So are you still interested in the job? As long as you keep your mouth shut, you can still get out of this and you won't have to see any of us again."

"Yes, I know; I can't tell a soul or expect any backup outside this room. Just us against the world, right?"

"Not exactly, Chris. There are Guardians spread out all around the nation and 4G agents all around the world, doing their part to make things better."

"Understood. Well, anyway, I'm definitely all in, but something tells me that you already knew that."

Both men smiled and nodded.

"See you Monday, Chris."

"See you Monday."

Chris exited the facility and walked to his loaner car in the nearby parking garage. He was promised his own make and model to come in the following week, as long as it wasn't too flashy and correlated with whatever cover existence that he had to make up.

Unbeknownst to Chris, the upcoming months were going to be filled with numerous challenges that would leave him both mentally and physically drained.

The more he would learn about his new world and way of life, the more he was going to spend countless hours seeking the answers. However, one lingering question resonated in his brain. As he was thrown into a world of gliders, power suits, and conspiracies, the question was by far the most simplistic. Yet it was the only one that kept him up in the late hours of the night.

That night, he had produced his staff for the first time from pure instinct. He wasn't coached to do it or had any practice time. For months to come, no matter how much stronger and wiser he would become, two questions haunted him: What if he hadn't blocked Tyrell's swing that night, and what if Ken hadn't walked in the room?

# CHAPTER 7

Two hundred miles south of China and six hundred miles west of Australia lay the small country of Bentai. The island flourished with virtually an unlimited supply of natural resources of gold, diamonds, and sapphires. However, the country was miniscule compared to its next door counterparts, with less than two million square feet in size and just about five hundred thousand inhabitants.

Once a month, representatives from the famous import/export Goomay Corporation, which was based in Kula Laumpur, Malaysia, traveled to Bentai to trade goods. The Bentains were humble people and lived a very simple lifestyle. There was no desire to travel outside the country and the most sophisticated product they owned were battery-operated fans. The anarchist society had no use for an established government or military force, for besides the cooperation, they were rarely visited.

Bentai was unknown to most of the world, which made people, especially the elders, very pleased. For generations they had lived a peaceful existence free of war, strife, starvation, and other types of suffering. Living in a society that was virtually crime free allowed mothers and children to wander the area at all hours, only use locking mechanisms for convenience, and establish a working barter system.

Throughout generations, corporations occasionally discovered the land by accident and saw the earning potential of the literally untouched gold mine, among other things. English became very fluent in the country, and although many had tried, Goomay was the first to grasp the culture well enough for an established trade system.

Instead of offering briefcases of cash and property deeds, which the Bentains only viewed as expensive burning paper, Goomay reps offered inexpensive gifts that the average consumer would scoff at. The Bentains happily traded raw metal and jewels for everyday comfort items, and agreed to make them and their affiliates their sole tradesmen in the foreseeable future. After numerous trial and error periods, the company had it down almost to a science as they delivered certain nonperishable foods, toilet paper, various types of perfumes, and something to wow them with, like fishing poles and radios.

The Goomay reps took their time to demonstrate the use and capability of every product and ensured they remained content, knowing that the agreement was nothing short of a steal. One faithful day, the four Goomay reps arrived with an additional two men that represented an affiliated U.S. import/⍰ export company. The company was looking to expand their business and the two reps were placed in charge to set up a deal with both Goomay and Bentai.

Knowing they stood to triple their profits by working with the men, Goomay actively greased the wheels with the elders to have the men assist with the next few trades. Everything went fine at first, but on the second run with the combined U.S. agreement, there was great unrest in the land. Both reps entered a world where the foundational rules of peace, tranquility, and love were quickly dissipating.

Both quickly learned of the unforgivable act that had triggered the spiral twelve short hours earlier: a local seventeen year old girl was missing and a good portion of people had blamed the twenty year old trouble maker last seen with her. With fear of escalation and a civil war that could potentially have them lose everything, reps from both companies decided to step in and mediate as best they could.

With such a heinous accusation in an otherwise peaceful country, the Bentains were overwhelmed, as no court or punishment system was conceived. Even in the rare occurrence of thievery or murder, the public unanimously agreed on the individual's guilt and punishment.

However, in this unprecedented case, the nation was divided as friends and family of the girl passionately pleaded for justice and his blood spilled by the end of the day, while his friends and family claimed the opposite.

The two Americans identified themselves as Barazza and Groves and jumped in to help establish an impromptu court system, where at least both sides could hear the other's side and give equal time. After much convincing, both sides agreed for the court to take place and that the accused's fate relied on whatever the majority agreed.

The Bentains of the feuding villages came together to create a makeshift court with leaves and branches, while the accused man named Tin Mai, remained out of sight. To make sure the process ran smoothly, Barazza and Groves took it upon themselves to represent sides, while the Goomay reps followed their lead to help uphold the peace.

As the trial began, the outsiders learned more of the backstory and why there was such opposing outrage. The name of the young girl missing was named Lu' Sa and she was loved by everyone in her village of roughly five thousand people. With countless fisherman and farmers, search parties were taken to corners of the sea and land, but there was no trace of Lu' Sa.

Her parents painted a picture of perfect saint that, like the other teens in her village, was constantly bullied by Tin Mai. He lived in a nearby village of seven thousand and seemed to find joy in making others miserable. On the day of Lu' Sa's disappearance, Tin Mai was seen pushing her down and laughing as she ran home crying. He was interrogated and beaten, but although he agreed with the lesser accusations, he stuck to not knowing where she went.

All the friends and family from Tin Mai's village backed up his story; although he was rude and inconsiderate, there was no way he was capable of doing serious bodily harm or death. Chaos irrupted as extended family and friends from both sides demanded justice. A brawl between the two villages ignited and only stopped when a village elder was mistakenly knocked down, taking a hut down with him.

The outsiders used their power of neutrality and convinced the crowd to disperse, only allowing the top three village elders from both villages to determine the young man's fate. All seven were whisked away to an undisclosed location and after much deliberation, the elders found it best for their country for Tin Mai to live out the rest of his days, if he would treat every individual with dignity and respect. Tin Mai was sent back to his village with his elders after they agreed to meet the next day to unify their search efforts for the missing girl.

However, hours before the meeting took place, Tin Mai was found dead in his village with multiple wounds and a stone dagger sticking out from his chest. Lu' Sa quickly became an afterthought as the villagers declared revenge for the man who was just declared innocent. All accusations quickly pointed to Lu' Sa's father, who had threatened Tin Mai's life several times before the court dispersed. The villagers demanded for him to be handed over within twenty-four hours, or they would engage war.

Both sides reached out to surrounding villages and the word spread like Ebola. In no time, countryman knew the story and as they debated their opposing views, the country was divided by nightfall.

Fearful that their lives were in danger from an unavoidable civil war, the Goomay reps quickly packed up and decided to head home before leaving was no longer an option. The U.S. reps, however, refused to go. They explained that they could still make a difference and would get a ride from their people when done. The reps tried to talk them out of it, but wasted little time, soon after leaving them behind.

With Goomay out of the picture, Barazza and Groves gathered the same three elders to gauge the seriousness, and just like Goomay, they feared war was inevitable. In that moment, Barazza explained how their names both had "agent" in front of them.

"We are part of the CIA. I know you don't know what that is, but all you need to know is we're going to help you. We would like to do business with your country one day in the future, and civil war is never good for either side. We are going to help you the best we can and we are uniquely qualified to do that. I will act like an advisor for your and Tin Mai's village and my partner Groves will be an advisor for Lu' Sa's. Our job is to get you whatever you want to expedite peace and make sure your people don't suffer. We will stay in your villages, but keep in mind we are not in charge. You all are in charge. Just tell us what you want and we will get it."

The village elders returned to their homes to pass the word as Barazza joined one village and Groves joined the other. Both held onto satellite phones to update progress and fulfill orders of their respective village by calling the nearby Japanese branch.

When settled in, one of the village elders led Barazza to Tin Mai's corpse, which still had the makeshift dagger buried inside his body. Barazza's eyes widened as he looked down at the helpless body.

"My God!"

The elder nodded his head in agreement.

"What you call this?" the elder asked as he yanked out the bloody object and held it in his hand.

"A dagger. Or a knife."

"Knife," the elder repeated.

"Reminds me of the phrase 'Don't bring a knife to a gunfight.' Sorry, I don't know why I just said that."

"What is gunfight?"

"You know? Gun?"

Barazza made the motions and sounds while the elder maintained a confused look.

"Is it as strong as knife?"

Barazza scoffed.

"It's much stronger than a knife! But you don't want that; too powerful, too dangerous."

"We need gun. You can get?"

"Yes, I can get it, but it's dangerous."

"We need gun!" the elder repeated.

"You help?"

Barazza sighed. "Sure, I'll give you guns, but only to protect yourselves. I'll give you handguns. Something small."

The elder looked overjoyed as he smiled and continuously nodded his head.

"Thank you. Good man! You good man!"

# CHAPTER 8

Three weeks had passed since Chris had first entered the doors of the Headquarters and was introduced as the newest Guardian on the roster. It might as well have been a lifetime ago. Before then, he never considered himself unhealthy or uneducated. He worked out from time to time and turned on the news when he ate breakfast on most days. However, in three short weeks, he was already in the best shape of his life and for a while it felt like every day was like an Easter Bunny or Santa Clause talk all over again.

Piece by piece, Chris learned how common truths were fabricated and that multiple incidents were covered up. Especially when dealing with crime. He was often reminded of an A-list movie star in training for an upcoming blockbuster, with the coaches and resources to prove it. Experts from various ranges of expertise took turns to teach him their disciplines.

Whether it was a form of martial arts, skateboarding, kendo, escape art, parkour, boxing, MMA, and numerous other types, the expert taught him on an individual basis wherever the person felt most comfortable. His cover was an entitled rich kid who preferred his privacy and not one instructor was willing to sacrifice the money they were earning just for being nosy.

Just like every Guardian before him, Chris was bombarded with an unimaginable amount of combat and combat related disciplines until he embraced the ones that felt right to him. Chris held onto these disciplines as he stood alone in his training room, completely exhausted and drenched with sweat, as if he had just escaped a torrential downpour. His back leaned against the wall as he made an effort to catch his breath.

There was no coach or other human soul in sight, and yet he was in the fight of his life. He wearily panted as he watched the five Trainers casually walk towards him from different directions. He couldn't help but smirk as the slightly creepy black mannequin looking items approached.

Weeks ago, he couldn't figure out why mannequins would be in his training area or why they all possessed the same militant stance, and unfortunately for Chris, Tyrell was the one to introduce him to why. It was his third day as a Guardian and while he practiced strikes, grabs, and tosses, Tyrell stormed in with a wide grin plastered on his face.

"Hey, man, how's your training going?"

"Good. I think I'm finally getting some of this stuff down pretty well."

"Oh, okay. Have you used your Trainer yet? They're a lot of help as well."

Chris flashed a puzzled look as he shook his head.

"Really? Come here and let me show you how it all works. These things are essentially built like chess programs; when activated, they're only thought is to outmaneuver and beat you. As you can see, there are ten in total and the control panel is behind the Lead Trainer. You can always tell the lead, because it's the only one that has this."

Tyrell stood in front of one of them and pointed out that it was the only one with a small white button at the center of the chest on the otherwise all-black exterior.

Tyrell had Chris follow him to the back of the head, which had a series of touch screen functions embedded on the flat surface.

"The intensity level ranges from one to ten, so the number level coincides with how many you'll have to fight, but it's not that simple. Every increased Trainer also increases the skill for all involved, which means you'll have a harder time winning. Don't worry though, they won't kill you; as soon as you're down on the floor for at least five seconds, they consider that a victory and retreat back to their locations. Are you ready?"

"Whoa, hold on a second. How do I win?"

"Oh yeah, my bad. Every Trainer has pressure point sensors and if you hit enough points, they will deactivate and retreat to their spot. Also, if you manage to hit the white button, then you deactivate all of them and you win automatically. Far warning though: they guard the leader like crazy. Any more questions? No? Okay, what level do you want to start with? I was thinking—"

"I guess level one," Chris interrupted.

"I can learn how it all works and just build myself up from there."

"Oh my God! Stop being a punk, you are in charge of us, aren't you? You better start at least at level three."

"Fine. Whatever!"

"Cool, oh, and you shouldn't even think about wearing your uniform until you're past level five."

Chris watched as he placed the settings at three on the Bluetooth enabled device and then instructed Chris to press the flashing start button. As Chris slowly pressed the button, Tyrell smiled and nodded his head in agreement as he stepped back. The Trainers didn't allow for a second to pass before the leader retreated and one of the other three sucker punched Chris in the jaw and stormed forward for more.

"Uh, oh! You did it now!" Tyrell yelled as he laughed with his arms folded, standing near the doorway. As Chris ducked and dodged follow up hits from his opponent, the third Trainer charged him and slammed him against the wall. As he winced in pain, Chris looked up to see the leader all alone, the white button beckoning him and giving him the motivation to give it another try.

He sprinted towards the Leader, but was immediately stopped by a baseball slide from the first Trainer. Chris immediately tumbled with his back hitting the floor. As the second Trainer straddled atop him and punched, Chris continued to block until three seconds passed. Suddenly all three Trainers stopped and stood up, retreating to their original spots. Before becoming stagnant, they balled their fists and lowered their heads to mirror their counterparts.

Tyrell looked overjoyed as Chris made is way to his feet.

"Damn, you got your ass kicked. You don't be so scared of them! Just think of them like the dolls you always played with when you had your tea parties back in the day. Hell, what am I talking about? You probably still play with them now!"

Tyrell let out a hearty chuckle as Chris rolled his eyes and shook his head. He was getting really tired of Tyrell always finding some way to provoke him when he had done nothing to deserve it. Chris wanted to be considered a valuable member of the team, and knew that the others had a history and already went through things he wasn't around for.

He still felt very much like an outsider and a burden, but worked hard to be considered valuable and an equal to his partners. Everyone seemed willing to at least give him a shot at this. Except Tyrell.

Throughout the weeks, Chris drastically increased his skills, strength, and knowledge as he moved up the levels for the Trainers. According to both Tyrell and Ava, it was a policy for him to beat level five before doing any field missions, and it was a challenge.

As he stood in his training room weeks later, he was in the fight of his life at level five. When prepared and free of distractions, level three wasn't too much of a challenge. Just as he thought he had figured it all out, he moved to level four. That added a Trainer and it seemed that all of the Trainer's skills nearly doubled in ability.

Unlike the level before, they could apparently drop kick now, and even though they never talked, their teamwork was on point. He spent an entire week of getting beat up every day until he developed a solid strategy to win. Once he won a couple of times, he knew it was time to progress to his current level: five.

It had taken five weeks, but now he stood in his training room in the middle of the fight of his life and refusing to give up. Completely exasperated, he leaned on the wall as he focused on the past failures and how this day would be different. Trainers used the walls like skilled parkour athletes, as the Leader and second Trainer remained in the background.

He wanted an extra couple of seconds, but the unforgiving machines charged him head on. He ducked the kick off the wall from one and sidestepped a second Trainer. He dropkicked the third in the chest and increased a little more distance between them. He landed a few solid hits before the Leader and the fourth Trainer punched and kicked from both sides, slamming him against the sidewall.

The glowing white button momentarily taunted him and as he foolishly reached to end the level, the second Trainer grabbed his arm and landed a swift punch to his gut. He then rotated his body and Chris slammed hard on the floor. He was just about to get up when he glanced towards the door way and saw Ava's surprised and concerned face looking down at him.

He remained still and five seconds later, the Trainers returned back to their positions. As Chris stood to his feet, Ava walked to him in the center of the room and spoke first.

"Wow, I guess you just want to go all out on this training, huh?"

"What you mean? I'm just trying to beat this stupid level five, which is literally kicking my ass, as you saw."

"Yeah, anything above level three is really complicated without using your suit. Heck, I don't even think I can beat level five without it. That's brave. It might be a little more of something else, but we'll stick with brave!"

Ava smiled and Chris flashed a puzzled look.

"I don't understand. I was told you have to beat level five without the suit to go to the field."

Ava chuckled.

"Level five yes, but I wouldn't recommend it without the suit, especially with you just starting! Who told you that!? Wait, let me guess, Tyrell?"

Chris's silence and pestered look was all that she needed.

"Man! He really doesn't like you, does he? I don't think he even made it past level five without using the suit, but even if he did, I know he certainly didn't on his first month!"

Chris shook his head in silence. There was nothing to say. Once again Tyrell had set him up for failure in an effort to make him look like a chump.

"Hey, don't worry about it. I promise you there are a lot of cool aspects about being a Guardian, when you get past all of the training and actually make a difference out there. I'm sure you're a lot like us in that way, because we probably wouldn't be having this conversation if not.

From what I've heard, Project 4G is pretty selective on whom they actually choose as a Guardian, since there are so many options to choose from. Well, theoretically at least. I tell you what, I'll even go out with you your first time to make sure certain people don't guide you into an epic turf war your first time out."

Chris was brimming with anger and Ava seemed the perfect person to calm him down. It's like she already knew what was needed to be said and what inspired him. Also, the fact that she was gorgeous and had a beautiful and warm smile didn't hurt matters at all. He agreed to her offer and was more focused than ever to get past level five.

He had used the suit a couple of times before, but always tried to avoid it, thinking it would stifle his success, not realizing until now that the very same training was designed for use with it.

The following day, Chris stormed into the training room and stood in front the Lead Trainer for a second, as if old enemies. He quickly initiated level five and walked back towards the front door.

He made it to the hallway when the three Trainers chased after him had caught up. Like before, the fourth Trainer and leader stayed back. He glared at the three, lifted his right leg in the air, and hopped on the glider waiting for him. He quickly floated back to the front door as the Trainers trudged forward.

Chris closed his eyes, balled his fists. A second later, his blue and white sneakers transformed into black athletic boots, and his grey shorts replaced with black, breathable leather looking pants. His shirt matched his pants, a black hoodie was draped over his head and a grey mask covered his face. Within a couple of seconds, Chris Andrews had changed into Black Guardian. Just like Red and Purple, one color dominated the majority of the uniform, except for the glossy grey hockey looking mask.

Like the other Guardians, the face was covered except for the slits for where the eyes were and pen-sized holes where the mouth sat. The hood sat perfectly on top his head and bonded with the mask; there was no gap in between for exposed skin. The same thing applied with his gloves and sleeves. Black Guardian opened his eyes, ready to finish the job started by Chris.

Black instantly felt an increased sense of power and agility. Moments before he had already been powerful, but now he felt unstoppable as he gleamed at the Lead Trainer. Without a moment's notice, he rushed directly towards the solo Trainer, grabbed its left arm and slammed it against the nearby wall using the Trainer's momentum.

After a couple of swift knees to the face, it was out of commission, which was just in time to duck the roundhouse kick of the second Trainer. Black quickly returned the favor of the attempted roundhouse by using the wall to jump off. With both the surprise and leverage, the Trainer was shortly sent back to its position as well.

As Black landed on his feet, he wasted no time to pull out his staff. A month ago, he would've been hesitant to have the powerful stick materialize just from the act of thinking about it, but on this day, he was ready for it. The suit and all of its accessories were part of him. For better or worse, they were not parting ways anytime soon, and using all of his tools was the best way of survivability.

The other Trainer landed a few punches, and although painful, they hurt substantially less than before.

He hopped on his glider as he slowly moved towards the fourth Trainer and Lead, as the third Trainer chased after him.

At the right moment, he easily ducked the wild punch from the fourth Trainer, hopped off the glider, and ran full sprint towards the Lead. As he attempted a slide, Black jumped over his head and quickly turned around to attack. With the Lead a little quicker, Black switched to the defensive role as he ducked, dodged, and sidestepped the flurry of attacks.

One Trainer closed in on a tackle while the other was inches away from landing a punch, when he finally found his opening and pushed the white button. In an instant, all three stopped, stood to their feet, and joined the other seven at their original locations. Black quickly transformed back to Chris, with a huge smile on his face. He had just beaten level five, which now gave him permission to go out and play.

Chris exited his training room and walked towards Ava's, which was on the opposite end of the colorful row of equally sized structures. Even after weeks had gone by, he was still in awe on how beautiful the entire facility was, especially the training rooms. As he exited his black glass structure and quickly walked past the red and blue structures, Chris was reminded of some sort of futuristic upscale racquetball court, with glass too dense to crack with the swing of a racquet or slam of a body.

Also, the design made it impossible for people to look in or out. When Chris had made it to Ava's purple structure, he pressed he chrome button next to the doorway, which each room contained to allow entry. As the doors slid open, Chris walked into the room, and opposed to being greeted by her hazel eyes and warm smile, he witnessed the intimidating artistry of Purple Guardian hard at work. She was in a fight with seven Trainers, and she seemed to be having a hard time as they appeared more advanced and quicker than the already skilled level fives.

Instead of experimenting with their surroundings, these Trainers fully embraced usage of the walls around them and organized like he had never seen. They kicked off the walls in tandem so if she blocked one, the backup could still finish the job. They also began to use one another as tools and balled up, throwing and rolling objects as others followed up with attacks, all the while making it look as simple as playing a game of hopscotch.

She seemed weary from battle as she breathed heavily and leaned her back on the wall. She placed her left foot against the glass and continued to hold on to her ribs on the right. As she watched them approach in a V shape with the leader in the far back, Purple Guardian maintained a certain calmness and poise through her adversity and seemed prepared as they lunged towards her.

She planted both feet firmly on the ground and her legs, arms, and hands went into a defensive stance. She placed her empty right hand in front of her body and in an instant, her palm was holding a five foot long purple staff. She lifted her left hand to grab the other end as she focused on a target. The fact that she was moments away from being jumped didn't seem to faze her; she moved off the wall and waited.

As they approached, she effortlessly sidestepped the first two, ducked under the one that performed a roundhouse kick off the wall, jumped over the one that attempted a baseball slide to take her legs from under her, and ran past another to face her target: Lead Trainer. As all other Trainers played catch up, one stood in her way to block her path, and as the remaining five closed in, she charged.

The inanimate object showed no fear and no hesitation to get in a stance and await her arrival. When in striking distance, the Trainer clinched its fists and cocked back to swing, but instead of confrontation, Purple shoved her staff in its chest forcing it to lean back. With support of the staff and unwilling aid of the Trainer, she performed a flawless front flip leaving both the Trainer and staff behind.

Finally face-to-face with the Leader, Purple gave him little time to react as she placed both palms on its shoulders, and used them to position herself above its head. For an instant, her body stood perfectly still with feet facing north directly above the Trainer, using its own body as support. Suddenly, her hands and arms rotated 180 degrees, taking its head and neck with her.

As the body went down, Purple landed on her feet as effortlessly as performing a somersault. Just like that, level seven was complete and as the Trainers returned to their spots, Chris was beyond impressed.

"Whoa," he impulsively uttered as he remained near the doorway.

Purple snapped her head towards Chris and her masked face met his enthralled stare.

Suddenly she rotated the mask upwards where it rested somewhere in between her head and the hood.

"Hey, Chris. Sorry, didn't notice you. I was kind of in my zone."

"Yeah, thanks for that. Just when I thought I was getting somewhere, you just proved that I'm nothing compared to your awesomeness."

She placed her hands on her hips and gave him a concerned look.

"Well, you know. It is my job to make you men look bad."

She immediately cracked a smile as Chris snickered.

"Just give me time, Purple. Give me time."

She glanced down and looked at her gloved hands and suit.

"Oh, yeah."

In that instant, her purple leather suit transformed into a cotton workout set, with bright colored sneakers and her long hair tied in a ponytail.

"So I'm guessing you passed level five then?"

Chris nodded his head in agreement.

After witnessing her path of destruction, he was certain that getting past level five was like saying that he could pee pee and poo poo all by himself, but he was wrong. Elated with joy, Ava congratulated and fist bumped him.

"So I guess want to get your taste of the real world, huh?"

Chris nodded his head.

"I couldn't think of anyone better to pop my training cherry."

"Aww!" Ava replied in a high-pitched voice as she sarcastically placed her hand over her chest, as if genuinely touched. They both laughed it off immediately.

"Meet you here at 4:30pm tomorrow? You can join me for a party."

"A party?" Chris looked skeptical.

"Yeah, it's a college party that the Temple chapter this fraternity hosts every quarter. It's actually part of the initiation process for their sister sorority and they head out to the Poconos, rent out a cabin and...well, I'll tell you more about it later. Interested?"

Chris hesitated.

"Sure."

"Don't worry; it'll be fun, trust me. Just meet me at 4:30. I'll give you the full rundown and you can decide if you want to ride together or not.

It should take about an hour to get there."

"Well, I don't have a car."

"Oh! They didn't talk to you about transportation yet?" Ava asked.

Chris flashed a puzzled look as Ava shook her head.

"It's G4's job to provide that kind of stuff. You just tell them the car you want, and they'll take care of it. Usually a car is the first thing they coordinate with you. They must be slacking. Sorry."

Ava explained to him how the main justification of the Guardians' existence was to accomplish missions. A mission was categorized as a planned attack that local forces either couldn't handle or would be forced to risk a great deal of lives. Project 4G didn't take the term lightly because in these rare occasions, one hundred percent participation was mandatory and failure wasn't an option. They were the unsung heroes of a national last line of defense in which losing would cause a catastrophic domino effect.

To stay sharp and be ready when the time mattered the most, it was mandatory for every Guardian to complete five Training Sessions a month. A training session was considered anything in which they stopped bad people from doing bad things. Whether the training session was a bank robbery, mugging, murder, or countless other heinous offenses that existed, each Guardian played their part to make the city a better place, bit by bit.

Chris could barely contain his excitement as he agreed to meet her in two days and left her to do her post-workout stretch. Weeks ago, he was given explicit instructions not to start a Training Session until he successfully completed level five, and now he could finally partake in his seemingly overdue session.

On Friday, Chris met Ava at HQ. She wore a beautifully bright colored summer dress and her long, flowing hair reminded him of a Tresemme shampoo commercial. She led him to the computers, sat down, and opened up a program as she started to give a quick tutorial.

"This program is installed on your cellphone as well, hence the reason why you would need both a finger scan and password to use it. Like I told you before, we are supposed to complete at least five Training Sessions a month and we are supposed to input the details into this program."

Ava maneuvered through the touch screen monitor with her index finger, which contained a colorful and user-friendly array of options to choose from. Animated icons scattered across the screen, each containing its individually colored circular background. Each selection came to life as the various stick figures portrayed images of stopping muggers, putting out fires, rescuing children, and many others.

Ava randomly selected an icon of a stick figure yanking another from what could only be the grim reaper, which Chris assumed was saving a life. A fresh screen popped up, which gave her the option to input the details surrounding that action, and the option to save at the bottom.

"Every session needs to be labeled. All you need to do is identify if it's a Training Session or Mission and the number you're on. The number refreshes every month. In other words, since you're about to start your first session in the month of May, you will label it as TS 05-01. The next will be TS 05-02, and so on, until June. Then you'd start over with TS 06-01, and the same rules apply for Missions. Does that make sense?"

Chris nodded his head.

"Yeah, it all sounds pretty idiot proof."

"We try. The best Guardian isn't always the brightest. Or the strongest, for that matter. Are you ready to go?"

Chris followed Ava to their shared garage.

A few minutes later, they entered the underground garage where two more G4 Agents sat. As Chris followed Ava to her new purple Chevy Camaro ZL1, he made his best attempt to avoid contact with the two agents that were hard at work inside the little enclosed shack adjacent to the garage. He went to them the same day that Ava had recommended, and they immediately handed a tablet with an opened digital form so he could detail his exact vehicular desires.

The man briefly described that they typically match the color of the vehicle with his uniform color, and if he wanted it different, he could just specify. Chris frowned as the man quickly went back to his computer and continued his work. Surely there had to be limitations on what he could get, and yet he was given very miniscule direction.

Just like the other agents, the G4 Agents seemed uptight, and at that moment Chris decided to change that. First he requested his realistic option of Infinity G37, and grinned as he listed a second vehicle. The vehicle was the first that came to mind when he thought about high budget, car chase, action movies, and added features that the lone wolf super-heroes would have in their cars. He figured this would force a long awaited laugh, as well as an explanation of the "do's and don'ts" for requesting a vehicle.

Unbeknownst to Chris, the two were waiting for him to finish, and as soon as he did, they sat the tablet down, escorted him out, and locked the shack so they could make the scheduled meeting on time.

Chris felt guilty, but felt much worse on Friday as he entered the facility. Greeted by the frazzled and apologetic team, he was led to the garage in which he was introduced to a brand new Infinity G37 and the Aston Martin Vanquish Coupe that was priced well over $200,000.

"We are so sorry, sir. The G37 is good to go, but we're still trying to figure out some logistics for the Aston Martin. The car works and we managed to attach the twin machine guns, but we still are having problems trying to figure out a rocket launcher and seat ejection. I know you requested it for today and we've been up for days trying to figure it out. If you just give us a little bit of time, we can figure it out."

"Don't worry about it. We're good."

"Are you sure, sir? I'm still waiting on a call from some consultants."

Chris nodded his head.

"Uh, huh."

Chris's heart fluttered, and he was virtually speechless. He wasn't serious about the Aston Martin and had no idea he would waste so much time, effort and resources on a stupid joke. He thanked them and left to meet Ava. While she explained the computer system, Chris hoped that she would volunteer to drive until he got everything sorted. As they walked towards Ava's purple Camaro, Chris made sure to keep his head down and walk faster as they moved past the G4 shack and kept his keys in his pockets.

The hour long drive to the cabin gave Ava plenty of time to tell Chris all about the party, and the monumental event that was about to take place. The Tri Sigma sorority was one of the most elite organizations at Temple University, and for good reason. To be one of them meant you had a great deal of power and influence within, and well beyond, the campus grounds. Within the school, Tri Sigma was often envied, idolized, and imitated.

Most girls would give and say anything for the opportunity to be one, while most guys would do anything to be with one. Every year, the sorority hosted an exclusive pledge party at a log cabin in the Poconos, and an invite was the only small window of opportunity given for all potentials. No invite meant you didn't make the cut and better luck next year. Initially, Chris couldn't fathom on what his role could possibly be at a sorority party, but as Ava continued to explain, the more he understood.

"This party has been going on for decades, but only recently has it turned into something ugly. These girls all meet up at the cabin with notions of joining a sisterhood and meet all the girls already in. They have music, drinks, and hors d'oeuvres as the pledges feel the pressure to impress and make themselves stand out as viable candidates.

Sometime during the night, the hosts plan for all of the power to go out and the sorority girls gives each pledge a flashlight. They explain that the real party is a half-mile away at a bonfire next to the lake, and that if they make it to the bonfire, they would be considered real pledges. If not, then they would be instantly exiled and won't ever be reconsidered.

"The pledges have to go through the woods to get to the bonfire, but I'm certain that they invite a couple to solely act as a sacrifice to their sick game.

The hosts leave out that their brother fraternity sponsors the party, and many student and alumni representatives scatter in the woods to prey on the predetermined unsuspecting victim. Some of these pigs are even registered sex offenders and have a publicized history of violence, but on this night they all come together as family and are encouraged to embrace their true nature."

Chris's eyes narrowed as he looked towards Ava.

"What exactly happens out there?"

"What do you think? Whatever they want!" Ava glared.

They momentarily sat in silence as Chris cringed at the thought, and Ava tightly gripped the steering wheel as she increased her speed.

"I don't understand though. How are they even getting away with it?"

The question appeared to strike a nerve with Ava as she pursed her lips and took a deep breath.

"Because the world can sometimes be an evil and limitless cesspool.

Some of the victims felt like it was their fault, because they had been drinking and it was their decision to enter the woods in the first place. Others were fearful; they knew that the offender was either a respected member of society or was connected to people that were, and it would take more than the testimony of some nobody to bring them down. Some even moved on and continued to pledge."

Chris shook his head in disgust. "So no one ever tried to stop them."

"Actually, not true. In the past couple of years, there were two separate occasions where a woman went against all odds and tried to pursue legal action. In both cases, the whole situation was quickly dismissed and brushed aside before it gained any traction. You have to think, these are not stupid men; they handpick a victim or two out of the crowd that meet the right criteria.

Typically, the victim would be severely lacking as far as connections to influential people, and after being tricked to consume mind altering substances, their testimony would become questionable at best. However, the best trick is the fact that the majority of girls would run through the same woods and nothing would happen to them, besides a possible scare with the use of a hiding spot, or playful taunts that weren't remotely threatening.

"These are the same girls that bonded together and discredited the 'black sheep" that tried to go against the organization. After a day or two of investigation, both accusers were viewed as jealous and bitter liars that wanted payback from banishment. Hefty sums of money are donated to the cops, which would encourage them to look away even if evidence landed on their doorstep."

"Which means it's up to us to stop them," Chris chimed in.

Ava nodded her head in agreement and took the upcoming exit.

The McConnell family lodge was an immaculate log cabin in the Poconos owned for generations by the prestigious McConnell family. Most weeks out of the year, they rented out the enormous five bedroom, three bath log cabin to tourists for nice profits, which simply added on to their seemingly endless pot. The owners could typically coordinate any date throughout the year, except for three particular weeks. The first was the week of Thanksgiving, where the extended McConnell family would gather and celebrate with a traditional rustic

style feast. Besides the similar setup for Christmas, the last
remaining day was reserved for the annual Tri Sigma pledge
party. The sorority set themselves apart by having minimal
involvement in the annual "rush week" festivities.

There was no point in attracting potentials, because everyone that had a shot in joining was already well aware of their
existence. Legacies and other "shoe-ins" were already contacted and they thoroughly researched and analyzed all potentials
that deserved a shot. They constantly referred to the other
organizations as the dancing monkeys, since they felt the need
to impress clientele with some dance, chant, or rhetoric on
why they were the best.

The pledge party date varied every year, and this year it
would be held about a month after pledge week as a test of
faith and commitment. If a girl showed any alliance to another
sorority, they would be automatically disqualified. All pledges
were given a week's notice of the date and time, and as twenty-
four chosen few grew both nervous and excited, the remaining
hundreds were crushed as the silence indicated "better luck
next year."

Ava was one of the selected few, and although it seemed like
an obvious choice to the majority, Ava worked like hell to be
noticed by them, let alone being chosen as a potential sister.
She came from a middle class family, which meant she didn't
have an automatic in and she had to compete for a spot. However, unlike the rest, she had no desire of ever becoming a part
of Tri Sigma.

Surely, the organization as a whole was legit, but the current Temple chapter sickened her. The spoiled bunch of new
age debutantes knowingly organized a group full of corruption
and an unknown line of victims that would never see justice.
The exclusively secret society would never open up to Ava
unless she became one of them, and for months she worked on
exactly that.

Being a Guardian made it too easy for her to change her
identity and instantaneously become a student at the university. For the past few months, she had worked diligently
on being noticed by the group of girls, while simultaneously
accomplishing Training Sessions at the school. She frequented
parties, games, and other public events and easily blended into
the crowds when need be.

Unfortunately, it seemed that the people up no good had the
same capabilities, but they stood out to Ava like a beacon.

Her physical beauty and extroverted, cheerful personality opened the door for a lot of party invitations of all types. Typically all alone, she was always cautious, and smart with every action made as she sought out her target. Although always the hunter, she allowed for her alias "Beth" to play quite the opposite role. At parties, Beth was reckless, dangerous, and irrational. She never brought a wingman, and yet openly downed cups of Coke and Sprite while pretending they all contained alcohol.

Every offered drink she received either led to a declaration of her hatred for beer, or a disappearing act to trade her mixed drink with something a hundred percent weaker. Much to her surprise, there were a larger number of people around with good souls. Both sexes tried to befriend and watch out for her, with some legitimately offering her a ride home, which they felt she desperately needed.

Internally, the selflessness inspired her, but she pushed them away, as they were not what she sought out. Hordes of men saw the wild party girl as an easy target and openly flirted with her in hopes that she would lose all control of her inhibitions. She increasingly played a role of being sloppy and out of control, which annoyed the majority of men that eventually left her alone.

The ones that stuck around and hung with her, past all of her stumbling, falling and slurring, were the ones that looked past all of her red flags and still saw a potential hook up. It usually meant she had finally found what she was looking for.

The predators, always tried to lead her away from the party to a secluded area, whether it was an empty bedroom, garage, car, or to their place. Most gave her a cheesy line about letting her relax, getting some air, or checking out some sort of collection or listening to music. She made sure to never consume an offered drink and was certain that a handful of men even tried to drug her. While others gave off a line, some simply grinned as she pretended to finish the offered drink as they happily accepted her virtually falling body into their arms and escorted her out.

Every time she was moved to the isolated area, she had to contain her mixed emotions; pure rage for their actions and gleaming excitement from what was going to happen in a few minutes. Each and every one eventually made their move, and although a few accepted her distinct words of refusal, most were to a point that they no longer cared.

Sometimes the guys had accomplices, but with no one around to help her, they felt it was their obligation to take advantage.

Ava embraced her inner actress and reacted to whatever moved her. Sometimes she pretended to cry and scream, while with others she would chant "no" and furiously shake her head. However, before they laid a finger on her or harmed her in any way, "Beth" was instantly assassinated and all that was left was Ava. Her heart pounded with excitement as her cries often turned into laughs and her seemingly submitted body suddenly dished out devastating blows, which would forever change the predators and their views on life.

During her Training Sessions, she learned more and more about the "greater evil" Tri Sigma, and that this was one party she couldn't just stumble into. With the help of G4 and a few well timed and placed scenarios around campus, she quickly stood out amongst the sisters.

For months, she had hoped she was making the right impact, but nothing was validated until the moment she opened her invitation letter. Ava glanced in the mirror and laughed at her excited face, as it surely matched the faces of the true potential sisters. She had been tossing around ideas for months, but with the confirmation that she was invited, Ava worked every logistic to maximize the potential of the elaborate Training Session.

The plan was a two person job and she thought before she may have to beg Tyrell or Max to be a part of it. As she sat in the car with Chris, she was content there was no sales pitch needed for his involvement. He had blind trust in his teammates and their willingness to make the world a better place to live, which she admired.

# CHAPTER 9

Ava was all alone as she parked her Camaro in between a Ford Expedition and Chevy Malibu in the open field adjacent to the immense lodge. It was getting late in the afternoon, but lights from the patio were already illuminated to prepare for the approaching sunset. Before exiting the vehicle, she quickly checked her hair and makeup.

Unlike some of the other girls, she rarely found a need to put on a lot of makeup, if any at all. She always felt sorry for the ones that took hours to get ready and needed an array of tools and aids to feel remotely pretty. Ava quickly brushed her hair and two more vehicles approached the lot as she exited and headed towards the front steps.

Two young and muscular men dressed in tuxedos stood at the doorway to greet her. She quickly recognized the two as part of the football team as well as the brother fraternity, and as she approached, one of the men pulled out a sheet of paper and politely asked for her name.

"Beth Murdock," Ava replied timidly as she continuously looked at the ground.

The man immediately used his white gloved index finger to scan the paper and seconds later responded: "Ah, here we go," as he used a pen to cross out. The second man grabbed her invitation, opened the door for her, and said, "Have a good time," as she entered the doorway.

As soon as she passed the threshold, Ava was instantly greeted by an elegantly dressed tall blonde. Her diamond necklace and earrings sparkled and dazzled under the light of the chandelier as she moved in to give Ava a hug. Ava followed suit to give air kisses to the left and right of her face.

"Welcome. My name is Sophie and I'm the charter president. Whom do I have the pleasure of meeting?"

"Beth. Beth Murdock," Ava responded quietly.

"Ah, well, welcome, Beth."

Ava answered Sophie's questions, like where she was from, why she chose Temple, and what her major was. Then Sophie gave her a quick rundown of the food, drinks, and how all the men were there to cater towards them and make sure they were having a good time. After less than two minutes of conversation, Sophie let her go and remained still to greet the next guest.

As Ava walked towards the lavish spread of hors d'oeuvres and chilled cocktails, she pretended not to notice the door greeter rush towards Sophie and start a conversation that led to them both glancing and pointing Ava's direction a couple of times. Soon after, they nodded their heads in agreement and the man wrote something on the guest list, then returned to his post.

Including Ava, there were twenty-two women in the house and counting the doormen, there were ten men. They wore matching black tuxedos with white gloves and all appeared to be young, muscular students from the fraternity. As the women sought out ways to kill time, the men walked the area and struck up conversations. Most of the women had already banded together and found a common ground with other attendees.

Many endlessly chattered about their life growing up and shared hobbies, and some took advantage of the music and danced together in circles. The majority of the men easily embedded themselves in the social circles, which seemed to increase the laughter and conversation.

Just like one other girl, Ava purposely stayed in the background and as expected, two males quickly broke off to give both special attention.

"Hi, I'm Brad," the man's pearly whites greeted Ava.

"Beth."

"You're pretty, Beth. Would you like to dance?"

"Oh. I'm not sure if I want to."

"It's okay, Beth. C'mon, just one dance."

He immediately grabbed Ava's arm and assertively escorted her towards the dance floor. When in motion, the man transferred his hand to the small of her back as he walked side by side with her, and by the time they reached the dance floor, his hand had slipped down to gently caress her ass.

Ava would have never allowed herself to be tugged along like some helpless child and it took everything in her power to not rotate his friendly hand until he begged for mercy in front of all of his peers. Ava had an extremely low tolerance for such disrespect, but she was no longer Ava; she was Beth.

Brad saw her silence as an invitation and his hand slipped two more times during the song. Both times she raised his hands to the small of her back and ordered him to stop in a shy, faint voice. He apologized on both occasions and after his third slip, she stopped dancing and thanked him for the dance before she walked away.

Brad appeared amused as he happily walked to Sophie as she greeted the remainder of the guests. As Sophie repeated her introduction, and sent the girl to mingle, Brad walked up and whispered in her ear. She glanced towards Ava and nodded her head, and Brad walked directly towards to the doorman and had him write down something. Ava joined in a couple of conversations, determined to never break character.

Bored with stories of the spoiled and over privileged, Ava observed her surroundings while pretending to be engaged. In a room full of twenty-one other women all in their own world, she cringed as she watched the other accompanied loner, and the man who constantly disrespected her. The quiet natured girl calmly and repeatedly pushed his hands back after he groped her large breasts. A few minutes later he repeated the actions of Ava's escort by visiting the president and the door-man.

When the same actions happened to a third seemingly timid girl, Ava's eyes narrowed as she was certain she had discovered the absurd system that was set in place. The entire time she had figured that all the predators were men, but it was apparent that they all followed their orders from the sorority president.

As the third escort reported to Sophie after groping the third victim, it was apparent they were "testing the waters" and received permission before they officially marked ⬚ the victims. The men were perfect gentlemen to the rest of the outspoken and confident women, and kept their hands to themselves as they refilled drinks and added comical insight to stories. Unlike the quiet ones, minimal physical contact was given on the dance floor and their hands remained above the waist at all times.

Her heart raced with excitement, as her acting skills had landed her the role of the helpless prey. Once again, she was forced to swallow her pride and bury the yearning to lay out the majority of the crowd that either were in on this setup, or too self-centered to see what was going on before their eyes. She quietly meandered around the room and waited for the party to change.

An hour later, all the power went out. The sun had set and a couple of girls shrieked from the complete darkness. All of the men and Tri Sigma sisters lit a flashlight and lined up to light a path towards the front door. Sophie stood in the middle of the path with her flashlight in hand.

"Pledges, if you want to live forever as a Tri Sigma sister, then follow me!"

Some girls whooped with joy as all the girls followed Sophie and lined up on the dark porch. Everyone else with flashlights followed her, and the men were the first to hand a flashlight off to the pledges and walk away into the darkness of the adjacent woods with smirks on their faces.

The sisters followed suit and handed out flashlights, until every pledge had one in hand. The remaining few turned theirs off until only Sophie and her pledges had flashlights on. As the sisters took a step back, Sophie paced back and forth in front of her pledges like a Four Star Army General.

"You are all standing here because you were chosen for the distinct honor and privilege of becoming a Tri Sigma sister. To be one us, you must possess a certain intelligence, bravery, and inner-strength we just can't teach. We shouldn't have to tell you how great and powerful we are, so I won't. If you want to be one of us, then you must party like one of us."

Sophie turned around and pointed her flashlight straight towards the wooded area.

"Straight ahead, there is a bonfire party awaiting a half a mile away for anyone who is serious about being a Tri Sigma. If you make it, you will be considered one of us. If not then... well, you know. Every year we have to make a sacrifice and there are dangerous wolves out there, ready to choose their victims."

At the end of her sentence, a ripped, shirtless man emerged from the wooded area wearing a wolf mask that reminded Ava of the Michael Jackson "Thriller" music video. All formal wear was replaced with jogging shorts and sneakers. The man scanned the group of ladies still silenced by the sudden change of events and in awe of his perfectly chiseled body. Most gave him adoring gazes as he turned around to face the woods and bellowed a long-winded howl.

Numerous men echoed from multiple directions and the man sprinted back into the darkness.

A couple of the girls looked uncomfortable, but the majority grinned and yelped with excitement. A small table on the patio contained shot glasses with each pledge's name taped on the side. The glasses were halfway filled with a dark liquid, and each sister cheerfully read their name as they handed the pledge their respected glass. Sophie was the last to grab one.

"Lift your shots in the air and repeat after me: I am a brave warrior, fierce from head to feet. In a world built for the strong, there's no place for the weak. Shower us with blessings, may we show them the way. And may God forgive us for our sacrifices today."

Every woman repeated each line without hesitation, and the majority giggled and cheered as they quickly downed the shot.

"I'm releasing you all, but one more thing: although Tri Sigma is a sisterhood, you are not sisters yet. You are individuals, and therefore if any of you are seen working together or even in close proximity, all involved parties will be disqualified! Ladies, I'll see you on the other side."

Sophie smiled as she walked off the patio with her sorority sisters. The women entered one of the several cars that were lined up and drove off on a path adjacent to the woods. As headlights headed to the same direction as the announced bonfire party, the pledges exited the patio and faced the woods.

Suddenly one girl spoke up.

"Uh, I'm dressed way too nice and look too damn good to be forced to play some outdoor games. My father is the D.A. and I'm already a big deal, so it's really their loss. I'm out, bitches."

As the women watched in silence as she entered her Porsche Boxster and drove away, unbeknownst to her at the time, she would be begging for a second chance to prove herself within a week, and would get earfuls from both parents for wasting such an opportunity for months to come. Ava used the distraction to spit out the liquid substance that she kept resonating in her mouth.

"Well, she's stupid!" a South American supermodel-looking brunette cheerfully announced as she watched the headlights disappear down the winding road.

"Anyone with half a brain cell can see that this is a lesson in humility and to show that none of us is above the sorority. Leave if you want, but for all of the smart ones, I will see you at the party. Just stay away from me until then. Ciao!"

The brunette lifted her dress and carefully entered the woods, as the other girls followed her lead. The girls scattered out and created their own path to get to the same destination. They stayed clear of anything with a flashlight and sought out fire.

Wrapped up in their own world, no one noticed or cared that Ava walked away from the tree line and stood back on the porch. She looked around to make sure she was all alone and turned to face the door for extra security. In an instant, her hazel eyes had become completely purple as she stood in silence and focused on the only accomplice in the vicinity. As she acquired a clear mental image of him, she was also able to mentally establish a line of communication.

"Black, can you hear me?"

"Man, that's eerie," Black Guardian responded nowhere in sight of her.

"You'll get used to it. Listen, they just started, and I'm pretty sure whom the chosen victims are. Including myself, there's a total of four, which means you'll have to rescue all three of them alone. If you need any help, I'll jump in, but I'm counting on you. We cannot let anything happen to these women!"

"How can I tell which ones are chosen?"

"If my theory is correct, it should be relatively easy. One girl has a black dress and one has red, and both are headed towards the far left of the lodge. However, focus on the one with a sky blue dress that's headed towards the middle first. Just looked for the girls that look extremely drunk."

"Or drugged!" Black exclaimed.

"Or drugged," Ava repeated.

"I'm headed in now, good luck to you."

"You as well."

Just as quickly as they changed, Ava's eyes returned to normal and communication was ended as she headed into the woods. She jumped at a sudden loud scream that was followed by laughter. Ava trudged on as she carefully kept an ear out for the screams that didn't end with joy and playful banter.

As Ava followed the path of the two remaining victims, she heard continuous howls, screams, and laughter from all directions. As more pledges made it to their destination, the noise died down tremendously. Eventually, all signs of life subsided in the woods as the party picked up at the bonfire party. Music blared and women cheered in celebration as four women were forgotten and left behind.

Ava bumped into the black dressed pledge and could instantly see why she was stuck in the woods. She could barely stand as she stumbled and clung on from tree to tree. It appeared that she was utterly plastered from alcohol, but Ava knew better.

Like many of the girls, Ava observed her intake and knew she only had a club soda the entire night. The only thing that could've put her in such a state so quickly was the mysterious shot that Ava spat out.

"You have to get out of here," Ava whispered to her, and she looked up with shock and fell on her buttocks, trying to back away.

"Stay away from me!" the woman slurred.

"I wanned na be Tri Simma my whole life! You'll gimme disquified!"

Ava frowned, and reached down to help her up and the woman slapped her hand away.

"Goway! Go away!"

Ava sighed and turned around to see if she could spot the other chosen victim, but instead immediately spotted the "wolf" closing in on them. Unlike the one before, the man seemed much older and shorter. His shirtless body made it impossible to conceal his hairy chest or ginormous beer belly. Ava backed up to stand near the girl as beer belly helped establish a circle around the two with his backup.

"Great," Ava muttered to herself, right before her eyes widened and she began to tremble on cue.

Seeing Ava standing next to her yet again gave the girl enough sobriety to find an opening between the eight shirtless men standing around them and she sprinted past them with heels in hand. Two of the closest men began to giggle as they saw her burst of energy wear off a few steps later and she began to stumble. They calmly followed behind her, and Ava walked towards her direction as well.

"Where do you think you're going, sweetie?" a man asked while he grabbed Ava's arm and yanked her back towards the middle of the circle. All four men watched in delight as she fell on her butt and involuntarily widened her legs to catch herself. Nothing was exposed, but that didn't stop the four from showing boyish grins as they stared in the same general area. Embarrassed and fearful for her black dress, Ava narrowed her eyes and immediately stood to her feet.

She was moments away from pushing past them by force, when she saw the two return empty handed.

"What happened to the other one!?" pot belly demanded.

The two buff looking students shrugged their shoulders.

"We were right behind her, and she just...disappeared. It was the weirdest thing! What about the other two girls?"

"I was trying to get ahold of them on the walkie, but no response. See, this is exactly why we have a plan and a rendez-vous point! How many of us are we missing? Six? They probably got greedy and wanted to keep the girls to themselves. Instead of sharing."

Another man in the group spoke up. One look at him almost made Ava sick to her stomach. Like the rest, he wore a wolf mask to conceal his face, but his shirtless body and wrinkled skin easily placed him in an age group with her grandparents. He made eye contact with Ava and in a disappointed tone said, "Great, so the rest of us are left to share this one girl? I'm going to have a talk with you know who when we get back."

"Please, just let me go. I just want to go to the party," Ava interrupted.

The majority looked at her in surprise, as if they had forgotten she could still speak and think on her own. One of the younger men leaned over towards the guy with the beer belly and whispered in his ear. Whatever was said was too silent for her to hear, but she nearly laughed as the man jumped from beer belly's immediate outburst.

"It doesn't really matter how drugged she is! Look around you. Who is she going to tell? Just watch and learn, boy."

Beer belly turned his attention to his group.

"Alright, fellas, I'll be the first to admit we had some minor setbacks; half our pack is missing and our genius football superstars managed to let a little girl that could barely walk disappear under their fingers. But none of that is going to ruin our Full Moon Party! The other guys are having their own fun while we're still gabbing! Anyone else see a problem with that? Don't worry, I'll get the party started."

A sinister grin emerged on his face as he inched closer to Ava and unbuckled his belt. Suddenly his eyes widened as he looked past Ava and beyond his circle of comrades. As his eyes fixated on the object he began to tremble.

"What the hell is that!?"

One look from the sheer terror in his eyes made the others turn their heads to take a look.

For the first time they laid eyes on Black Guardian, who stood silently in the dark. There was no telling how long he had been there or what he heard.

"Who are you!?" one of the students asked in a demanding voice, but Black only shook his head.

As Ava shrieked and used the distraction to run in the opposite direction, three other men followed her as the five others tried to make sense of what they were looking at. Under his mask, Black silently chuckled at Ava's shenanigans. Her plan to infiltrate the group as a harmless victim had gone flawlessly. The moment she saw him, she knew that he had successfully rescued the three others and took care of the missing members of the "wolf pack" without her needing to get involved. However, there was no point in pretending any longer, as the remainder was already concentrated in one spot.

He also was fully aware that she had waited months for this very moment, and there was no way he was going to spoil any of her fun. He watched as the three men followed her to their inevitable doom and he focused on the remaining five before him.

The oldest in the group tried to influence and encourage the rest of the members.

"You are world class athletes and he's one man dressed like a freak, for God's sake! Spread out and take care of him!"

"Yeah, gentlemen, listen to grandpa! I'm only one man."

The men narrowed their eyes and did as he ordered. They created a V shape facing him, but before they could figure out a plan, Black Guardian smirked as he materialized his Glider in front of him. Two inches off the ground, the board remained stagnant as if an obedient servant awaiting orders.

Black immediately floated inside the formation and aimed for the man that trembled the furthest away from him. The board made a loud hissing sound as if two king cobras were having a heated debate as he moved in closer towards his target. Neither his feet nor the Glider touched the ground as the board hovered. Using the momentum, he lifted and carried the man with him.

The athlete soared towards a nearby tree and as his back slammed against the base, he winced in pain. He used the same tree for support as his body slid down and his ass made contact with the ground. Completely seated, the man looked up at the hovering masked figure which automatically encouraged him to remove his own.

With his face exposed, the man defensively placed his hands in the air.

"I'm sorry. I don't know what you're after, but you can have it!"

"Shut the hell up! What is wrong with you!?" interrupted a man that appeared to be in his 40's.

"Don't you think I have a contingency plan for these things, you idiot!"

Black turned his head to the man as he pulled out a knife.

"I advise you to walk away before I gut you like a fish. When I get pissed off, I get surgical with this thing, and lucky for you I'm still in a descent mood. Walk away now and no one gets hurt!" His speech was bold, but every word was shaky as his knife hand trembled.

Black chuckled and shrugged his shoulders.

"Sure, I guess you can always try."

He walked towards the man and glanced at the younger partners as they moved in closer. The Glider was gone and was replaced with the black staff that he held firmly in his hand.

The resistance almost felt like slow motion for Black, as he virtually anticipated every move. As he effortlessly dodged and deflected the desperate knife lunges, he sidestepped and countered the double tackle from both sides. The only surprise was the gun the old wrinkly man hid behind his back. Instead of fighting, he waited for a clear shot, which turned out to be when Black was going for his third knockout blow.

As grandpa pulled the trigger, Black Guardian initially jumped. The man had closed in to shoot him in the temple, and as the loud bang went off close to his ears, Black immediately chuckled after his reaction. He had been informed several times on the ineffectiveness of firearms to Guardians, and trained that very same way, but he found it hard to unlearn something that was embedded in his head his entire life.

The old man was the last one standing and was shivering uncontrollably as he clung to the gun. Black casually walked towards him and Grandpa let off another loud bang, then a third right before he tripped over a tree stump. Black hovered over him as the man froze in fear.

"I...I'm harmless. I was just about to stop them, you know!"

"Right," Black said as he straddled on top of him.

One gentle punch in the face was all that was needed to put him out of commission.

Ava made it about a quarter mile before one of the men tackled her from behind. She continuously screamed as both of them hit the ground.

"Oh, I'll give you something to scream about, baby. Just you wait."

He made several attempts to grab and rip off a piece of her garment, but every reach was met with a swift a violent kick. As the man increased his efforts, the more violent her hit became. Every scream began to match her attack, and before his two friends realized that he was in any trouble, it was too late; the man was knocked unconscious. Ava went to her knees and began to cry as the two shocked men moved in closer.

Suddenly her cries turned into laughter and her bright and dirty dress transformed into a pristine purple garment. As she stood to her feet, the two young star athletes were face to face with Purple Guardian. One spoke up in an effort to encourage his friend, as much as himself.

"We can take her! I don't care what the hell she is. She's a girl and we outweigh her by like, a hundred pounds! C'mon, let's go! Let's get her!"

It seemed to take forever for either one to make a move, as Purple placed her hand on her hip and sighed.

"Well, boys, I have time, but I don't have all night. Don't tell me the two of you big, strong men are scared to fight a girl. Oh! I know what you're waiting for."

Purple enthusiastically plopped her body down on the ground as she stared at their fearful eyes through her mask. Her hoodie remained perfectly intact on her head.

"This is how you cowards like your women, right?"

Fed up with the taunts, one eventually charged as the other backed him up. Purple happily obliged as she slowly dissected the duo with increasingly devastating kicks, punches, and flips. Taking them through a clinic of impressive moves and hits, she made sure to take her time. Black had finished long before her, but made sure to watch from afar as the men unsuccessfully sought out attempts to gain the upper hand.

Twenty minutes later, all fourteen members of the wolf pack were gathered up and bound together. There were four generations of students and alumni that had been scattered around the woods with wolf masks.

"So, do we call G4 to take care of this?"

"No. We call them for logistical needs. This is more of a public affairs issue, which makes it G3. G3 has to be the shadiest between all of those folks. It's their job to make sure we don't land on public websites and newspapers. From what I hear, they're pretty good at it.

I mean, think about it, how else do we get people like these perverts in any trouble if we're not allowed to go on the witness stand or fill out any testimony about our observations? G3 finds a way dish out the proper punishment without exposing us. Do you have your phone? I couldn't bring mine with this dress."

As Black unlocked the phone and handed it to Purple, she stood next to him to show him how to dial G3. After she made the call, they rested nearby.

"Well, that was fun, but kinda short. I hate when they have barely any fighting skills."

"Not me, I'm still trying to get used to all of this, so I'm perfectly fine with a quick victory, as long as I don't embarrass myself in the process."

Ava smiled.

"No, I think you were fine, especially for your first time. Thanks for the backup."

Black followed her lead and rotated the mask upward in between his head and hoodie, as they both gazed at the full moon above them.

"So I overheard one of those guys say that this is a full moon party. I guess they follow some kind of ritual for doing all of this. It makes me wonder how long these parties have been going on for."

Chris glanced at Ava's saddened face as she continued to look at the moon.

"We can only stop what we can, but at least we stopped it for good tonight. Even if I'm wrong, we'll just keep an eye out and do what we did tonight. Unless you're above this all now."

"Hell, no."

They both looked at each other and smiled.

G3 arrived about fifteen minutes later and asked a few preliminary questions before taking over custody of all of the men. The two explained the attempted crimes and everyone involved before leaving the agents to do their part.

Chris yearned to ask questions on the next stage, but he was instructed not to. A few days later, he was watching the ten o'clock news and it all made sense to him.

He saw some of the same faces that he had pummeled being whisked away by authorities with a caption reading "Eight Men Arrested for Tax Evasion Scam." He realized that it didn't matter what the media header read, because the majority wouldn't question it.

They would serve their sentences for a long time, which would match the length of their actual crimes. He wasn't sure what G3 had done, and his advisors were right; he didn't want to know. However, he felt grateful that they were on the same side.

# CHAPTER 10

Chris returned to his apartment a little past midnight tired and completely drained from his first training session at the sorority party. Although the men were amateur fighters, he had expended a great deal of time and energy playing protector, while remaining hidden until the right moment. He was always a moderate fighter, but the session had showed how much he had drastically improved in the past few weeks.

Even outnumbered, he was without fear; the suit made him feel stronger, faster, and more agile than his already improved body. As his confidence skyrocketed, he felt more bold and daring and didn't think twice when he lurked in the shadows or individually confronted a group of some of the city's most powerful citizens.

The bad guys were sent away, and besides his Training Session log, there was no paperwork to fill out. He felt empowered to lock up anyone that he saw as a menace, probably even kill if it came to it. There were no rights to read, laws to research, or judge to coordinate with. The typically overcomplicated system of justice was much more simplified for the Guardians; they stopped bad people. Period.

As he got ready for bed, his spirits remained at an all-time high. After hours of extensively complicated training, he had finally completed his first session and felt validated. Surely there was room for improvement, but he felt that he performed out of the gate at the expert level everyone seemed to expect from him, with little time and minimal supervision. He had his doubts, but no longer. When he was finished getting ready, he turned off the light, climbed into bed, and snuggled under his warm blankets. Comfy and relaxed, Chris quickly dozed off.

He awoke to the cool air of a barren land hitting his skin. He opened his eyes to find his bed was replaced with a bed of sand. He frantically stood to his feet as the scene looked all too familiar. He was positioned the same distance away from the massive ruin that stood before him, as the same dilapidated highway road remained behind him.

"Aww, c'mon! Not this again!" Chris cried to the dark skies, but he was all alone.

This was the fourth time he was visiting the strange land, and he still had no idea on what triggered it. Ever since he became a Guardian, most of his night's rest remained the same, but every once in a while he was dragged back to the unfamiliar territory. As usual, the main attraction remained the massive ruin, as the peak's bright light beckoned him in the otherwise gloomy world.

"Forget this! Wake up! Wake up! Wake up!" Chris bellowed as he simultaneously slapped his face a few times.

As he rubbed his sore cheeks to soothe the pain, he accepted that it wouldn't be that easy to get out. He felt like a video-game character restarting at the game's save point, as the once distant ruin virtually stood right in front of him. The scenery was just as desolate as he left it and there appeared to be no signs of life still.

Each time he was pulled in, the same host greeted him before he would return to the sanctuary of his bed. The last time he ran into the black robed figure was about two weeks earlier, when he had visited the lands. He was there for only a few minutes before he heard his name called in the distance by a pleasant voice, as if old friends.

As he turned around, Chris could see the black robed man approach him. As usual, the black hoodie hovered over the empty space where a face should be. Within a minute he stood before Chris and immediately pointed out that he wasn't alone this time. The robed man pointed out that two figures dressed just like him approached from the east.

As Chris tried to make sense out of all of it, he was convinced that these beings were coming out of nowhere. Surely he would've spotted two black specks standing out in the vast desert area if they were there a few minutes before. The two looked identical, except one was shorter and smaller in size, while the other bigger and wider. Wasting no time, the biggest of the three walked up to Chris and looked him up and down, using the darkness within his hoodie.

"Chris, now that we're all friends, you need to do something for us: stop this Guardian crap TODAY!"

Chris's eyes doubled in size as he filtered all of the questions going in his head.

"Why? Why do you care?"

The smaller one chimed in and her soft feminine voice was a major contrast to the deep bass he had just heard. She seemed much more calm and rational as she addressed Chris, and the big man gave her space.

"Look, it doesn't really matter why; it's for your benefit anyway. I mean, think about it, what would you really be giving up? You would miss out on risking your life and making sacrifices for ungrateful people that will never respect you? Hell, most of them won't even know you exist and follow whatever trend that allowed their weak asses to be in danger in the first place. Your life would be full of secrets and deception, and you can forget about building a relationship or starting a family. Not to mention, you're working for your government, which means you'll be surrounded by liars and hypocrites on a daily basis.

"Trust me, you will lead a much better life than the path you're going down now. First off, you get the peace of mind of not dealing with us." The female moved in closer and placed her small, white-gloved hand on his shoulder. Like the others, her white arm sleeves helped cover every part of her body as the hooded dark abyss looked up at his face.

"We like you, Chris. We don't want to hurt you. You are a good person and you should live the rest of your life without the fear of meeting us again, or coming back to this place. No more suit means no more visits. However, if you do make it back here, then you've ignored this warning and we will destroy you!"

The female grabbed a pressure point on the side of his neck and drove in her fingers, which sent Chris to his knees in agonizing pain. As he yelled and tried to get her off, the other two surrounded him on both sides and each held an arm back as the female drove in deeper.

"Don't ever come here again! This is our land! Next time, we will not be so friendly!"

A few minutes later, Chris awoke in his warm bed once again. It was morning time and although his body felt rested, his mind was racing with thoughts.

The pain in his neck had instantly subsided as he switched from one world to the next, and there was no sign of ruins, desert, or robed individuals anywhere nearby. His claims to any physician or health professional would easily have him committed at the nearest psych ward to be thoroughly studied. There were no signs of struggle or conflict, and as he propped his back against the headboard, he scoffed on how ridiculous his Freddy Kruger like situation sounded in his head.

As he turned on the TV, the answer to his ultimatum became evident within seconds. The reporter tearfully reported on the innocent young couple that was gunned down a week away from their wedding. As the story unfolded about the unlucky duo at the wrong place and time, Chris knew that he could never cope with himself, knowing he once had the power to make a difference and gave it all up from fear and selfishness.

Later that day, Chris entered HQ and walked directly to Ava and Max, who were sitting on opposite ends of the couch. Engulfed in Headline News on the television, both seemed equally amused as they deciphered which were legitimate and fabricated stories. Knowing he would add seriousness to the mix, Chris waited for the commercial break to interject and stood by as the two alternated joyous banter with the inanimate object.

As the reporter detailed a supposed gas leak which evacuated hundreds, Max painted a different picture of hundreds that were evacuated to stop a terrorist from releasing a powerful nerve agent in the northwestern city. Ava shook her head as a different reporter covered a story of a lone college student that shot and killed his ex-girlfriend on campus, before turning the gun on himself.

The truth was it was a twenty man militia that attempted to make a statement to the world by holding the entire faculty and student body hostage. Chris stood in disbelief as it was evident how much Project 4G and the Guardians were needed in society. As a lovable dog and actress with a big bag of dog food invaded the screen, the three exchanged greetings and Ava asked how he was adjusting.

Chris responded that everything was fine and made sure he had both of their attention before discussing his dreams. No shrink or doctor could help him, but since they started at the same time he became a Guardian, maybe this was a side effect from wearing the suit.

The ones that could clarify one way or the other would be his fellow teammates. He desperately wanted to know, but told the story about the dreams and asked as if these experiences were shared, maintaining a normal generalized conversation. Instead of nods of agreement, his questions led to shared puzzled looks on both of their faces.

Max crossed his arms across his massive chest, which covered the usual two dog tags, one black and one blue, that dangled from his neck. He sat in silence as he pondered every word then followed with:

"No, sorry, man. I haven't heard of anything like that. It's definitely not a Guardian thing."

"Me either. Sorry," Ava repeated.

"It's okay," Chris said. He was interrupted by a loud voice from across the room.

"AAAAAAAAAAAAAAAAAAWWWWWWWWW!!!"

All three looked over to see Tyrell's widely grinning face as he approached. His eyes remained glued on Chris until he was a couple of feet away from him. Tyrell pouted his lips and began to talk in the most patronizing baby talk he could muster.

"Poor Chrissy Wissey had a bad dweam!?"

Un-phased by Chris's silence and irritated stare, Tyrell alternated between sniveling and outbursts of laughter as he continued to pout.

"Whenever I was scared of the boogeyman and monsters I just turned on my nightlight! The last time I used it I was eight, but I can see if my mom still has it."

Tyrell couldn't hold back any longer and burst out into laughter.

At that moment Chris figured that whatever was going on with him was his burden and he would need to face it alone. Whatever the dreams were, he was the only Guardian going through it, and for that reason decided not to ever bring it up to anyone again. His anger was piqued and Tyrell showed no signs of leveling out. Chris rolled his eyes and muttered "whatever" as he retreated to his training room and endured one of the most intense workouts to date. He could still hear Tyrell's taunts as he stormed off.

"Aww, Chris, don't go like that! Bring your sensitive ass back here and let me help you! What do you need, man? A cuddle buddy?" Tyrell snickered.

"Hey, how about if G4 makes you some specially designed Guardian Pull-Ups?

You don't have to worry about wetting the bed anymore!"

As Chris vigorously thrashed around the Trainers, Tyrell stood in silence with a satisfied look on his face. Neither Ava nor Max were amused as they looked up at the gloating man.

"And that, ladies and gentlemen, is our new leader!"

A unified "shut up" was directed toward Tyrell as Max and Ava took turns getting onto him for not giving Chris a chance.

"Obviously, this is something new for him, just like being a Guardian. How are you so sure the two aren't connected, and why are you hell-bent on giving him a hard time?" Ava asked and Max nodded in agreement.

"You should focus more on helping the dude than tearing him down. You can't expect him to perform like a leader if you don't want to take the time to train him to be one," Max said.

"Oh, whatever! If he has such potential to be a leader, then he can take a joke or two! If he can't handle it, the he shouldn't be one! What the hell are you two ganging up on me for!? I'm outta here!" Tyrell yelled as he stormed off.

That day, Chris knew that he was all in and there was no turning back from his duties. He would train and work harder to become one of the greatest Guardians the world had ever seen. He also knew such a declaration would inevitably reunite him with the robed trio that surely wouldn't be happy with his decision.

Two weeks later, the weary Chris had yet again found himself in the sandy and desolate dream world, with no foreseeable method of escape. He decided to continue his trek to the ruin as he awaited to be greeted yet again. Five minutes later he stood at the foot of the enormous structure that stood about one hundred feet tall.

He moved to the center of the nearest side, which started the series of stone steps that narrowed to the centralized peak. The beautiful and inviting light of the eight foot archway still glowed brightly and Chris wasted little time trying to climb to the top.

Instead of being slim and narrow, there was plenty of space for his size thirteen shoes to comfortably stand on each step without fear of tumbling. Although the structure appeared ancient, the steps appeared in mint condition, completely intact and free of cracks, holes, and dents. As he made it to the third step, he heard a familiar voice from behind him.

"Chris! Get down here!" female robe scolded from the sand, like a mother prepared to place him in time out.

Chris turned around and looked at the trio. The two males had their arms crossed in front of their chests, and the female stood in front and in between the two, with her hands on her hips. Even though there was no facial expression to see, Chris could instantly tell that they were in a particularly foul mood. He gave them a friendly smile and waved at them as if they were old friends.

"Hey, y'all! Yeah, I'll be there in a second, I'm just going to check something out real quick."

He turned back around to face the archway and continued to climb much faster and with greater purpose.

"Chris! Chris!!!"

That was the last thing he heard before quick and heavy footsteps came from behind him. He was fully aware that they were dangerous individuals with the capability of harming him. He also knew that he had just hurled a huge rock at an already unstable hornet's nest, but he no longer cared.

As Chris reached his halfway point, he could hear the trio directly behind him. Over his shoulder he said, "It's okay, guys. I'll be right back, just wait there for a second," as he slowed down and timed his steps against theirs. The moment one was in reaching distance, Chris suddenly stopped, planted his feet, turned around, and dished out a swift sidekick to the nearest person.

His face showed amusement as the bigger male tumbled backwards and rolled down a flight of stairs like a bowling ball from The Flintstones era. The glow of the nearby light made the atmosphere feel slightly warmer, which made him feel even more relaxed. He continued the climb as if the other two weren't directly behind him until a swift blow to the small of his back immediately stopped him.

"I don't think so!" exclaimed the female robe.

Chris grimaced in pain as his right hand held onto the affected area and he raised his left arm in the air as if he had surrendered.

"Okay, okay. At least tell me what that arch is all about."

"Something you can never touch. Go back down so we can talk about your actions! We can do this the easy way or the hard way, and please say the hard way. I'm really wanting to kick some ass--"

Her tough talk was cut short as he jumped down to their level and kneed her in the right collar bone before landing.

As she tumbled backwards, the smaller male jumped in and violently punched Chris in the face multiple times. Moments later, the female jumped in as well, but the ever-determined Chris fought off the onslaught. He had landed a good punch or two when he found an opening. He smirked at the evenly matched bout, which once again proved how much he had improved in the past weeks.

Whenever he was thrown into this bizarre land, it seemed the adversaries would always appear when he made a decision to climb the ruin. Surely the light would provide much needed answers for him and he was desperate to get to the top. The longer he simultaneously fought off the two adversaries, the more confidence he gained that he could do it.

He had grown as a fighter and he could take them. They were not going to force him to leave the land this time, but he would leave on his own accord, and only after getting the answers he sought. As his landed punches and kicks increased, the increasingly ineffective duo slowly backed up.

Chris completely focused on the two as they grew slower and weaker. Very soon, they would be done all together. His one-track mind allowed for the third robe to quickly maneuver directly behind him and with no time to think, the male sprinted and speared Chris's abdomen with his shoulder and they both fell to the floor. As the male stood to his feet, all three surrounded Chris as he remained still.

"Think you're really funny? We told you not to wear the damn suit anymore, didn't we? Didn't we!?"

He had tried to transform into Black Guardian as soon as they arrived, but nothing happened. He had tried to materialize his staff and glider, but nothing happened. He tried again as the female straddled across his chest and slapped him a few times.

Thriving in pain, Chris was unable to move a muscle as he saw a shoe forcefully descend on his face.

BEEP BEEP BEEP BEEP BEEP was the next thing he heard, as his alarm clock beckoned for him to wake up.

He awoke in his bed and it was morning again. He quickly looked himself over and felt for bruises, but they all existed in his head. His ego had suffered a massive beat down as the trio had proven to be too much for him. He felt a slight soreness around parts of his body, but he couldn't tell if it was physical damage or purely mental.

He balled up his fist and slammed it on his bed, then jumped up to turn off the relentless alarm clock. His body was well rested, but the mind was weary.

He knew they would meet again and he was determined to get better. He didn't care anymore about what made sense and what didn't. All he knew was that he refused to not only have his sleep disturbed, but also become embarrassed and bullied on top of that.

He grabbed the remote control and turned on the TV for the daily news. Even with Guardians, police, and many other protectors, there was just too much crime to stop it all. Every day the news in Philadelphia consisted of horrendous crimes from robberies to muggings to murders, and this day was no different. He felt like a starving kid at a buffet line and didn't know where to start. For him to help one, would be to also ignore countless others in need.

Suddenly, a yellow strip flashed on the bottom of the screen that read "Breaking News" as the somber newscaster told the story of a dangerous gang that had seized control of a nearby park. They had attacked their third victim, a tourist.

Most locals knew to stay out of that park at after dark, but unfortunately not every tourist received the warning in time. As the newscaster explained the gut-wrenching story of the eighteen year old kid from Iowa who visited his ailing grand-mother, she continued to frown as she explained how a casual jog at a nearby park had went horribly wrong. As she gave her heartfelt "hope is lost" conclusion, Chris smirked as he felt compelled to go for a run.

# CHAPTER 11

C hris descended down the stairway of the poorly lit and littered subway stop in the dark night. During his twenty minute ride, he could physically witness the decline of quality and safety of everything around him as the living areas worsened. As the car traveled from prominent to impoverished areas, added conveniences like security guards, information booths, and vendors quickly faded away. Shortly after the number of bums, hustlers, pickpockets, and other shady characters was at its peak, Chris had arrived at his destination: Friendship Heights.

Contrary to the title, the area was home to some of the worst slums in the city. Many emergency responders, including police and fire fighters, avoided the area at all costs. The brave few made sure to get in and out as quickly as possible. In Friendship Heights, such professions commanded as much respect as gas station attendants, and many responders' lives had been needlessly lost in everything from vendettas to gang initiations to Friday night boredom.

With police distress calls ignored, paramedic assistance avoided, and firefighters handpicking the fires to fight, Friendship Heights spiraled into a further decline of lawlessness. Gangs, drug dealers, and prostitutes ruled the streets as police looked the other way, and innocents ran, dodged, and hid to avoid it. Those with ambition moved away as soon as humanly possible, while those that couldn't afford to or were too stubborn to move were forgotten and left on their own.

For the crimes violent or worthy enough to make it in the news, local thugs often viewed them as a badge of honor, and without fear of repercussion, the culprit often trumpeted their exploits for anyone willing to hear. Such an occurrence had happened the night prior, as the Red Dragon Gang proudly accepted all blame for the disappearance of the out-of-state college kid that was visiting his ailing grandmother.

JOHNNY DUNCAN

He was last seen minutes before going for a jog inside Hope
Park, which was a few minutes away from his grandmother's
Friendship Heights address. Three days had already gone by,
the star athlete was missing and the media took turns to vil-
lainize the uninvolved cops that had briefly scoped the park
during the day and had yet to interview or suspect one person.

Earlier that day, Mayor John Parker held a press conference
on the subject. The mayor yelled into the microphone as the
half circle of representatives held onto their cameras, cam-
corders, and notepads.

"I am so tired of the city that I know and love spiraling out
of control like this! When a harmless young man visits his ailing grandmother, the last thing she should have to worry about
is him not returning from a night jog. The mayor before me
spent countless time, money, and resources to build the oasis
known as Hope Park.

Now only a few years later, what is supposed to be a staple
of change and betterment in Friendship Heights sits in ruins.
When law abiding local residents and our own police department are too afraid to enter the park after the sun sets, then
we have a problem! We've allowed thugs and all types of illegal
activity to take over the once promising area of Friendship
Heights, and especially Hope Park! Well, I say no more; the
time for change is now! We can clean up this city one neighborhood at a time!"

Mayor Parker clenched onto a small broom, gold in color,
and hoisted it high in the air while a small gathering of people
cheered and media reps embraced the photo opportunity.
The mayor momentarily stood in silence as he allowed for the
cheers and applause to settle.

"Citizens, I charge you to stand up and make a difference.
Don't just stand idly by and allow our city of Brotherly Love to
be taken over by low lives. In this technological age, there are
literally countless opportunities to contact your local authorities, so use them! First responders, I challenge you to step it
up! I encourage more patrols and police presence around areas
viewed as problem areas! You all have my unwavering support,
and anything I can do to help this process, say the word. We
can make Philadelphia a better place!"

The mayor hoisted the broom one last time and people
cheered and applauded as he left the stage. Chris had watched
the entire teleconference and he was fired up. He was certain
that the passionate speech wouldn't make a shred of difference

in people's lives, but he understood that it had to be done. The young, white star athlete had a bright future ahead of him, and was visiting the city with selfless intentions.

The public attention had forced the mayor's hand to publically announce his disapproval and show attempts to rectify the travesty. However, like most citizens, Chris knew that almost nothing would change in their everyday lives. Murders and robberies would continue to occur within Friendship Heights and all around the city.

The Red Dragon gang was a powerful and deadly self-contained unit and Hope Park was their home. For cops to storm in and attempt an arrest with just one of their members would be a declaration of a war that would end with a great deal of bloodshed. Every cop in the precinct knew that the Rules of Engagement would extend out to their families and loved ones as well, and no would dare take that risk.

Chris exited the train station and began to walk the darkened streets of Friendship Heights. With streetlights absent, neither the traffic lights nor lights of the distant low-income  apartment complexes helped. Luckily for Chris there was a full moon out, which shown through the black of the night. The streets were littered with trash and a few bums were sprawled out in dark corners.

The otherwise empty streets commanded an eerie presence as he made his way to Hope Park. Even as a Guardian, his heart raced from anxiety of the unknown and he quickly chuckled at himself as he realized the similarities of being on a blind date. Not only was he dually eager and nervous, but he took forever to get ready. In fact, earlier that day he visited the mall, only to pick out something that would impress the Dragons.

Ensuring that he would stand out, Chris picked out the most expensive and "eye popping" workout gear he could find. Shopping with a virtually unlimited government credit card made it the easiest shopping spree in history, as he literally grabbed the highest priced, brightest outfit he could find. The shoe store was the next stop in which he beat his previous record. As the salesman began to pick up steam on his speech on why the new celebrity endorsed KR12s were worth well over two hundred dollars, Chris cut him off to get rung up.

Hours later, Chris carelessly strolled down the street with his matching yellow workout suit with lime green shoes.

As he made it to the stone archway entrance, the illuminated "HOPE PARK" hovered in the center of the structure, with two bronze lions standing on both sides and facing outward. Although the sign was too high for anyone to tamper with, the statues were fair game. Chris saw the graffiti riddled lions as ▨ park ambassadors, which introduced him to a new standard. As he entered the park, Chris was initially surprised that the front of the park was in contrast to his expectations.

There were trees, flowerbeds, and street lamps that screamed beauty and sophistication. Chris immediately followed the perfectly intact concrete pathway that curved towards the right as soon as he entered the park. The brightly illuminated pathway caused by the lamp posts made the graffiti message easy to spot a quarter a mile down the trail.

"DRAGON TERRITORY. KEEP OUT. YOUR ONLY WARNING!" was accompanied with a vicious looking red dragon in the middle of the concrete path. The sign acted as an entrance to a completely different park, which was evident by many shattered, some bent, lampposts.

Trash was littered all around and a majority of the items seemed to be empty beer bottles and potato chip bags. As Chris looked around the park that had once signified promise for the area, he noticed a kid standing off next to a set of bushes. He barely noticed the raggedly clothed little boy that wore dark clothes and stayed out of the light. As the boy stared in awe of his new sneakers, his eyes immediately shot up as Chris addressed him.

"Oh, I didn't see you there, kid. What are you doing out here all by yourself?"

The kid shrugged his shoulders.

"Is everything okay?"

The kid nodded his head.

"Where are your parents?"

The kid shrugged his shoulders again.

As Chris inched closer, all his questions were answered as he saw a small dragon tattoo under the boys left eye. Every member of the gang bore the same emblem on their wrists, while recruits had temporary ones, like this kid.

"Good talk," Chris mumbled as he pulled out his newly-purchased top-of-the-line Bluetooth headphones and iPod and quickly drowned out his surroundings with music. He placed his jogging hoodie atop his head, flashed the kid a warm smile, and waved as he entered the dangerous territory.

As Chris trotted away, the boy shook his head in disappointment. Being twenty feet away and with his back turned to the boy, Chris glanced over his shoulder and observed him already on his walkie talkie reporting the newly inbound visitor. Satisfied, Chris faced forward and jogged away.

Generally, Chris enjoyed jogging; not only was it a good fitness tool, but it had a calming effect as well and gave him time to think. As the fast paced music blared in his eardrums, he allowed his mind to wander and in a couple minutes he had almost forgotten his real purpose for being there.

The increased broken lampposts and scattered debris, however, reminded him that he was not on sacred ground. Understanding that he couldn't afford to be caught off-guard, Chris remained alert and cognoscente of his surroundings.

At the half-mile mark he was greeted by the first self-proclaimed landowner. The slender built man appeared to be in his early 20's and proudly displayed the red dragon tattoo on his wrist, which he waved to Chris as he began to talk. Chris returned the wave as if on a casual jog around the neighborhood and continued his speed.

The man's cocky smile faded as Chris showed no signs of stopping. He could tell the man was trying to address him and his voice was growing louder to get his attention, but he didn't care. The man flashed an angry glare as Chris blew past him and he heard a faint "Hey! Heeeeey!!!" through the deep bass and high tempo of the music. The man attempted to give chase and in response, Chris increased his speed.

It wasn't more than a quarter mile down the road when he found three more Dragons waiting for him. Two blocked the path in the middle of the concrete trail and playfully taunted him with baseball bats in hand, while a third stood to the left in the grass with a big knife in hand. Without hesitation, Chris jogged on and headed towards the right.

As Chris blew past the enraged trio, they gave chase, much like the first man, but with the spur-of-the-moment run, the men found themselves ill prepared. Two had baggy pants that had to be continuously pulled up, while another was far too overweight to keep up. The fourth guy was somewhat athletic, but the street clothes, long chain, and baseball cap he seemed determined to cling to put him at a severe disadvantage.

Chris, on the other hand, was not only an avid runner, but he was fully decked out in the proper gear that gave them no chance of keeping up.

Chris chuckled as a thrown baseball bat landed near him as a last ditch effort. As angry threats continued to seep in on how much they were going destroy him when they finally caught up, Chris fought the urge to slow down and give them an opportunity to stay true to their promise. It was dually entertaining and annoying to hear them with such certainty on how they could end him, when the reality was they wouldn't last five seconds. Chris stayed the course and a few seconds later, he was out of their range completely.

Lit lampposts became scarcer and patches of darkness increased on the trail. He began to rely more on the moon and the color distinctions between the ground and path, when suddenly two bright beams of light lit up from behind. The music playing couldn't compare to the loud motorbikes behind him, and he paused the music, removed the earbuds, and stuffed everything in his pockets while he continued to move. One rode up on his left and maintained Chris's pace.

The man wasn't equipped with any protective gear, and with one glance at his deadly serious demeanor Chris slowed down. Chris and the driver stopped simultaneously, while the motorbike's passenger laughed hysterically and waved a machete. The second bike moved to Chris's right, and the four men he previously ignored closed in from behind.

Two more beams of light helped illuminate the area as two ATV's slowly approached side by side and blocked his path. Two men walked alongside the ATV's towards Chris. As Chris panted and caught his breath, men and machine from all angles boxed him in. As the multiple beams of light shone on him, he could see that almost every member held some type of weapon.

The looks ranged from pissed off to excited; either way, they all seemed determined to get started. Chris kept his head down and used the workout hoodie to conceal his face while being addressed. Chris's silence and composure seemed to rile the mob even further, as threats from all angles grew louder and more precise. One of the members facing Chris stood in the middle of the circle and instantly hushed the crowd.

"So you want to play games? Well, we can play games too. Give us all of your stuff or you die!"

Not letting out as much as a sigh, Chris raised both of his hands high in the air, as if being apprehended by police. Every beam of light from the ATV's and bikes were focused directly on him, and Chris was ten times more illuminated than any operational lamppost.

"What the hell are you doing!? Strip down, now! I want everything from that bright ass hoodie to your corny ass shoes! Don't stop until you're down into your underwear, unless you'd rather go up against a bat or knife. I usually don't like to get blood or holes in my new stuff, but since you had me run a damn marathon to get it, I may make an exception! Now strip!"

Chris remained silent, with arms suspended and head down.

The tension increased and the angry men were moments away from turning into a volatile and vicious mob, disregarding all potential loot in the process. Even with this stranger sorely outnumbered, he continued to disrespect them with silence.

"Strip or die!" bellowed out the leader.

Chris remained silent.

"Ok, then. Let's play," the man mumbled to himself.

He took his eyes off of Chris and looked around to determine his weapon of choice. Suddenly, he heard a loud, "Whoa! Where the hell did that come from!?" emitting from one of his men. As he turned to face him, the man's eyes were wide and his trembling finger pointed towards Chris. The leader turned his head back just in time to witness Chris's black gloved left hand and the right hand transitioning from bare skin to make it a matching set. The men stood in awe and fear as the loud tracksuit transformed to a sleek, black, and deadly design. The hoodie was the last to change, followed by the mask on his face. Black Guardian raised his head and immediately stared down the leader.

"What!? You think we're supposed to be afraid of you!? We're not! There's no magic trick in the world that good to scare us off! We're the Dragons! We run this area!" the leader announced loud and abruptly, and yet his voice and body trembled with every word.

Black nodded his head as he casually walked towards the leader, whom nervously looked around for backup, but everyone stood perfectly still. They stood face to face in momentary silence. The situation felt eerily familiar with the robed figures and Chris made sure to remain aware of all his surroundings. Although he didn't have welts and bruises to prove it, he distinctly recalled a vicious beat down from tunnel vision, which he would rather not repeat ever again.

As the leader trash talked, Black observed a man stealthy moving on his right side.

When the timing was right, he sidestepped and used his momentum to force his body to crash down to the concrete. The man was knocked out almost instantly, and the attempted signal to have everyone to jump in turned out be a warning for all contenders. The Dragons exchanged baffled looks and looked for guidance on what to do next. The leader shared the same expression, but quickly gathered some composure and attempted to manage some control of the situation.

"Don't just stand there! He can't take us all! We're the Red Dragons, and this is our land! We rush him at once! He can't take us all. Why do you think he's waiting for us to move!?"

Black Guardian chuckled and swung his black staff around a couple of times before he forcefully stood it up vertically in front of his body.

"What did you guys do with the kid from yesterday?" Black asked.

The leader chuckled from the question and addressed his men.

"Check it out, fellas; it looks like this freak wants to join our Dragon Cemetery. The first one that obliges him will take complete ownership of that new BMW we found the other day."

Black Guardian looked at rows of sticks that stood up out of the ground with a sequential number on each one. There seemed to be a dozen total, and must've been what the leader referred to as the cemetery. Black shook his head in amazement on how the untouchable crew felt no need to conceal their evil deeds, since they were within the park they claimed ownership over.

"Look, all you guys are going to be restrained and taken out of here. You have two options: lay your weapons down and sit by the tree until I'm done, or I will whoop your ass!" The group paused for a second, but strength in numbers and the prospect of a new car were enough to make a move. The Dragons all came at Black in their own way; some in tandem, some with knives and bats, and some relying on their fighting skills. One by one they all fell until there were only a couple left standing.

"Okay. Okay, man." The final two conceded with their arms raised and slowly plopped down by the nearest tree.

"Damn, that was easy," Black muttered to himself as he called G3. Black Guardian looked around to make sure there weren't any bystanders or curious minds lurking around, and when satisfied he began to round up the unconscious gang members. He used a few zip ties and a nearby tree to link the men's arms and circle them around the stump.

While waiting for G3, Black used his Glider to return to the entrance and scare the hell out of the kid. He yelled that he'd better stay out of trouble and stay in school. One slip up meant that he would return, and the kid would join the rest of his buddies in jail. He chuckled as the kid nearly peed his pants while running away in fright. While he waited, he logged the events of the Training Session using the app on his phone.

Unbeknownst to Black Guardian, every action and decision was being carefully monitored from the moment he entered the park. There were four people in total and neither had any affiliation with the Dragons or CIA. In fact, they saw both ⬚ organizations as a joke, as they consistently analyzed flaws and shortcomings. Given thorough instructions to not be seen, the four remained hidden within some of the further distanced tree line and observed every action with binoculars. The original guidance was to completely destroy the Red Dragons, but everything changed when Black Guardian had literally beaten them to the punch.

Their boss Nero was the one to give them instruction, and although they knew very little about him and that they could individually take him in a fight, they all knew it was in their best interest to follow every instruction without alteration or hesitation. He was a magnificent businessman and leader that seemed to have his hand in virtually every large scale criminal activity within the city.

Every crime boss knew to pass any major action through him and give him a kickback of the percentage. To keep him out of the loop would be a declaration of war, and every major crime boss knew that Nero's enemies didn't last long. His rise to power in just a little over a year was a mystery to everyone, but no one could deny him after his integral role in in the downfall of the top three gangs in the region.

With Nero as the authority, the bosses were unified under one regime, which led to greater profits for everyone and lower crime rates around the city. His power was rarely challenged, but every once in a while some arrogant and stupid gang would grow big enough to became an annoyance to him. For the past few months, this gang had increasingly been the Red Dragons.

The Dragons quickly rose to power in their area, and were made up of a couple of smaller and weaker gangs that merged and unified under one umbrella. As profits rose to a noticeable level, Nero attempted to reach out a few times, but was continuously disregarded. A few weeks later, the Dragons began to operate in ways that received too much public attention, and Nero sent one of his men to give the leader his one and only warning.

Too much public attention would force authorities to step up their game, which was bad for business. However, as news of the missing teen visiting his sick grandmother reached Nero's ears, the time for talking was over. That night, he sent his personal team to destroy any and every one remotely affiliated with the Red Dragons. As the four got into position, they realized that Black Guardian was already in the process of shutting them down.

They called Nero and followed his explicit guidance to observe, but not interfere. One of the four impatiently paced back and forth as Black gracefully maneuvered around bats, knives, punches, and kicks. The hulking man towered at seven feet eight inches and scowled at the whole scene with crossed arms. Not only was he itching for a fight, but he loved hurting people. He considered himself a specialist, as he thoroughly enjoyed the sounds of bones cracking and the sight of blood oozing from his victims as they screamed for mercy.

Besides the money aspect, hurting people and being rewarded instead of punished was one of the main reasons he joined Nero and his cause. While he was growing up, he had always been the biggest kid on the playground or the toughest kid in school. Even during his two semesters of college, before being expelled from excessive fighting and the nasty incident in which he hospitalized five classmates with his bare hands, he was the biggest on the football field.

Even the bravest linemen and blockers were terrified to go up against him, knowing his immense strength was matched with ruthlessness. The expulsion gained national attention and Nero recruited him with the promise of a substantial amount of money, even greater power, and most importantly the guarantee of never having to apologize for the people he harmed. Nero had held up to every part of his bargain, and the man saw destroying the Red Dragons as yet another wonderful perk of the job.

He had eagerly anticipated the opportunity all day, only for his present to be stolen by the meddling Black Guardian. As the others calmly viewed the entertainment, the man angrily stomped back and forth as all of his spoils dwindled into nothing.

The big man glared at his teammates as they watched Black Guardian with interest. He couldn't understand what the big deal was. Sure, he was the newest member and they hadn't watched him as much as the others, but it was the same thing they'd seen countless times before. They knew the extent of the Guardian's abilities and at this point, they probably knew more about Guardians than the Black Guardian himself.

Upon Nero's direction, they've been watching the four for months, and yet the others stood there like he was doing something new. The large man was the first of the four "game changers" as Nero kept calling them, and he was tired of being on the sidelines.

Tired of being the cheerleader to Black's fun, the big man nicknamed Crush let out a low growl and made a beeline to the action. He only made it ten steps down the hill before he suddenly lost control of his body. Every one of his bulging muscles were helpless by the sudden force that yanked him backwards to re-join the rest of the group.

A tall and slender man stood fifteen feet behind him, with his left arm stretched out and hand facing the small of Crush's back. As his hand slowly moved rearward, so did Crush's body and both stopped simultaneously with Crush standing a couple of feet behind where he started.

"Dammit, Skye, I told you before not to do that voodoo crap with me!"

"And what were you planning to do down there, genius? Clean house? Has that big head of yours already forgotten what Nero instructed? You should thank Crush before you piss him off and ruin all of our paydays! He wants us to see what this new guy is all about, so that's what we're going to do. Don't worry, you know our time will come soon; but you have to chill until then."

"Whatever!" Crush muttered as he pouted, folded his arms, and moved a few feet away from him. Skye rolled his eyes as he once again was forced to witness one of Crush's little kid tantrums. Moments like these made Skye all the more impressed by his boss.

Nero had to see some of this coming, when his first order of business after assembling the team was to publicly place Skye in charge and constantly pull him to the side to say "keep an eye on things" and "I'm especially counting on you" when they started a job. It was clear that Crush wasn't the sharpest tool in the shed, but then again, destructive sledgehammers were never designed that way.

The remaining two of Nero's group were too busy entertaining each other to be bothered with much else. The fraternal twins had been inseparable for the majority of their lives, and Nero signed them on the moment he found out about their unique fighting abilities. Individually, they were great fighters but combined, they were almost unstoppable, especially after Nero's gift to them. However, when not in combat, Skye often found their consistently childish and playful attitudes far more annoying than Crush.

Imported from Korea, the duo was only fluent in their native tongue, which made their bond even stronger. Yi was a shorter slender man, while his sister Ya was in equal height and slender build. As Skye looked over to check on them, his expectations were met as the two giggled and reenacted what they had just witnessed.

Yi puffed out his chest, flexed his muscles and let out a low growl as he began to walk down the hill. Ya yelled something in Korean while stretching out her arm. She jerked her hand back while Yi comically jumped backwards and screeched while he fell to the ground. They both laughed hysterically, and immediately caught Crush's attention.

"Shut up, Chinese Connection, before I give you something to really scream about!"

Yi stood to his feel and simultaneously faced Crush with a goofy fighting stance.

"Not Chinese," Yi started.

"Korean," Ya ended.

Crush stared back at them with rage. Skye was the only one with telekinetic capabilities, and as much Crush hated being tugged along, he hated people making fun about it even more. Yi and Ya had little regard for his feelings and could barely contain their laughter as they pretended to power their hands with energy.

"How about you all stop fooling around and focus on the one person we're here to see!" Skye interjected.

He made eye contact with the twins and pointed towards the park: "Guardian. Focus."

Without hesitation, the twins bowed and simultaneously bellowed, "Hi!" Skye desperately wanted to slap the goofy childish grins they shared as they stood up and turned to face the park, but he maintained his composure. They all turned their attention to Black Guardian just in time to watch the remaining two members cower under a tree.

They looked on as Black followed the same typical, overly predictable protocol they've seen many time before. They stuck around and didn't leave until the Red Dragons were carted away by G3, when Skye called to give Nero the update.

"Hi, sir, we watched him in action, and honestly I'm not impressed. I don't even think he's the strongest of the group, so he definitely won't interfere with our plans. Agreed. Yes, sir, will do."

Skye hung up the phone and passed on instructions for everyone to head back to camp. As they watched Black leave, Crush shook his head in disbelief.

"I don't get it; if this guy is our enemy and we'll end up crossing paths in the future, then why don't we just take him out now? There's four of us and one of him! We can do it in, like, five seconds flat!"

"That's not what Nero wants, is why. Not to mention I actually agree with him; if you looked at the big picture then you would too! Compared to us, their whole Guardian program is a joke. We outclass them in every way, and the sooner they realize and accept this, we can move on. He doesn't want to waste time with us going back and forth with them, trying to beat odds that are outright immeasurable for them.

Allowing them to fight on equal footing without any surprise attacks will avoid all of the wasted time and effort of strategizing and looking for some nonexistent weakness. They will be dismantled in one swoop and we can move on. Now, let's go."

As Skye looked for a reaction, the twins showed no interest in the conversation. They could only understand half of what came out of his mouth, but the twins often made out to be ideal employees. They would receive a task, have some fun while completing it, and get paid a hefty sum for their trouble. All of the in between planning was pointless to them. Crush, on the other hand, swelled with anger, but remained silent as he trampled towards his Hummer and drove off.

There was no point in confronting the messenger when Nero was the one making all of the calls. He decided not to waste his breath and talk to the man in charge instead.

Crush entered the luxurious twenty-two acre gated property and parked in his designated spot, then followed the well-lit stone path that led to the immense mansion. Although Nero had many under his employ, only his special four were allowed to share the estate. Nero otherwise lived alone and the place was big enough for him to share without the need of bumping into any them. The West Wing was Nero's territory and Crush stomped down the hallway to confront him.

Crush stood in front of the grand oak doors of the bedchambers, balled his fists and pounded four times as if he was Johnny Law himself. He waited a few seconds and pounded against the rattling door two more times until it was pulled open. Nero stood on the other end, unaffected by Crush's enormous size and heated attitude. He looked up at Crush with distain as he narrowed his eyes on him.

"Hey, Crush, what's wrong now?" he said, as if talking to an emotionally unstable child.

"Tonight was a waste of time for me! We just sat on the sidelines like a team of benched rookies!"

"And you think I expected a Guardian to show up?" Nero asked while his emotionless eyes remained fixated on Crush's.

"Look, Crush, you're an important asset to this team, but if you don't start looking at the big picture, you're going to drive me crazy. Who cares if he did your job for you? I promise there will be plenty more people to beat up on."

"But what about...."

"You all are too damn good to sneak attack one lowly Guardian. I only want you to deal with them at full strength. No excuses, no alibis, and no more Guardians."

Crush exhaled loudly.

"But when will...."

"Soon, Crush! Soon! Just be patient. This is chess, not checkers. Quite frankly, I'm tired of talking about this. I tell you what, since you're so fired up, why don't you fight a few of our beloved Minutemen? Let's say, fifty?"

Crush's eyes widened as his head involuntarily shook back and forth.

"No! No, I'm good."

"Fifty!" Nero repeated.

Crush shuttered at the idea of going against the soulless human replicas with only one design and purpose: destruction. Nero had complete control of the Minutemen, and Crush understood that they would be programmed to show no mercy. Even with Crush and his immense capabilities, they both knew that going against fifty would be a nearly impossible endurance race that he didn't want any part of.

As Crush flashed a look of disappointment, Nero left him with some departing words before giving him time to reflect on his backfired approach.

"Try not to question me, Crush. You should know by now that everything I do has a purpose behind it. We will hit the Guardians when the time is right, and I'm going to need you ready. In the meantime, just follow the instructions that I give you. Oh, and next time you come to my door, act like you have some damn sense!"

Nero slammed the door and Crush somberly walked away to prepare for his fight.

An hour after leaving Hope Park, Chris strolled into HQ. Ken was seated in front of his computer and typing on the keyboard, while Ava sat directly behind him with a poised back and her legs crossed. The blood orange skirt accentuated the beauty of her smooth and toned legs, while she used the center edge of the workstation table to look over Ken's shoulder. Chris walked towards the two and as he was spotted, they both stood up, smiled, and applauded.

"So how was your first session without your training wheels?" Ken asked.

Chris immediately smiled at the question.

"Loved it. It was such a rush to go out there and put an end to a growing problem in just one night. I knew the suit gave you more energy, but I had no idea that it regulates your temperature as well. One second I felt winded and sweaty and the next I had a boost and my body was cool and felt more refreshed."

"Ahh, to be brand new again."

Chris looked at Ava and mirrored her smile.

"So was your first solo session similar?"

"Oh, no, things were a little different back then. Steve wanted us to...."

Her smile quickly faded as her eyes looked down at the floor. "Who's Steve?"

Ken's eyes shot up and he looked at Chris with a worried look, right before Ava looked up and reestablished eye contact.

"Black Guardian," she said in a harsh, almost accusatory tone.

Ken quickly interjected, trying to change the conversation. "Hey, Chris, have you used any of your communication abilities with the suit yet? I know that freaks out people the first time they use it."

Chris quietly nodded his head as he attempted to regain composure and accept the bailout, but Ava's distant stare made it hard to focus. She was whisked away in her own world, where she no longer cared about playful banter or Chris's new discoveries.

Ken continued to talk as he nervously fought against the pending awkward silence.

"Uh, I'm not sure if I told you about emergency transmissions within this region that you can triangulate through the suit. We pick up on the signals from HQ and shoot them off to your suit, where you can turn it on or off at will. All you have to do is concentrate and open that path to your brain and you'll start hearing it. You can try it now, if you want. It's a pretty cool feature, but like I said, communication is probably what freaks people out the most."

As Chris opened his mouth to speak, Ava emitted a barely coherent "excuse me" and walked away. His mouth remained ajar as he watched her walk away and disappear into her training room. He desperately wanted to say something to take away the obvious pain she was feeling, but feared saying anything would only make it worse.

Ken continued to talk about the suit and the ability to use it as a distress call, but Chris's focus was gone. He maintained eye contact and nodded occasionally, but his mind was elsewhere. Eventually Ken caught on and paused and let out a loud exhale.

"Obviously Steve was the previous Black Guardian, and he died a little less than a year ago. He was--"

Ken was interrupted by the sound of the door closing and Max walked in the room with a grey hoodie, white sleeveless shirt, and blue athletic shorts.

Music blared though his headphones and the dog tags on his chest lightly jangled as he walked towards the two men. It didn't take him long to figure what was going on, and he hit pause and wrapped the headphones around his neck.

"First solo session, right?" Max asked as he shook Chris's hand.

Chris nodded his head.

"Cool, man. Good stuff."

"Thanks. I meant to tell you, by the way, like your dog tags. I see that you always have them on."

Chris intended to continue, but the mutual looks of shock and anger forced him to reconsider.

Max unknowingly reached for his dog tags and slowly rubbed them together while he mentally escaped to yet another world that Chris couldn't follow. Chris was silenced again as the man that barely said anything to him mumbled "yeah" in response.

This time Ken had no conversation piece in mind and all three awkwardly stood in momentary silence, until Max excused himself as well and entered his own Training Room.

Angry at himself, Chris narrowed his eyes and clenched his fists as both attempts to bond blew up in his face.

"You've got to be kidding me!" Chris muttered to himself as Max disappeared.

Ken placed his hand on his shoulder and flashed a sympathetic smile. "Don't worry about it; a lot of this is probably my fault. I should've prepped you better on your teammates emotional trigger. I never expected you to hit two in a row like that. Bottom line: being part of this crew comes with a lot of mental and emotional baggage. Hell, if there weren't, you all probably wouldn't have been chosen in the first place. Those emotions and experiences are what drive you and make you far greater heroes than most people in this city."

"Holy crap! Did little Chris actually finish his first Training Session all by himself!? Was it real people this time or another one of your bed wetting dreams?"

Chris cringed as he rolled his eyes and slowly turned his body towards the door. He frowned as Tyrell was already making his way to the two of them with a wide grin on his face.

"Aww, I'm sorry, that was our little secret, huh? Anyway, now that you're officially one of us and doing sessions, I think ⬚ it's about time that I cordially invite you to partake in the Traditional Guardian Invitational!"

"Which is?"

The question seemed to annoy Tyrell as he let out a loud exhale.

"It's nothing but a friendly sparring competition where you would face the reigning champion. It's a great way to learn about strengths and limitations within the group and would probably help with teambuilding."

"Careful, Chris, most of what he says is full of crap," Ken interrupted as Tyrell gasped at the accusation.

"We only sparred to test our capabilities and jive better as a team than when we first started. Tyrell was the only one that made it a competition and only wants to keep it going because he's the reigning champ. But don't get roped in, especially since as the leader you should run this as you see fit. He just wants to feed his ego."

Tyrell was no longer full of smiles as he folded his arms and glared at Ava.

"As I recall, my ego was good enough for you to beg to go out with me."

Ava chuckled. "Beg!? Is that what you tell yourself, Tyrell? First off, you were the one doing all of the begging until I agreed to have one dinner with you. Secondly, you couldn't even make it through one meal without confirming you were the sexist and conceited horn dog that I thought you to be."

Tyrell rolled his eyes and waved his hand dismissively. His grin reemerged as he turned his attention to Chris.

"She was so excited to skip to the fun stuff, she couldn't even finish her meal. Maybe I'll teach you about that one of these days, Chris."

Tyrell seemed entertained, but Ava wasn't in the slightest as she moved in closer to Chris with narrowed eyes.

"I excused myself to the bathroom, snuck out the back, and left him with the bill!"

She rotated her head and focused on Tyrell.

"Tyrell, you are a sexist dog; you treat women like crap and I will never go out with you. In fact, you turned me off from dating all coworkers. So keep dreaming."

" Ava, if you want me to give you another shot, just say so! I didn't know you still thought I was sexy." His grin stretched wider as he saw her appalled reaction.

Ava rolled her eyes and turned her attention back to Chris.

"So, how does it feel to be our new leader? Are you learning everything you need to take over this little operation?"

As anticipated, Tyrell's laughs were immediately silenced and his smile swiftly faded.

Chris shrugged his shoulders and said, "I'm just trying my hardest to get on your levels without slowing you down. Right now, I feel like you are all X-Men and I'm just some dude with a stick."

Ava smiled. "Hey, at least it's a strong stick."

They shared a laugh, which seemed to annoy Tyrell as he crossed his arms and flashed Chris a quick look of disgust before forcing a fake smile.

Ava flashed a satisfied smile and walked away to leave the room.

"So, fearless leader, where was your Training Session?"

"I went to Hope Park in Friendship Heights."

"Friendship Heights? Man, I know that area! They're weak as hell. I think most of them are tweakers. How many seemed like drug addicts to you!?"

Chris gave off a nonchalant shrug, but Tyrell had just started.

"I bet half of them could barely stand when you were doing your killer bed-wetter moves, but hey, to each his own."

Chris contemplated explaining all the details to his flaw-lessly executed plan and how he expertly strategized taking down an entire gang by baiting them in one concentrated spot, but figured there was no point. He no longer cared for the conversation, as it would never lead to anything positive. He was a second from dismissing himself before Tyrell asked another question.

"So, my training room, or yours?"

"Huh?"

"The Invitational. We have to spar it out. Don't worry, I'll be gentle."

Chris chuckled. "Nah, I think I'll pass. Maybe some other time."

"Look, I know what the girl said, but you don't have to act like one, Chris! Be a man and fight me!"

Chris smirked as he waved his hand and turned the other way. As Chris left the room, Tyrell bellowed out every insult he could conjure. From lack of testicles to mother insults, and the more he was ignored, the angrier he became until he was the only one left in the room.

In the weeks that followed, Chris continuously increased his skills, knowledge, and efforts to become a better Guardian.

The number of Training Sessions rose, as well as the countless number of innocent people at the wrong time and place. The Guardians grew as a team and all four quickly turned into a functional and cohesive unit.

Unbeknownst to any of them, each member was consistently watched individually and collectively. Nero's crew monitored every action and move, but made sure to stay away. All four anxiously bid their time and eagerly awaited the inevitable orders to take the Guardians out.

# CHAPTER 12

Thousands of miles away, the small island of Bentai was still in a great deal of turmoil. Heavy conflict ensued as the raging war showed little signs of slowing down. It had been a month since agents Barazza and Groves had set foot on the once beautiful and peaceful land in hopes of building a trade system. When all others had abandoned them, Barazza and Groves stayed with the Bentain citizens in an effort to help them settle differences and communicate.

The two remained on opposite sides of the land so that both sides could be represented. they acted as liaisons between the feuding territories. An invisible line was established which the other side couldn't cross without permission or escort by one of the agents. On a daily basis the agents provided updates and met with the leaders to find some sort of resolution.

Both men agreed to provide an unlimited supply of whatever resources their tribe needed for the fighting to end, but were adamant to remain at advisor capacity. They also explained how their assistance was strictly on a voluntary basis, and the moment either one felt any danger, they wouldn't hesitate to pull out of the country altogether.

With Lu' Sa still missing and Tin Mai murdered, Bentain citizens saw the adopted court system as a broken process and a waste of time. With no rules or laws established, citizens took it upon themselves to ensure justice was served the only way they knew how. Threats on Tin Mai's life from the missing young girl's father were witnessed by hundreds and soon after finding his corpse, friends and family demanded for his head.

It took the gun shipments two days to arrive and Tin Mai's village waited for that day to storm their uncooperative neighbors and exact their revenge. They were only fixated on killing one man that night, but ended up killing nine more that stood in their way and tried to stop them. An uncontrollable spiral of death and violence erupted the following weeks, as surrounding villages chose sides to align with.

The Barazza side elder was a man who was highly respected and his opinion mattered greatly to both sides. Fed up with the senseless killing, he enacted a crusade to re-unify the nation, and for two days the land was at peace. However, on the third day, he was found hanging by his neck, which immediately sent the Barazza tribe in a frenzy. There were no witnesses, so they naturally blamed his only enemy: the Groves tribe.

The members of the Groves tribe pled innocence and pushed for a path of peace, which quickly fell on deaf ears as violence reemerged. The violence grew to epic proportions, as both sides demanded increased armament to eradicate the murderers responsible and finally achieve true peace. Barazza and Groves tried to talk the Bentains out of it, but as both sides ensured the decision was absolute, the agents stuck to their agreement.

The caliber of weapons increased from handguns to automatic weapons to grenades and explosive rounds, and the death count on both sides continued to rise. Neither man, woman, or child was exempt from the horrors of war. A month after Lu' Sa was discovered missing, the population of Bentai had dwindled from five hundred thousand to a little under one hundred thousand.

The issue of the missing girl had long been forgotten about, and the majority of friends and family directly connected to both the victim and accused had long passed. However, chaos raged as new issues and affiliations surfaced. The members ⬜ of both sides were grouped together with family and lifelong friends.

Many had lost mothers, fathers, sons, and daughters, and the opposing side was solely responsible for that. Many yearned for revenge, and felt if they were to stop and give up without justice being served, then all those people would've died for nothing. With that sentiment, war raged on.

# CHAPTER 13

## Training Session 07_03

In the black of night, Black Guardian perched atop one of the tallest skyscrapers in a popular area of downtown. Street lamps illuminated the otherwise dark and empty streets, as all workers were gone for the day. In eight hours, the same desolate streets would be crowded with tourists, employees, and hustlers alike. The Galleria was one of the largest malls in the area and drew a large, dedicated crowd, no matter the weather or time of year.

Regardless of social status or budget concerns, there was something for shoppers of all walks of life. Peddlers and starving artists would occupy the street corners, fully prepared to amaze tourists with the latest card tricks, songs, or dance moves. Chris frequented the area himself and couldn't walk two feet without unintentionally eavesdropping on a conversation, or running into people like human bumper cars.

On this night, however, Black Guardian was experiencing a completely different world filled with peace and tranquility, which allowed him to appreciate the beauty. Glimmering lights hovered above the street of the nearby entrance below him, and he could see the amazing architecture of the various buildings at his eye level.

Suddenly, his peaceful moment was interrupted with a familiar voice: "What the hell are you looking at, creeper?"

Black instantly frowned as he turned around to greet Red Guardian, and waited for the subsequent smart ass remarks that would surely follow. Black smirked as he mentally enabled the internal emergency system.

He immediately began listening into emergency dispatches within the area and Red unknowingly continued to talk. Black could tell by the body language that he wasn't missing anything important as he looked past him and waited for a call worthy of intervention.

His heart nearly skipped as news of a car chase in progress made it to his ears. There were four armed and highly dangerous men in the vehicle, and apparently the cops were having a hard time after the criminals left two patrolmen in a bloody heap.

As Red continued his idiotic rants, Black focused on a spot on the ground a few feet away and moments later his glider instantly appeared. Black in color, the oval shaped glossy object hovered about a foot off the ground while remaining completely stationary, as if an obedient servant waiting for orders.

Red glanced downward and flashed Black a disappointed look.

"Do you not think they can handle this one, or do you just want something you can actually handle to make yourself feel good?"

Black looked up with a surprised expression.

"You were listening, too? Then you know they already attacked two cops. Why wouldn't I help prevent any more?'

"So they can get some payback. They're four dudes in a getaway car; I'm sure Philly's finest can handle it by themselves. Wouldn't you want an opportunity for revenge if some jackass offed a couple of your teammates? Well, then again you probably would get scared and wait for backup or something."

Black rolled his eyes and stepped on the glider. Never had Red witnessed him cower in a fight or do anything that resembled a cowardly action. Yet he felt the need to continuously break down Black's character and wear on his patience. He had learned weeks ago that correcting Red would be a waste of time and energy, and stooping to his level gave him too many middle school flashbacks.

The only viable option he could think of was to ignore most of what he had to say. As Red attempted to encourage him to stay out of it and to look for something more challenging, Black chuckled as he looked him in the eyes.

"Then stay here. You're acting like I invited you or something!"

Before Red could muster some witty comeback, Black Guardian floated towards the edge of the building and jumped off. He effortlessly moved down the side of the twenty-story building as his feet remained engaged on the board. As he made it down to the ground level, Black detached with the glider.

As he sped towards the direction of the fleeing car five miles away, he glanced over to find Red Guardian trailing behind.

Several police units were desperately on the lookout for the four robbers that had managed to break into a bank and escape with thousands of dollars. The planned breaking and entering took a serious turn for the worse when a random police patrol investigated the open door of the bank.

The robbers had spent a great deal of time and money to acquire the proper keys and codes to pull off such a low risk job, but dumb luck lead to a fire fight with one dead cop and one in critical care. Vengeful police units scurried in the streets, anxious to dish some localized justice with the legal process and courtroom bureaucracy as secondary considerations.

While the cops were anxious to find the perpetrators, the world-class professionals, including the top ranked driver, were just as anxious not to be captured. Just as police units closed in on their suspects, the driver forced a patrol unit to overturn and soon after, another crashed into a barrier, ensuring their getaway.

The police scrambled to pinpoint their location and collaborate about their last known whereabouts, but the trail was rapidly turning cold. Escape seemed inevitable for the men, as the vehicle's breakneck speed transformed into a steady pace. Without helicopters in sight and all cars left in the dust, they were home free as there was no one left to stop them. Or so they thought.

Black Guardian followed the path of destruction and tracked the once reckless vehicle that was now cruising at a casual speed. He flashed a pleased smile as the glider accelerated faster than ever before to catch up with the assailants. Just as he thought he was alone, Red Guardian's voice trumpeted in to break his concentration. Black gradually decelerated as he tried to make sense of the loud voice that directly entered his brain without reaching his eardrums.

"Please tell me that lame ass slow speed isn't the best you can do. Watch and learn, rookie!"

Red Guardian emerged from behind him and matched his speed. Black shrugged his shoulders and said, "I'm working on it," but immediately frowned and glared with envy as Red gave a two-finger salute off his temple and sped off. Black was a hard worker and strived to better himself and had come a long way in the past few months, yet Red treated him like it was day one and he was nothing short of steaming hot garbage.

It was no wonder that Red was faster; he had a year of practice over him. But those factors seemed to be overlooked. He didn't care if he would only get some kind of sarcastic response; he wanted to confront him!

Black narrowed his eyes and focused on catching up to the man before him. He scaled up the side of the building and zoomed from rooftop to rooftop as he closed in on the distance between the two of them. Black was a few inches behind when both noticed an overturned patrol car and a second car immobilized by a barrier.

One officer managed to open his door and slowly crawl ▨ towards his radio that had been ejected with other debris. As they tried to assess if the rest of the patrolmen were stuck, unconscious, or dead, the situation drastically elevated when fuel began to spew from the overturned car.

"I'll handle this, you follow the gunmen," Red stated.

Black nodded his head in agreement as Red moved towards the edge. Just as he thought they may finally be on the same page, Red left him saying, "Besides, as slow as you are, I'll have plenty of time to take care of this and still catch up before you find them." He laughed as he flashed a peace sign and jumped off the roof with the glider under his feet. Black was slightly embarrassed and jealous, but he was mainly pissed off.

Black stood alone with a newfound purpose as Red's departing words echoed in his head. He no longer cared how much faster or stronger Red could be. He wasn't concerned with how many training sessions he had over him or what his beef was against him. In that moment, the only thing he cared about was ending the threat before Red realized his own predictions and deemed Black Guardian as utterly worthless.

Black picked up a tremendous boost as his glider leapt onto the adjacent rooftop towards the direction of the fleeing vehicle. With increased motivation and tunnel vision, he had no idea that his increased speed quickly surpassed two local street racers and they momentarily shared the same direction. As the reckless teens turned a corner, he continued forward and within a few minutes found the getaway car.

Black drastically slowed down his speed to match the car's and tactically descended off the side of the building. He kept his head and body low as he crept up from the rear and grabbed hold of the spoiler. With all adversaries out of sight, the criminals thought there was no longer a need to look behind them.

As the radio softly played in the background, all four sat in silence until they heard the loud commanding voice from behind.

"Stop the car! Now!"

Three of the four men immediately turned around and the front passenger dropped his smartphone in the process. The man behind him slammed his back on the passenger's chair as he began to tremble. He wasn't an easily scared man, and he had witnessed many things from his rough teenage years to his brief stint in prison.

He refused to go back and rationalized every bad action as means for survival. He was cold, calculated, and he was rarely surprised. However, on this night, he showed fear and uncertainty as he tried to make out what was peering into the rear window.

He had seen all types of enforcement agencies from police to DEA to FBI, and yet none of them managed to creep up behind a moving vehicle undetected. The eerie ensemble of the black suit, hoodie, and mask were the added measures that took away his will to fight altogether. With eyes wide open and mouth ajar, he managed to only utter one repeated syllable: "Wh-wh-wh-wh...."

"Stop the car now or I'll force you to do it! But I promise you, I won't be gentle!"

Unsure on what else to do, all three looked to the driver for guidance. He sped and rocked the car with unwavering contempt. As Black held on to the car, the driver turned his attention on the shaking passenger next to him.

"Shoot him."

As the passenger flashed a dumbfounded look, the driver repeated with a louder tone:

"Shoot him! Now, idiot!"

One by one, passengers' eyes lit up as they were reminded that they were the bigger threat that had already taken out four police officers, not him. As the nearest man reached ⍰ for his weapon, so did Black. With one hand on the spoiler, he used the other to swing his staff as hard as he could at the back windshield.

The glass shattered and the two in the backseat immediately ducked for cover. As the staff connected with the windshield for a second time and left a gaping hole, the front seat passenger unloaded a clip from his UZI.

The bullets pelted everything on Black's body, from upper torso and higher. The shooter didn't stop until the fifth time of hearing the loud audible click, which informed him that his bullets were expended. Black fell forward on the trunk, still holding on to the spoiler. The driver smirked as the men flashed dumbfounded looks at each other and the immobile body of Black Guardian.

The driver pulled over to the side and stopped the car and he began to chuckle.

"See, what did I tell you? He's probably some old magician that went crazy a long time ago and just escaped the crazy house. You idiots were acting like you forgot how to use a gun or something. Now one of you get this moran off my car!"

The men nodded in agreement as the man directly behind them cracked a smile and exited the vehicle. As the man moved in closer, he felt it odd that there was no blood and his suit was completely intact, but he wasn't given much time to weigh his options.

He had already lost a great deal of dignity and needed as many "tough guy" points that he could acquire. Witnessing the billow of smoke and deafening loud rattle that accompanied the hurling bullets towards the intruder had built his confidence. Without fear of retaliation, the man walked up to the stagnant body with confidence. He grabbed the shoulder of Black Guardian's body and peered into the gaping hole of the back window.

"Man, I wish this freak wasn't already dead! I would've whooped his ass for breaking the window and making the rest of the ride home breezy and uncomfortable!"

As he carelessly yanked at the supposed corpse, the passenger's body unwillingly jerked closer in. As his eyes widened and body trembled, Black Guardian's eyes shot open.

"Wish granted, genius!"

The man screamed while the others stared in shock. Regaining his composure, the driver put the car in gear and sped away. The last thing they saw before turning the corner was the passenger being thrown to the ground and punched repeatedly. The driver moved faster and maneuvered better than ever before.

His true skills surfaced as he did all he could to distance his team away from Black. He no longer cared about his destination or the man left behind; he only wanted to get away from whatever was back there.

He cut corners, ran red lights, maneuvered around sporadic vehicles on the road, and at times sped down the wrong side of the street to accomplish his goal. After a couple of minutes, he calmed down and decelerated from his breakneck speed. The thought of overcoming every obstacle in his way only to be caught by something trivial like speeding was too tragic of a thought; like Al Capone going to jail for tax evasion.

His heart rate stabilized to a steady beat as the men continuously scanned different sectors of the street. This moment of calm was very short lived as they heard a loud thump on top of the roof. Without hesitation, the men in the backseat crouched down and began to shoot as the driver sped up. Holes were riddled throughout the roof as the muzzle flash lit up the interior like a strobe light.

Like the one before him, the gunman only stopped when he ran out of bullets. With bewildered eyes, he lowered the weapon and placed it on the seat next to him. His eyes met with the other passenger.

"Did we get him?"

"I think we had to. The roof looks like a damn slice of Swiss cheese."

CRACK!

As the black staff connected, the front windshield splintered into a crack ten feet in diameter. The driver shifted his body to see the road and the car kept moving. The passenger let the gun go off on a couple of five second bursts, but he lacked planning and direction. The roof was already demolished and their stalker should've perished long ago, but he lived. In a last ditch effort, the driver swerved like a maniac while fluctuating his speed in hopes to throw him off.

As the driver made his fourth wild turn, Black Guardian's upside-down mask peered into the windshield and for added measure, gave off an enthusiastic wave before disappearing again. Irate and embarrassed, the driver yelled as he swerved into a nearby alleyway and sped up again. The driver slammed on the brakes and Black Guardian was sent flying off the hood. As the three men watched him tumble about thirty feet in front of the car, a menacing grin surfaced on the driver's face.

The other two cheered as Black took his time to hobble to his feet, while focusing on the driver. "Mow him down!" one yelled, while the other chimed, "Finish him off!" The driver nodded in agreement and without hesitation, floored the gas pedal and rushed the car directly towards the man in black.

Black Guardian stood perfectly still and squinted his eyes at the impending headlights. Suddenly, Black used his glider to charge the car, which only encouraged the driver to pick up more speed. Black Guardian stayed in line with the direction of the car, and moments before impact, he hopped on the hood and effortlessly floated towards to trunk.

He hopped off just as easily and turned around just in time to watch the driver brake uncontrollably into the wall in front of them, rendering them all unconscious or injured. After checking their vitals, Black started making phone calls. The accomplishment automatically put him in a better mood, but spiked to a state of euphoria as Red Guardian arrived on scene a few minutes later.

Everything was already taken care of and there was no mess to clean up or assistance needed. Black had done well, and there was no logical insult that Red could possibly dish out. As Black continued his phone call with G3, Red remained silent with his arms folded. He looked around the area, then back at Black Guardian as he got off the phone.

"Wow, looks like you got lucky and actually managed not to screw this up! I'm going to head out."

Black smiled and shook his head and Red hopped on his glider and left the area. He accepted the comment as a compliment, knowing that was probably the closest he would ever come to receiving one from the ever pessimistic Red Guardian.

## Training Session 07_39

The night started pretty calm for Black Guardian. He had spent hours patrolling different areas and the greatest threats to society were an adolescent pickpocket and irate drunk. He decided to call it a night and give some attention to his long neglected television. As usual, the DVR was filled to the max with shows and news broadcasts that he intended to eventually watch.

Being a government asset forced him to constantly embrace his time management skills and remain faithful to tasks that were more important. However, he was constantly reminded of the many perks of the job. Shortly after becoming a Guardian, he moved to a place more conducive for his night job.

The apartment was an expensive high-rise that he couldn't have afforded working double shifts at the movie rental store, yet on a daily basis he was reminded how the beautifully constructed modern building was worth every penny. As he entered the gated community with his brand new Audi A8 W12 on the cobblestone driveway, two large stone lions greeted him as a soft orange glow of steady water spat from their mouths into the fountains before them.

Chris was never a materialistic person and didn't care about having the best stuff. Although his car and apartment were both top of the line, it was a matter of efficiency as opposed 🮲 to desire. Living in the high-rise, Chris had greater opportunities of inconspicuously departing at odd hours and head to the rooftop. People were pretty well off and felt relatively safe. Most residents stayed to themselves and were lost in their own worlds, which made Chris mutually happy for the situation, but concerned with society as a whole.

As he exited the parked car and headed to the entrance, the front doors automatically swung open and the night clerk at the front desk looked up and greeted him with a warm, cheerful smile. The clerk had no idea what his name was, or any other detail about Chris, just the fact that he belonged in the building.

"Welcome back, sir. I hope you had a great night."

Chris nodded his head as he moved to the elevator and pressed the button. Two minutes later, he entered his fifteenth floor apartment and propped his feet up as he used the remote control to turn on the TV.

Filtering through his recordings, he debated between a sitcom and a recently released movie, when all the sudden his vision grew dim as if he had just put on some high-powered sunglasses. The shade grew darker until he felt as if he was in the middle of a blackout, although he knew every light was perfectly fine. Unlike his first encounter, he knew exactly what was going on and remained seated as he placed the remote on his lap.

He was being summoned and if he looked in the mirror, he would see a pair of completely black eyes staring back at him. With no distinction between pupil, sclera, and iris, it would feel as though he were looking into a deep abyss of nothingness. Getting freaked out by his own reflection was something he didn't want to repeat. Like before, the darkness lasted thirty seconds and his eyes returned back to normal. However, before they did, a voice entered his brain that screamed out one word:

"GUARDIANS!"

He immediately stood to his feet and rushed towards the nearby window. The call came from Ava, or most assuredly Purple Guardian at the moment, which could only mean this was a distress call. Wherever she was, and for whatever reason, she need help, ASAP.

Whenever summoned either by a Guardian or for a mission, the left eye acted like a next generation GPS that pinpointed exactly where the caller was located. As the system looked beyond dozens of buildings, streets, and other stationary objects, it quickly honed in her position, which gave him a route of travel.

There was no annoying electronic lady to instruct him on his quickest route or repeatedly jabber about U-turns and recalculations. All he had was a destination and it was up to him how and when he would get there. As he climbed to the rooftop, he quickly dismissed the thought of following the roads displayed on the navigation system.

The internal GPS adjusted to the elevation, and gave him a clear view of which direction to go. He took off using rooftops, sides of buildings, his staff and glider to improvise his route, and within a few minutes, he arrived in record speed.

The seemingly immeasurable limitations of the suit continued to amaze him as he continued to increase his speed, strength, and agility. It appeared that the more he was affected mentally and emotionally, the better the suit increased. Purple's distress call had just allowed him to move at a speed he didn't think was in him.

As Black made it to the crowded warehouse and tactically moved into position, he felt virtually unstoppable. Unbeknownst to him at the time, Purple Guardian wasn't bound and gagged like his mind had tried to convince him. In fact, she wasn't in any remote danger at all, but had realized this fact too late and had already made the call.

She was irritated at the people around her, but not nearly as much than at herself for overreacting. Purple Guardian sat on a table on the bottom floor of a huge two-story construction building, accompanied by fifty disgruntled men all around.

The building appeared to have been out of commission for years, as it contained trash, broken windows, and scattered equipment parts. Purple sat on the large work bench with her crossed legs swinging nonchalantly back and forth, as about twenty of the men surrounded her.

From crowbars and bats, to guns and knives, the majority of the angry mob brandished some form of weapon as they maliciously focused on the threat. Others stood guard or patrolled in various areas. Three unconscious men lay at her feet, and the floored weapons in close proximity told the story on how the rest of the group became so hesitant to attack.

"You know, boys, someone is eventually going to have to make some sort of move. I mean, I'm only one girl and my friends are coming soon."

"No one's afraid of you, bitch!" exclaimed the shirtless man directly in front of her. "I think you forgot that I cut you and made you bleed. How's that hand of yours!? Huh?"

Purple sighed, "Actually, not as bad as you think. Let's just say I have magical healing capabilities."

As she spoke, Purple placed her hands in front of her chest and wiggled her fingers as if performing a trick. She exposed the flesh of her perfectly intact right hand and the man's eyes widened as he expected to see a wounded ligament. Immediately following the reaction, she covered the hand back up mentally, which once again blended with the rest of the suit.

"To be honest, the cut wasn't that deep to begin with. Sorry, but kudos for sneaking up on me like that. I honestly thought that you, well, all of you had much more fight in you than, well, this!"

The man's malicious smirk faded and he was rendered speechless, as his attempt to rally his people had backfired.

"Sorry, didn't mean to hurt your feelings. I was just saying, as much time as you all stood still and tried to intimidate me, you all could've tried to make a move, especially when I was injured. Now I'm back to full power."

When she looked around the room, Purple was as equally disappointed as the men's faces. She exhaled a deep breath as she momentarily closed her eyes and shook her head. A select few had gun muzzles pointed on her body, even though countless rounds had already been ineffectively expended. The majority had accepted this fact, though the last of the most stubborn members couldn't get past it.

"Wow, then again, I see that some of you really aren't that bright, huh? You had your chance to attack me all at once from all angles, and maybe you would've had a chance, but it looks like time is about up. My backup is here, and now that I see you wimps won't put up much of a fight, I wasted my time calling them."

Purple Guardian took a long sigh.

"I tell you what, since I have nothing to lose at this point, I'll give you boys one final countdown to hopefully prove me wrong. After that it's game over. Okay, so five."

The men looked at each other, and the front man with the bloody knife nervously raised it to her eye level. He mustered a shaky laugh before saying, "Are you forgetting about this!? You can't intimidate us with lies."

"Four," Purple interrupted as she raised the gloved right hand that was cut and opened and closed her fingers to signify there was too much talking.

"Three."

The leader let out loud war cry and lunged towards her. Purple sighed as she shifted her position and kicked him repeatedly without the need to stand. As the leader fell to the ground, two others opened fire and once again Purple remained seated.

Purple waited for the men to expend the remainder of their rounds. After she heard the clicks of both guns, she sighed one last time and stood to her feet.

"Well, I guess time's up."

Blue Guardian hurled a massive rock at the far right side window and walked through. About one-third of the thugs turned their attention to him as he produced his blue staff and gently placed it on his shoulder, as if he was about to knock out a few practice swings on the baseball diamond. He comfortably strutted his way inside the room and smirked as the nearest gang member anxiously attacked.

Blue ducked the swing of the man's baseball bat and countered with his own, which sent him flying backwards a few feet as it connected to his face. The one hit turned into a homerun derby as the men lined up to take him down and failed miserably.

Red was already inside at the bottom left side and as the fighting started, he ran straight towards the group closest to him. As the three men spotted the inbound Red Guardian at full sprint, they responded by charging him with their two axes and a crowbar.

When close to striking distance to the first man, Red leapt in the air and jumped over the heads of the first two and effortlessly dropkicked the un-expecting third man. Red turned around in time to sidestep and duck a few axe swings from both directions.

When he found the opening, Red grabbed the handle and kneed one in the gut and quickly finished him with a few well-placed punches as the man doubled over. He heel kicked the first man that tried to sneak up from behind and made quick work of him as well.

Black was on the second floor, safely positioned in a dark corner. He had already quietly taken out people in his area, but since the fighting started, there was no longer a point in concealing it. He quickly put the remaining two on his floor out of commission and descended to the first floor and crouched.

Thrown into the chaos, Black looked around to choose his next spot, when three approaching men chose him instead. Each brandished a different weapon: crowbar, bat, and knife, and attacked from different directions. In response, Black produced his black staff in the right hand that was placed behind his back.

He stood up to block the swings of the first man trying to reach him, and countered by sending his bat flying one direction and his body another. There wasn't time to celebrate the perfect execution, as he rolled out of the way from a descending crowbar swing and used the staff to sweep the man's legs from underneath. Black got to his feet as the final man contemplated what to do with his large blade.

His three-on-one advantage had quickly shifted to even numbers and seeing how quickly his friends were decimated, his fighting spirit was fading rapidly. Black stared at the man as his whole body trembled. Regardless of what would happen to him that night, the sheer look of his face told the story of a forever changed man.

Black Guardian dropped his staff, flailed his arms in the air and yelled out, "Booga Booga Booga!!!" as he moved in the man's direction. He couldn't help but laugh as the man dropped his crowbar and took a full sprint in the opposite direction. As he maintained a few chuckles, Black kicked and punched the men that followed up, who were at least brave enough to attack him.

Purple stood on the table when the chaos from all sides divided her crowd. The setup reminded her of a music festival in which the fans could choose which stage hosted the band they wanted to hear the most. Although many in the back had trailed off to a different location, she still had plenty to deal with.

She scanned the room and watched the other three in their own zone and rolled her eyes as Red acted as a guru at a martial arts demonstration. He took his time with each one and only finished with them after he made fun of them and belittled every action.

She wasn't going to hear the end of it when it was finished. Being the only female, he would most assuredly make some type of damsel in distress comment or two and how he was the brave and conquering hero of the story. The fact that they weren't much of a challenge would only add on to the claim, and the more she would show any hint of annoyance, the stronger he would feel compelled to continue.

He was already well aware of her anger towards the average man that assumed they had the advantage just because of their birthrights. No level of training or techniques would convince them otherwise, until she had to prove them wrong on a personal level. She shook off the negative thoughts and muttered, "Oh well, it is what it is now."

Purple Guardian turned her attention toward the crowd of bitter men, and without warning, performed a devastating aerial attack that left one unconscious and one barely coherent by the time her feet hit the ground. She began to hip throw the first few men to try and take a swing at her, then upgraded to kicks and flips.

All four Guardians shared the idea of migrating any adversary that lasted long enough towards the center. As they made it to the center of the room, there were only three members of the gang still standing. The trio was frozen with fear as each Guardian blocked all potential escape paths. Evidence of their work was scattered all around the room, and all hopes of overcoming the odds was diminished.

Red Guardian moved in closer as he focused on the men and immediately spoke up, as if the host of a game show. "Alright, fellas, check it out. We're the Guardians. Tell your mom, your sisters, your cousins; it's real. Just like we did with everyone else in this room, we are seconds away from whooping your asses and having you all hauled off to jail."

Their expressions barely changed, as their threshold for fear was already maximized. Black was about to instruct them to drop their weapons and sit on their hands, but Red continued.

"Now that I'm thinking about it, there is one way to avoid all of this; no jail time and you would go home tonight looking like heroes to your crew.

All you have to do is get past one of us. I know it's a long shot, but hell, if I were in your shoes I would take it."

Everyone, including his teammates, shared puzzled looks, and with the captivated audience, he continued.

"Don't focus on all of us; you really only have to get past one of us. So I would recommend the weakest link of the group. You see that Black Guardian over there? I would aim in that direction."

"What the hell is your problem?" Black yelled.

"You are so foul!" Purple said.

"You need to chill," Blue said.

Red shrugged his shoulders at his critics.

"Hey, just one man's opinion. Am I not entitled to have my own?"

Red turned his attention back to the men and addressed them in an uncharacteristically monotone voice.

"No, they're right, guys. I guess you are all going to jail and there's nothing you can do about it. Maybe you can get a fresh start after twenty years or so."

Before there was any more time to respond, they rushed Black one by one and he effortlessly took them down while concentrating on Red. When they were all down, he stormed to Red Guardian and gave him a hard shove.

"And what the hell makes you all high and mighty? You're not better than me!"

Red Guardian quickly scanned the area one last time before he removed the mask on his face. He portrayed an amused expression as he closed in the distance caused by the push.

"How about you not put your hands on me again? Unless, of course, you finally want to man up and do our sparring exhibition at HQ."

"I'm not going to be part of some stupid game just to add to your overly inflated ego!"

Red smiled and nodded his head dismissively.

"Whatever you say, punk ass."

"How about you boys stop with your pee-pee match and just leave? Our job is done and Blue and I can wait for G3," Purple stated.

"Cool. Peace!" Red kept his two fingers suspended as he hopped on his glider and floated away.

Without a word said, Black forcefully jumped on his glider and rushed the opposite direction.

As he headed home, he fought against every desire to call up Red and invite him to HQ for some hands-on training. However, knowing that he would take the whole thing on a personal level, he figured it best to ignore desires and do what was best for the team.

As he made it home, he had yet to calm down and suddenly it hit him why. Red talked a lot of needless crap, which he was always able to bypass. However, Purple Guardian was a different story. She had lumped them together in the same category, that both had contributed in their spat.

He was unsure if that was her intention, but Red had already ruined any potential date or hangout with the girl Black was infatuated with. He was essentially rejected before he could even ask the question, and he refused to show anyone that he was remotely like the man responsible. He went to bed angry, ready to restart to a new day.

# CHAPTER 14

It was a warm, sunny afternoon with a mild breeze when Chris was summoned for his first mission. At the time he was mall shopping with his newfound friend Ashley, although he only used the word "friend" to be nice and eliminate confusion. In reality, she was a constant annoyance that roped him into things he had no interest in.

The culinary professor was new to the city and had recently moved into the same apartment complex as him. He was immediately drawn to the beautiful redhead with her long curly hair, brown eyes, freckled nose, and a fit body that contradicted his imagination of a "food expert" in every way.

A few weeks ago, Chris had come home to find her struggling to move boxes into her apartment and he immediately jumped in to assist. Thirty minutes later, Ashley was all moved in and offered Chris dinner, which he happily accepted. Later that night, the two dined out, patrolled the city, and shared two romantic kisses with the city's beauty as a backdrop.

Weeks later, he was regretting every one of those decisions as he tried his hardest to avoid her. She was a nice woman and he enjoyed talking to her, but her overbearing personality and lack of friends sent her over unannounced all of the time. At least twice a week she incessantly knocked and returned until he would taste whatever concoction that she created.

The food was always delicious, but he wasn't always hungry. Sometimes she would catch him right after he ate, which never mattered to her. She wasn't satisfied until he had a couple of tastings of her work and raved on the spot.

Although Chris wasn't home a lot, he had to walk past her apartment to get to his own, and in many cases he was bombarded with tastings and endless chattering before he would get his door open. Privacy and personal time was a concept lost on a girl that didn't even come close to reaching "girlfriend" status.

Weeks later, Ashley wanted to go shopping for new supplies and Chris couldn't think of an excuse fast enough to block her fast-paced thoughts.

Chris followed Ashley from store to store like a lost puppy, all the while trying to think of an excuse believable enough to get him out of there, but sincere enough for him not to come off like a jerk. Either way he looked at it, Ashley lived in his apartment and if she put in so much energy just to see him as a friend, he was terrified to find out what she would do as a jilted enemy with extra time on her hands.

They had only been on one date, and yet weeks later she seemed to be holding onto the kiss like a declaration of love. Chris often wondered how long she would she hold onto hurt and rejected feelings if it came down to it and concluded that he'd rather not find out if he could help it. He had broken the cardinal rule of not trying to date people he had to live with and now he was paying for it.

As Ashley babbled about the past week and her debate on making restaurant quality French toast, Chris let out an occasional "uh huh," which was more than satisfying for her. Although she was a nice girl, she was a little ditzy, little self-absorbed, and completely not his type.

Suddenly Chris's eyes began to darken and he quickly closed them right before they turned completely black. He used both index and middle fingers to rub the sides of his head while reading the message that came across his left eye.

The short and concise message instructed him to report to HQ and thirty seconds later he could feel his eyes turning back to normal. He opened his eyes to find his pretend headache was unnecessary, as Ashley had continued talking about frying pans. Only after he missed one of his cues did Ashley turn to look at him.

"Are you okay?"

Chris looked shocked as he yanked out his cellphone and pretended to be late for work. The excuse was weak by itself, but he made sure to add, "I can't believe how much you made me lose track of time."

Ashley immediately grinned from ear to ear.

"Oh, okay. I understand; I don't think you ever told me what you did, by the way."

"Secret Agent," Chris smiled as she let out a soft chuckle.

"Yeah, right. That reminds me of this one time I went to England."

"Story for later? I have to get going."

Ashley nodded her head in agreement.

"Go save the world for now, Mr. Bond. Next time I want to know what you really do."

Chris nodded in agreement.

"Sure, I'll tell you all about it when I have a little more time."

Chris flashed one last warm smile and waved goodbye as he turned away. With his back turned he muttered a deep-rooted "Not!" and headed for the door.

"Wait, but I drove you here. How are you doing to get to work?" she yelled towards his back.

He stopped and looked over his shoulder with a smile. "I'll find a way."

Ava was sharing lunch with an old friend when she received the call. Although assumed by some that they were best friends, they hardly had anything in common. Minimizing interaction was the best way to not allow the awkwardness to set in. Her name was Crystal and she walked a completely different path than Ava in almost every way. She would've ended all communication long ago if it weren't for their one and only shared interest and a promise Ava had made to herself.

Ava had met Crystal when Ava was a high school junior, which was the same year of the tragic and unforgettable incident that would bond them forever. It all started and ended with a boy named Desmond. Unlike Crystal, Desmond was in the same graduating class as Ava and she made a point to avoid him like a penicillin shot to the eye.

At this point, she had known Desmond for years and as far back as she could remember, he had a crush on her. Although the feelings were never returned, she made a point to always be nice to him, since over half the student body made fun of him on a daily basis.

She was not blind to his quirky personality and the consistently weird things he did that set him apart from the majority. He flashed a satisfied smile and took a long whiff of her hair whenever she walked by and shamelessly attempted to kiss her shoes whenever she mistakenly crossed his path or bumped into him. Although taken aback by his actions, she never felt them justified for him to be bullied as he was.

One fateful day Desmond decided to proclaim his undying love to her during lunch period. As a cheerleader, a member of the volleyball team, and a local ballet group, Ava was vastly popular. However, the fact that she had a contagiously friendly personality, combined with the majority of classmates finding her gorgeous, placed her on a whole new level.

Desmond, on the other hand, was a declared loser, a nobody, an embarrassment. On the day of his declaration of love, people took offense to him having the audacity to speak her name, let alone declaring his feelings about her. As if he even had a chance with her.

From that moment on, his hazing intensified drastically as he was jeered, ridiculed, and beaten until he was eventually forced to move schools. He departed right before midterms and Ava was grateful. She no longer cared about how he made her feel; she just wanted him to not suffer anymore.

Although he was strange, she felt that no kid should've endured so much in their pursuit of education. He was big in stature and had probably done some damage, but never sought out revenge on his attackers. Not even the smaller ones when he found them alone.

When he eventually moved schools, Ava thought that the story of Desmond would soon come to an end, as the sheep would flock to a new favorite subject. She was mistaken. His story became legend as it quickly spun out of proportion. The number of storytellers increased and extended to classmates who weren't present for any of it; a few weren't even students at the school.

Different versions of the seemingly firsthand accounts spread around the school; the story of the weird kid unwisely confessing his crush transformed into a story of a helpless girl being stalked by a monster of a person.

The ever-changing narrators spun the story until it appeared that Desmond would've more than likely tried to rape and strangle Ava if the good citizens hadn't stepped in to save the day and whisk away the bad guy. People who never met him originated catchphrases like "Don't go all Desmond on me," and "Chill, don't be a Desmond," which quickly spread around the school.

The week after Desmond moved away, Ava sat in the cafeteria with friends during lunch. She happily nibbled on carrot sticks while she talked over a few routines when she overheard some of the jocks at a nearby table retelling the infamous story of Desmond. The kid was new to the school, but his "star athlete" status automatically placed him with the "in crowd" after making Varsity. He had a captivated audience as the jock talked about Desmond's obsession with collecting cheerleader's hair strands so he could weave a doll and carry it around school.

As the crowd roared with combined sounds of disgust and entertainment, another jock chimed in about Desmond's commitment to sacrifice live animals for the sake of his Wiccan beliefs. As the shock value increased, so did the entertained responses of the listeners. Suddenly Ava narrowed her eyes, slammed her hand on the table in front of her, and stood on top of the lunch table.

She politely flashed a smile, waved around the room and yelled: "My fellow classmates!"

That was all that was needed for the room to erupt in cheers and whistles as the popular kids began to chant, "Ava! Ava! Ava!"

She lifted and slowly lowered her palms towards the ground indicating everyone to quiet down. She smiled a bit wider as she exhibited a cheerful attitude normally seen at Pep Rallies and Homecoming games.

"How many of you think that Desmond guy was a creepy ass freak who will hopefully get locked up or run over by a bus so we all can make the world a better place?" She received a few displeased and angry looks, but the majority erupted in cheers and laughter as some began to re-chant, "Ava! Ava! Ava!"

"Then you're all freaking morons!" She shouted.

Her charming smile disappeared as the cheering section was instantly silenced and the room became quiet.

"Most of you never even met him, and know nothing about him, so how dare you pass judgment on him! He was a little off and strange, but what gave you people the right to cast judgment and bully him? You already forced him to move schools and now you want to spread lies and make up stories For what? To make yourselves feel better and look cool? Let the man be!"

Ava sat back down in her seat and continued to eat her lunch as if she didn't just embarrass half the room, completely unaffected that her own social status could be endangered. As her day ended, Ava's only regret was waiting so long to speak her mind and allowing things to go as far as they did.

In the days that followed, Ava happily embraced the expected backlash from her peer's mixed reactions, as some said she possessed an "honest and brave soul" while others proclaimed her to be a "stuck up bitch." This was the same time that Ava had met Crystal, and a five minute conversation was all it took for her actions to be validated and gain a friend for life.

Unlike Ava and Desmond, Crystal was a freshman and one of the newest cheerleaders at the school. After practice, she waited for everyone to leave the locker room before she approached Ava. After she scanned the room for stragglers, Crystal thanked her for sticking up for Desmond. Before Ava could respond, Crystal's eyes began to swell as she explained how Desmond had a pretty raw deal in life, and not once did anyone defend him the way she did.

Ava stood in silence as Crystal painted the picture of a reckless woman, abandoned by her family at a young age and the boyfriend that knocked her up.

"She was a selfish woman, and tried to escape from all her responsibilities and disappoints by turning to drugs and alcohol. The majority of the time that she carried Desmond, she was on something and the moment he was born he had to struggle with disabilities.

From an early age, he knew something was different with him and he busted his ass to appear as normal as possible. His concentration and learning issues forced him to spend hours on material that most kids only had to skim over, but he did it! He even practiced in the mirror daily on ways to act and sound normal. No matter how hard he tried, he still struggled with grades and was labeled a freak by his peers."

Tears streamed down Crystal's face as it became more and more apparent that she was more than an intuitive and concerned classmate; she was his sister. Thoughts crossed Ava's mind on why she wasn't the one to stand up for her big brother, but the more she unveiled, the more it all became clear.

Unlike Ava, Crystal wasn't strong enough and it was eating her up inside. She was making friends and had just joined the cheerleading squad, which showed much promise, but to stand in Desmond's corner was social suicide.

Fear of public scrutiny and alienation convinced Crystal not to acknowledge her brother under any circumstance; which forced her to watch him suffer. Not wanting his sister to share his fate, Desmond was on board with the secret without a shred of animosity or hard feelings.

However, the fact that he was so accepting made Crystal feel even worse. Tears continued to flow and Crystal bawled and sobbed uncontrollably. Ava didn't approve of Crystal's actions, but she understood it all. In that moment, she made a solemn promise to always look after her and Desmond as best she could.

It was apparent that Chrystal had no real adult or legal guardian to watch over her. Although the mom had straightened out her habits before Chrystal was conceived, she was still very much about herself. She was absent on most nights and had very little involvement in her kid's lives.

With Ava watching over her, Crystal gladly obeyed instructions to get homework assignments done on time and avoid dating the numerous promiscuous football players that found interest in her. Her grades were up, and for the first time she considered the possibility of being the first in her family to go to college.

Everything changed a year later when Desmond decided to take his own life.

He had chosen the bleachers of his new school to carry it out and Ava was completely devastated by the news. Questions plagued her mind as she guilted herself for not doing more for him, but none of it compared to Crystal's self-blame. Crystal shortly spiraled out to levels she could no longer maintain. Unable to cope with what she felt solely responsible for, she resorted to any and everything she could find to escape reality.

By the time Ava had reached graduation, Crystal was nearly unrecognizable. Her beautiful, flawless skin turned into a sickly complexion with dark circles around her bloodshot eyes. Her arms looked like a human pincushion. She used rope to keep the shorts and pants up on her frail and skinny body. She had replaced her once-healthy and full-figured body with something frightful to most, and she didn't care.

Any form of future ambition was long gone for her as she constantly skipped school and associated herself with people that she wouldn't have shared the same street with in the past.

After many failed attempts to divert Crystal off the destructive path, Ava was just about to give up until she found out that Crystal had another sibling; a younger sister named April that would be entering high school the following year. In that moment, she revamped her vow to focus solely on April and to always look out for her.

She had already failed both Desmond and Crystal. There was no way in hell that she was going to allow April to follow any of her sibling's footsteps!

For years, Ava kept her promise and stayed in touch with both Crystal and April. April admired Ava and constantly played around with the idea of her being an honorary big sister. Crystal was just as flattered and content with the idea as Ava. As an adult herself, she had many regrets that neither one of them wanted April to repeat. Although still a train wreck, Crystal happily assisted Ava in keeping tabs on her little sister.

As they sat at the table in the crowded restaurant, Crystal boasted on how she was three months sober and how she was working hard to clean up her act. After a few encouraging words, both transitioned to their favorite subject, and talked about how well April was doing in school and ideas for birthday gifts.

As Ava's world began to gain a purple tint, she immediately closed her eyes and pretended to have a sudden headache. Crystal was looking directly at her in time and caught a split second glimpse of the transformation before they were closed to her. Crystal let off a faint gasp as she leaned in closer towards Ava.

"Are you okay?"

"Yeah, just a slight headache or something. It'll pass in a second."

"Yeah, but Ava, open your eyes for a second!"

Ava remained silent.

"Seriously, I swear I saw something."

Ava opened her eyes with a baffled look as Crystal gazed deeply into a sea of hazel.

"Something what?"

A look of surprise flashed across Crystal's face followed by a look of confusion.

"Sorry, I could've sworn there was something weird with... never mind."

Ava knew exactly what she had meant and witnessed, but continued to play it off like she was speaking gibberish.

"How long were you sober again?"

Ava immediately cringed as Crystal narrowed her eyes in silence form the insincere comment.

"Sorry, bad joke," Ava muttered as she stood to her feet.

"But, hey, I have to get going and take care of some errands. As usual, it's always good to see you.

We should meet soon to do some shopping for April."

Crystal agreed and the two girls hugged before Ava headed for the door in route to HQ.

Max was at a local gym when he received the call. He constantly moved from gym to gym, never to claim one as a home or allow anyone to become familiar with him. There was no desire to develop a friendship, not even workout buddies. The opportunity to build his name and reputation meant nothing to him as he visited the places with one intention in mind: to get better.

From wrestling to boxing to MMA, Max frequented the places and conformed to the rules of the sport. He took on any opponent that was willing to give their personal best in the ring. Most were self-motivated, since Max was a stranger; a surprise unwanted guest that was visiting their house. To be beaten so easily by some random nobody on their home turf screamed like an embarrassment.

Max walked inside the busy gym and headed straight for the middle section, where a large, gated octagonal ring housed two fighters wearing only trunks and gloves. He stood next to the ring with arms folded.

He didn't say a word, but a few perfectly timed scoffs and headshakes was enough to capture the attention of the fighting alpha dog as he sent his opponent crashing down and forced him to submit in under a minute.

As the opponent remained on the ground and squirmed from the pain, the big man in red trunks strutted towards Max and stopped directly in front of the wire mesh fence that separated them.

"Since you want to stand out there like some kind of expert, why don't you come in here and teach me something!"

"Because if I go in there, I'm going to embarrass the hell out of you in front of all of your little friends. Trust me, you don't want that."

The fighter helped his old opponent up to his feet and ushered him out of the octagon as quickly as possible. As he wobbled away, red trunks remained alone in the octagon with the door wide open. He stared at Max with balled fists.

"Bring your bitch ass in here, boy!"

Max sighed and said: "Last chance to back out and save face."

The man became increasingly livid and Max fought hard to conceal his excitement. With every exploration of the different arenas, the more he found that almost everyone had a hothead ready and willing to fight. Subtle trash talk was all that was needed to motivate his opponents, and the man before him was no different.

Max began to remove his shoes as the man hopped from side to side like an excited little kid about to head to the playground. Suddenly, he stopped and looked disappointed as a small and frail older man stormed over to Max. He had grey hair, wrinkled skin, and a worn out golf cap that matched his cardigan sweater and khaki pants. From behind, Max felt a tug at his shirt, and as he turned around, the old man wagged his accusatory index finger at his face.

"Kid, what the hell are you trying to do!? This man is the undefeated heavyweight champion and he's an absolute maniac. The guy he just fought only agreed after knowing he would get paid and that he had complete medical coverage! Trust me when I say you do not want any part of this man!"

The fighter's disappointed voice bellowed from the background. "C'mon, Marvin! Let the man fight! He looks old enough to think for himself!"

"Shut your mouth, Stone! You want another lawsuit on your hands?"

"I don't care about that!" Stone crossed his arms and pouted like an oversized spoiled child.

Max smirked and yanked off his shirt as the man turned his attention back to him with shock in his eyes.

"Are you really? Fine! Fine! If you really want to go through with this, you damn well will sign a consent from and I'm going to copy your identification. It's your funeral!"

A couple of minutes later, Max joined Stone in the octagon with nothing but his workout shorts on. His clothes were folded neatly on the nearby bench, with shoes underneath on the floor and his chain with the two dog tags on top. Through the fence Max stared intensely at the black and blue dog tags, temporarily lost in thought.

"Nobody's going to steal your cheap ass jewelry. You need to focus on me, Blondie!"

Max turned his head to face Stone as the referee asked if they were both ready.

"Fight!"

Max immediately went on the offensive and Stone easily ducked the few initial punches and countered with a few powerful kicks to his front leg. Max was a far superior fighter than the previously defeated fighter, and it was evident that playtime was over for Stone.

With increased speed and power, Stone came out like a defending prizefighter with his championship belt on the line. There was no more smack talk or snide comments, only action. Max tried desperately to keep up, but found it hard with the man's skillet pan-like punches and crazy quick feet.

Fighters, visitors, and managers began to circle the cage and cheer their champion on as he performed a clinic for Max. As their cheers grew louder and called for Stone to finish the job, he became even more quick and vicious with his hits. After a few failed takedown attempts, Stone eventually charged and lifted Max, only to slam him on his back.

Everyone cheered as they felt the end was near, but Max fought out of the follow-up attacks and made his way back to his feet. Although he was banged up and a bit wobbly, Max was still standing, which felt like a direct insult to Stone and he felt the need to retaliate verbally.

Moments before Stone hoisted Max in the air and slammed him for a second time, Stone made fun of the dog tags that he wore all of the time.

"Take that fake shit back to your mom's and tell her to stop calling me!" was the last comment that Max heard before his body connected with the mat. As Stone closed in on Max with his finishing blow, something snapped within Max and he had a new level of rage from within.

Max ignored the two elbows that connected his face and found a way to turn his body around to pin Stone's shoulders on the mat. Everyone looked on in shock as Max returned the favor by grounding and pounding, until the referee shoved him off and the mangers rushed inside. Bloody and dazed, Stone scrambled to his feet and made it to a corner as medical professionals and others attended their prize investment. The old man returned to Max with shock in his eyes.

"Who the hell are you?"

Max smirked as he exited the ring and started putting his clothes back on. The old man followed.

"Don't ignore me, kid. I'm going to make you rich and famous. You should fight for us, and we will treat you well.

I can promise you that."

When fully dressed, Max flashed a smile and politely shook his head as he made his way to the exit. This wasn't the first time he received an offer to be a pro fighter, and surely it wouldn't be the last time. However, he had other obligations that were far more important and paid much better, so he continued to ignore the man and the others that began to speak up. In perfect timing, Max's eyes turned completely blue as he pushed the door to leave and he headed to HQ.

Tyrell sped in his brand new red new Mustang GT500 on the highway, wearing shades to block the effects of the sunny afternoon. Music blared from the speakers as he maneuvered around cars with great disregard for turn signals and personal space. Whenever Tyrell couldn't get around, he trailed the car in front of him at a nearly kissable distance and flashed his lights until the person sped up to move to the other lane.

If these actions didn't occur within the timeline he wanted, then he had no problem laying down the horn until the person caved in. Tyrell arrived at a quiet cul-de-sac with houses of equal height sandwiched together on the block.

Each house had its own set of steps with a railing and porch attached, but there was no sign of greenery in sight. The neighborhood was relatively safe, but Tyrell still hid his belongings and locked the door as he exited the vehicle and walked three houses down. He approached the steps and a beautiful woman in her early twenties immediately stormed out. She had long black hair with brown eyes, tanned skin, and full lips.

She slammed the door on her way out and folded her arms as she narrowed her eyes on Tyrell. The light and calm afternoon breeze gently kept the bottom of her summer dress in motion, while she remained stagnant. She spoke to him in her thick Brazilian accent as he ascended with a wide grin on his face.

"What are you doing here?"

"I'm here to see you, baby! You know you're all I can think about."

The woman rolled her eyes.

"I've been calling all week, ever since I got back. Why haven't you returned any of my calls or texts?"

Tyrell frowned.

"I'm sorry, baby, I've been really busy with work and stuff.

How was your gig at fashion week?"

She looked surprised as she nodded and responded in a passive aggressive tone.

"Oh, it was great. The director liked me and said he would hire me for future shoots. I also met this other model named Isabel from Guatemala and we became good friends. We were talking about our time in America and our boyfriends."

Realizing where this was going, Tyrell removed the shades from his face, hung them on the neckline of his shirt, and attempted to grab for the woman's hand.

"Don't touch me...you...you pig! She told me that you took her on a date two days ago. Two days ago!"

He stood in silence as she pulled out her phone and flipped through pictures that showed him and Isabel as a happy couple. After the fifth picture, Tyrell snatched the phone and placed it in his back pocket.

"Give me my phone back! Give me my phone!" she protested as Tyrell slowly moved closer and hugged her.

Her protests became fainter as Tyrell softly whispered in her ear.

"I'm so sorry. I'm sorry, I really, really care about you and I don't want to leave like this. You are the only person I care about in this world. You are so beautiful and smart and funny and wonderful. No one can replace you."

The woman matched his low voice and said, "But what about Isabel?"

"Forget about Isabel; she doesn't have what you have. You're the only special lady in my life. Don't you know that?"

Tyrell continued to hold onto her and gently rocked side to side and she let out a few soft sobs. He was about to release when his world turned a sudden shade of red and beckoned him to report to HQ. He wasn't in the mood for a mission and let out an inadvertent sigh, which the woman heard and reacted by clenching a bit tighter to him as they continued to rock.

With his head next to hers, he glanced her direction and rolled his eyes before he continued his act.

"I'm sorry to put you though this, but you don't ever have to doubt my love for you. It's so vast that I can't even explain it. I have to go for now, but we should meet up later."

The woman nodded her head in understanding.

"Okay, maybe we can go out later and do something?"

Tyrell frowned.

"I would love to, but unfortunately I'm going to have to work late tonight. Maybe I can stop by afterwards though; maybe around midnight?"

The woman lowered her eyes and nodded and agreement, and Tyrell gave her a long kiss before he placed the glasses back on his face. He moved down the steps and headed to his car while he bragged on how beautiful and wonderful she was. Tyrell turned on the car and sped off as the woman went back inside.

Tyrell stopped at nearby stoplight, and as the white Toyota Camry pulled up next to him, he quickly took notice of the gorgeous female that sat behind the steering wheel. She had smooth, flawless mocha skin and was wearing a tight shirt that exposed her large breasts.

Tyrell continuously revved up his car until he had her full attention, then directed her to roll down the window. She rolled down the window and turned down the music as she cracked a smile to expose her straight, pearly white teeth.

"My God! You are beautiful. I'm not kidding; I think you must be one of the finest women I've ever seen, which makes this a momentous occasion. How about you let me buy you a drink sometime tonight? Don't worry, no funny business; just a celebration drink. Trust me, you deserve a celebration with looks like that! Interested?"

# CHAPTER 15

## MISSION 08_01

Max was the first to enter HQ. He walked towards Ken, who remained busy gathering information. Without his eyes leaving the computer screen, Ken walked towards him and preemptively placed his hand in the air. He briefly instructed him to wait for the rest of the team before he continued to compile information.

The message had provided limited information, but he knew that their mission involved some type of retrieval job. Max retreated to the couches to wait for the rest of his teammates.

Ava and Tyrell walked in the door about the same time and Chris followed a few minutes later. Although no more than two minutes had passed, Tyrell sarcastically applauded Chris as he walked through the door.

Chris faced Tyrell and cracked a smile as he bowed.

"Thank you, thank you. But don't worry, you'll get on my level one day. You'll just have to keep practicing," Chris said.

Ava and Max snickered as Tyrell scowled and muttered, "Yeah right." He otherwise remained silent which, Chris viewed as a small victory. Before he had time to sit down, Ken announced: "Alright, guys, gather around so I can give you the rundown."

Ken sat on top of his desk as all four gathered around him. With remote in hand, he turned to the enormous freestanding tablet that stood nearby and displayed the image of an overweight and bald, dark skinned black man with a few gold chains around his neck. The still image depicted a disgruntled man in a dimly lit room.

"This was taken at Tabu Nightclub yesterday and on the streets he's known as Panda, but don't let the goofy name fool you. He is a drug Kingpin and has been for over fifteen years; he is extremely good at what he does. He's into all types of bad things and never received as much as a speeding ticket.

He's cold, calculated, and never acts out of anger or revenge. So what makes him so special to us, right? He's actually not from here; he runs New Jersey, not Philadelphia. Yet without a moment's notice he decided to uproot, along with the majority of his crew. He used a great deal of muscle and resources to set up shop here and we want to know why.

His practices are pretty ruthless and with enough thugged-out stakeholders, bloodshed could increase expeditiously. There's a theory that someone is purposely trying to stir up trouble in this city, just like when you stopped the Red Dragons gang, Chris."

Tyrell scoffed and rolled his eyes as Ken continued.

"We find it curious that they picked the one person that would attract the most media attention instead of targeting any of the locals, whose disappearance wouldn't even cause an inquiry."

"I thought it was just because none of the locals would dare enter that park at night." Chris said.

Ken nodded his head.

"Maybe, maybe not. Either way, your mission is to pick up Panda, blindfold him, and bring him to a nearby facility be investigated by G3. He's the only one of interest, and make sure you don't harm him in the process."

Tyrell crossed his arms and shook his head. "Really? All of this to get one dude?"

"There's like one hundred dangerous men standing in between that one dude, so yes! Anything else?"

After momentary silence, Ken nodded his head, jumped up and pressed the small button underneath the desk. Chris watched as a few nearby tiles went out on the otherwise lit floor. Moments later he saw the tiles slide out of the way as a long, black metallic rack arose and locked into place.

The rack contained various sized pouches and hooks that housed an arsenal of weapons that ranged from grenades and smoke bombs, to swords and sledgehammers, to automatic and semi-automatic guns. Chris's heart pounded with excitement, but fought to match the nonchalant facial expressions of the rest of his team.

Chris struggled to contain his surprise and excitement and as Ava looked his direction, she flashed a smile.

"Oh, yeah, I forgot; it's your first mission. Follow me."

As they both moved in front of the rack, she pointed out some of the different goodies they got to play with when a mission was initiated.

"It's always best to research as much as possible, so you grab whatever tool you feel you may need. If you don't think you'll need it, then don't grab it. Unlike Training Sessions, there will always be a few G4 members in close proximity for logistical support if you need it. I believe seven minutes is the time they are supposed to respond in."

She picked up a long, black, flat metallic stick that reminded Chris of an elongated and oversized car slim jim. Two hook shapes were carved into the metal and faced upwards to the left and right. Two more shapes did the same in the opposite direction and the pattern repeated all around the six foot long, one foot wide metal piece.

The small bumps that sat between every hook set allowed Ava to easily bend the piece and wrap it around her body like a sash. She effortlessly rotated two of the hooks at the ends of the former stick inward and secured the piece over her left shoulder an around her right waist. The appearance looked like something a beauty pageant contestant would wear at a gun show, but Chris remained silent to allow Ava to explain.

"This thing is lightweight and obviously extremely flexible. We use it to keep our toys nice and secured." Responding to his perplexed look, she grabbed what looked like a can of mace and used the affixed holes at the top and bottom to hold the ⬚ item in place. She picked up a pouch and once again used affixed holes to hold it on the sash.

She grabbed a small pocketknife, compass, and flashlight, then placed them in the pouch and snapped it shut. Ava lifted her hands in the air and gave the "it's that easy" pose seen in infomercials and trade shows.

"Even in the suit, there's something about this metal that keeps everything in place so you can use it when convenient. I personally haven't tried hanging grenades from my body, but apparently others have. Everything here is custom designed so we won't blow ourselves up like a damn Acme commercial. That would be embarrassing."

Chris nodded his head in agreement. "Do you think we should get something for this mission?"

Ava shook her head. "No, we only have to grab one guy and fight off his minions. I'm not going to bother, but feel free to help yourself."

Chris watched as she placed the items back and turned the sash back into a flushed metal piece and put it back on the rack. They all headed out a couple of minutes later. All four Guardians used the elevator to head straight to the rooftop, and with no one around transformed into Guardians. The internal GPS immediately honed in on where exactly they needed to be and they all turned to face the correct direction.

Standing in front of the rest of them, Black Guardian turned around to face the others as they looked outward into the city.

"Hey, before we do this, let me say something really quick: I know I'm the designated leader, but I'm obviously still learning a lot from you all. I think it may be pointless to designate one, as long as we work together and treat one another with respect. I mean, we're all equals in this."

Red broke his speech with an outburst of laughter. "Uh, you are not my equal! Far from it, actually! Of course you would already know this if you found the balls to accept my challenge. Finally want to step up after this, fearless leader?"

Blue Guardian exhaled a deep breath. "We don't have time for this! We're on a mission, remember? But since you're so willing to compete, I have a competition for you: let's race to our destination. Loser buys dinner. Get ready."

The other three only had a moment to assess if he was being serious or not before he said, "Get Set."

There was no time to argue or discuss stipulations. All four rushed to their personal edge of rooftop and positioned themselves at different angles just in time for Blue to finish off with, "Goooooooooo!"

All four Guardians rushed off to their goal from their respective stationary positions. Purple used her extended staff to sprint and pole vault on the adjacent rooftop. Blue turned around and floated full speed on his Glider. With his high trajectory, he made it to a nearby telephone wire, where he rode the cables as effortlessly as driving down an uninhabited straight roadway.

Black and Red had similar ideas as they both used their Gliders to descend off the opposite sides of the building at breakneck speeds. While maintaining the speeds needed, they leapt on adjacent rooftops with gliders attached and accelerated forward. Although a small street divided them, both Guardians momentarily floated side by side and there was a quick stare down.

Reminiscent of an epic samurai pre-duel battle, neither man broke eye contact until they simultaneously reached the edge and headed separate directions. Both men focused and embraced the surge of energy and speed as they rushed towards their destination.

No street, rooftop, telephone wire, building, or other manmade or naturally forged item was off limits and all four arrived in record speed. Each member trickled in satisfied, as the thrill of the ride far surpassed any feeling of victory or defeat.

However, no smile was as wide as Red's as he had the pleasure to witness everyone fall in line behind him from Black, to Purple, and then Blue. Nothing was said as all four Guardians reunited and Blue nodded as he looked at his comrades.

"Yeah, I'm going to need a rematch one day, but for now I suppose it's time to get down to work."

All three nodded their heads in agreement and discussed a plan to infiltrate the five story apartment complex that they stood on. According to their data, Panda had recently run off squatters and addicts from the condemned building, unless they were customers.

After making a few modifications with some of the interior, he and his guys set up shop. The lopsided foundation, corroded walls, and faulty wiring deterred most citizens from stepping foot in the building the city had deemed unfit in the months prior.

With poor illumination within and around the building, the Guardians moved around with ease as they gained entry. As Black entered the top floor, he was amazed at the lax of security, which contradicted their reputation. He had expected some type of resistance from the top and front door entrances, but all four had successfully entered without any resistance whatsoever.

Black and Red simultaneously entered from topside, while Blue and Purple went through at the ground floor. They were uncertain where Panda was exactly, and attacking from all fronts made the most sense to them. Black was the first to confirm that something was definitely off as he pushed open the already ajar graffiti-riddled door near the rooftop.

He stood for a few seconds as his eyes adjusted to the dim, flickering light that displayed the two unconscious bodies that greeted him on the vinyl floor. As his eyes scanned the area further out, he discovered a new collapsed and stationary body every few feet or so.

They were all part of Panda's gang, and it appeared that someone had beaten them to the job. Right before Black updated, Red Guardian had beaten him to the game-changing punch.

"Wow, there are bodies, guns, and bullet casings everywhere. We must've missed one hell of a good fight."

The others agreed to the same testimony and after they searched their areas, the Guardians agreed to meet back on the rooftop. They didn't find even one member to talk to.

"Wow, didn't see that coming. How in the world do we find this Panda guy now?" Purple Guardian asked.

"What the hell is going on over there?" Blue interjected.

As the other three turned to him, he used his staff to point to a nearby playground no more than two thousand feet from the building. Next to the playground was a basketball court and the Guardians were immediately drawn to the four fifteen-foot light fixtures that illuminated the area. There appeared to be about six people in the area, and near the center of the court was the man they were looking for.

On his knees and bound, the once tyrannical Panda appeared pitiful and helpless as five others were spread out around him and stood perfectly still. His eyes were narrowed as his gagged mouth desperately tried to speak, but no one paid any attention.

"Minutemen!" Red Guardian yelled out as he hopped on his glider and rushed towards the court. The trio immediately followed and stopped alongside Red, a few feet from the nearest man standing post. The black of the night didn't stop the man from wearing dark shades. He was dressed in worn out, faded clothes that looked two sizes too big for his body and was draped with an old dingy trench coat and a tightly tied rope to keep up his wrinkled jeans.

Red Guardian stormed up to him as the man maintained an emotionless expression. As Black Guardian looked at the rest of his team, there was a silent shared look of hatred.

"Okay, I'm obviously missing something. Does anyone care to clue me in?"

Red materialized his staff and walked forward in an attempt to stroll past the man and walk directly to Panda. Once side-by-side, the man balled his fists and attacked Red Guardian with speed and intensity. Red ducked the punch and side-stepped from the impending kick.

With the man lunged forward and off balance, Red cocked the staff over his head and aggressively swung downward towards his neck as if he was attempting a decapitation.

Black stood in awe as his worry of the man's impending death quickly shifted to shock and confusion as the man instantly turned into dust. His clothes quickly plopped to the ground as the wind carried off what was left of his body.

Black stood wide-eyed with his mouth gaped as the rest of the Guardians stood with composure and certainty. As the other men faced Red and stood in between him and Panda, Blue explained the situation to Black as the trio remained fixated on Red and his upcoming opponents.

"You know how we have our Trainers back at HQ? Well, think of these to be in the same family. They're called Minutemen, and like Trainers, they can't think or talk for themselves; they're only programmed. They are much weaker than Trainers and there's mechanical pressure points all over their bodies.

If you hit one hard enough, well, you just saw what happens. They can be programmed for anything to obviously include fighting. Alone they're decent fighters, but nothing you can't handle. The problem is, these things are clones and mass produced at some undisclosed location.

"So they kidnap people and make them clones?"

"Actually, no. In order for the system to work, they must acquire an obedient and submissive essence in order for the clone to be that way. In other words, it only works for volunteers willing and open with the process. Once it starts, a bit of life is drained to create every clone and eventually the human dies."

"What kind of person would be willing to accept a fate like that!?"

"A person with nothing to lose and no will to live. Trust me, they exist!"

The four remaining Minutemen stood defiantly between Red Guardian and his target. He clenched onto his staff as he moved in closer, when suddenly two large beams of light sped towards him accompanied by the sound of a revved engine.

The pulsating light grew bigger as the Guardians squinted to see the inbound dark vehicle. When next to the court, the van's headlights turned to face the opposite direction. While everyone turned their attention to the vehicle, the Minuteman remained focused on the potential threat.

After the van had come to a full stop and the engine cut off, a tall, slender man exited from the driver seat. His trench coat looked to be in much better quality than the raggedy one that currently lay nearby on the ground. He had short black hair with sideburns that came down to his ear upper ear lobes and stubble under his chin.

A Hummer H2 pulled up and parked behind the van as a side door opened. Two slender Asians, one male and one female both similar in size, exited the van as a huge muscle-bound man exited the Hummer. Following the man in the trench coat, all three headed to the court and remained on the edge as he headed towards Panda.

"Turn and face me," the man in the trench coat said.

As instructed, the Minutemen turned to face him with no hesitation, which increased the anger of the already enraged Red Guardian.

"Grab him and place him in the far back left side of the van. We're leaving in a few minutes."

Without hesitation, all four Minutemen grabbed a leg or arm and lifted Panda like a piece of cargo as he protested and whimpered through his gag. As the Minutemen began to clear the court, the man turned to face the rest of his crew as Red exhaled loudly and the rest quickly stepped up to join him.

"Hey, bad news; we need that guy. So we're going to cancel that order. On the bright side though, we're about to make three clones disappear if you want to see a magic trick! Who the hell are you guys, anyway?"

The big man erupted into laughter as he took a step forward. He opened his mouth to speak, but trench coat raised his hand and the big man stood there and crossed his arms. The smug look on his face remained and he seemed overjoyed, like a kid ready to open his Christmas presents. His cargo shorts and a sleeveless white t-shirt exposed every bulging muscle; he possessed the unique ability to make the muscular Blue Guardian appear much smaller than normal. As he remained silent, the man in the trench coat quickly glanced over his shoulder.

"You might just want to consider this one a loss and stay out of this, Guardians! For your own sakes!"

"How about you have five seconds to bring him back or we'll grab him ourselves!" yelled Blue Guardian.

"Look, both my employer and my colleagues would love to teach you all a lesson in power and humility, but it doesn't have to come down to this." Trench coat said.

"We both have our orders to follow from our respective authorities. In this case, we're wanting the same thing: we are trying to figure out why this crime boss decided to uproot his gang and move to an already highly trafficked city like Phila-⬛delphia."

"You know nothing about us," Black stated. "It's our job to--"

"Protect the good citizens in the city as best as you can. We know all about you, Black Guardian. And by the way, welcome to the team. We know much more than you would think; just like if we were to use the name Nero, you would be the only one not to freak out."

Just as he predicted, the situation instantly grew more intense and the man took a step back as he focused his gaze on Black.

"See, right now your friends are looking at me with hatred because of our boss. He is ultimately in charge of Minutemen and they're convinced that he is somehow the cause of their past leader's untimely death. I wasn't there, but I heard the story and know enough about Nero to believe it was the classic case of wrong time, wrong place."

As Red Guardian scoffed, the man redirected his focus.

"Nero is a businessman; he cares about numbers and results. He's virtually monopolized the drug industry and there are now rules in this city; dealers are prohibited from operating in schools and to minors, period. Before he came, it was a damn free-for-all here.

Also, that stupid stunt that the Red Dragons pulled to that poor kid, he hated it just as much as you guys. We were given instruction to shut down their whole operation the night that you literally beat us to the punch, Black Guardian. He doesn't have time to hold petty squabbles or seek revenge, and trust me when I say having your guy go like that wasn't best for business.

Nero is ready and willing to move on from the whole matter, and I figured that two sections are charged with upholding the peace, they could surely find some common ground. I've compiled the names and addresses of some horrible establishments within the city. You probably don't even want to know the half of what they're all about, but I guarantee you that you'll save a lot of lives and put away some vile individuals."

Black Guardian took a step forward and said, "Look, if you don't want to see this escalate, then the first step is to hand us Panda and allow us to do our job. Then maybe we can figure something out after that. I'll give you one minute to bring him back out here on the court."

The man's eye's widened as he shook his head in disbelief.

"I am so sorry. I didn't mean for you to think that we're scared of you. In fact, the guys behind me are itching to beat your asses. I was just hoping to avoid it and find an alternate solution."

"Hell no, Skye! They want to fight too, look at their faces! I call dibs on the so-called muscle of the group. You better start warming up, Blue Guardian! I'm coming for your punk ass!" the big man bellowed and grinned with excitement.

As the Asian twins giggled, the man in the trench coat took another sigh and stuffed his hands in his front pants pockets.

"Well, since this all seems inevitable, we felt it only right to give you all a heads up on who we are and what we can do. In a few minutes, you all won't be standing and when that happens, I refuse to let you start coming up with excuses about being blindsided and coming up with ways to prepare for the next time."

"God! Do you always talk this much?" Red Guardian yelled out as he crossed his arms.

The man's eyes narrowed as they stared into Red's.

"Oh, trust me, you're going to want to hear this. Don't worry, very soon you'll be on your back, regretting those words. As my colleague stated, my name is Skye and I'm the leader of this group we usually call Nero's Crew, or The Crew. Doesn't really matter, I suppose. Nero hired us months ago and instructed us to watch you all.

I'm sure you know by now that an injected serum is what turned you all into Guardians. Knowing whatever government agency you work for, I'm sure that they conveniently hid that your version of the serum isn't the only one around. Long story short, your serums gave you your abilities and Nero's gave us ours."

Skye paused and smirked as he looked at the shocked faces of the Guardians.

"Let me guess, now you're interested. Your powers work internally, and ours work externally. For example."

Skye's right hand reached for his back pocket and pulled out a faded and worn out baseball cap.

The bill shadowed his forehead, eyes, and eyebrows as he snuggly placed the cap on his head.

"This cap gives me the ability to use telekinesis, but only in my right hand for some reason."

The Guardians were capable of performing impossible feats on a daily basis and yet each of their faces showed skepticism as they watched him.

"You do what with a teletubby?" Red exclaimed.

Skye chuckled as he turned around and outstretched his right arm towards the van. Suddenly, the van began to levitate and reached about five feet off the ground before being gently lowered back down. The van was still once again and Skye turned back around.

"I tell you what, I'll show you all about it in a few minutes, Red. The overly eager big man behind me is Crush, and with the gloves he wears, he is one scary individual."

Right on cue, Crush reached in his back pockets and pulled out a pair of gloves reminiscent of weight lifting ones and placed them on his hands. With a wide grin on his face he made his right hand into a fist and pounded it a couple of times into his open hand. As Blue Guardian crossed his arms across his chest, Crush looked at him and winked.

"These two are Yi and Ya; twins from Korea. With the rings on their fingers, they are virtually unstoppable and unpredictable in a fight."

The twins smiled as they each pulled out a ring with a golden gem and platinum band from their front pockets and simultaneously placed it on their index fingers. They happily began to speak in their native language and pointed back and forth between Purple and Black Guardians. Suddenly both turned their attention to Purple Guardian and simultaneously bowed with wide and malicious grins on their faces.

Skye placed his hands behind his back as he alternated looks between the Guardians.

"Well, that's it, Red Guardian; introductions are over. You can feel free to get started whenever you feel like it."

"Shit! You don't have to tell me twice! Come here, you damn Smurf!" Crush bellowed as he ran towards Blue. Blue instinctively moved back to give himself a little more space and his opponent happily followed.

Skye's eyes momentarily followed Crush, but quickly regained focus on Red Guardian.

"Minutemen, hurry over here and fight the Guardians. Your main objective is to find and destroy the Black Guardian!"

He reached for his ear, pulled out what appeared to be a high-tech Bluetooth device and placed it inside his interior jacket pocket. There was no need to turn around as nine Minutemen exited the van and Hummer.

Not even taking the time to shut the door behind them, the clone warriors all sprinted for Black Guardian. Black scoffed and he immediately ran to meet them halfway, giving the rest of his team the chance to fight without interference.

"Whenever you're ready to get started, I'll be over here, Red." Skye said.

As Skye strolled towards the nearby lamppost, Red Guardian quickly followed, which left Purple Guardian and the twins near the center of the court.

Unbeknownst to them at the time, Skye's predictions were moments away from turning into reality and all Guardian opposition lasted no more than five minutes.

Black was the first to be attacked as he confronted the Minutemen.

"Before we get started why don't--," was the extent of what Black Guardian could get out before being punched in the gut. He winced in pain as he took a step backwards, but quickly recovered to defend himself and turned the first attacker into dust before his eyes.

As the clothes of the missing Minuteman made their way to the ground, Black briefly scanned the area to witness the newly transformed battlefield. Fears of his recent blunder quickly dissipated as he saw that each Guardian was too engaged in their own world to mock him.

As Blue Guardian stood in front of Crush, he saw nothing but yet another opponent with a big mouth and oversized ego. He was quite used to the personality trait at this point, as it seemed that every alpha dog possessed it. After the opponent would realize the inevitable truth that they couldn't win, then the insults would start flowing to compensate.

In his experience, the louder they barked, the more fearful they were of losing. However, as he stood in front of Crush, he had a different impression. Without a doubt, he had to be one of the most vocal and confident opponents, but unlike the majority, there wasn't a shred of doubt. Crush walked with determination and his face was filled with so much certainty that Blue couldn't match.

"So, Little Boy Blue, you ready to get your ass whooped?"

Blue Guardian sized up the man that contained a greater height advantage and muscle mass and he remained silent. As their eyes met momentarily, Crush cracked a wide smile.

"Okay, I guess I'll take that as a yes."

With his right foot planted, Crushed bent down and leaned forward as the weight of his left foot when to the ball.

Blue flashed a puzzled look as Crush yelled, "Down. Set."

Suddenly Crush sprinted and shoulder tackled the unsuspecting Guardian, forcing him to land on his butt. Engaged and embarrassed, Blue quickly jumped to his feet, charged from behind and put his arms around Crush's hips. As soon as he clamped down, Blue arched his body backwards and suplex slammed Crush back first to the ground. Blue let go and Crush rolled out the way and took a knee with a smile still plastered on his face.

"That one was a freebie, Suzie."

Blue narrowed his eyes and charged a second time while Crush was still taking a knee. With built momentum, Blue lifted his left foot to punt the giant's face back to the ground, but Crush had other plans. Without warning, Crush charged him a second time and his feet left the ground as he tackled Blue's midsection.

As Blue writhed in pain, Crush reached down to grab a fistful of uniform and punched him a couple of times before he chucked him several feet in the opposite direction. Blue wearily stood to his feet and mustered all of the energy he could to counterattack. Crush gladly endured a few solid punches and kicks before he countered with a few of his own.

Hit by hit, Blue felt the effects of the sledgehammer-like punches and kicks that were incomparable to any fighter he had ever faced. Blue continued to fall to the ground and his response time delayed more and more until he was unable to stand at all. Blue shared the same fate as many of his victims in the past: he was rendered unconscious.

Red and his opponent mutually glared at one another with confidence.

"Look, man, I don't want to embarrass you in front of your people, especially after you gave that nice little speech. I'll tell you what; just pretend that you forgot about some important job that you all have to do now. Maybe you can catch a game, since you have that dirty ass baseball cap on your head. I don't care, I won't tell anyone."

"Humph, and you thought I talked too much." Skye responded as he rested his hands inside his coat pockets. The brim of his cap shaded his eyes as he maintained his calm and assertive demeanor.

"I'm so sorry if I played any part of your overdeveloped false sense of confidence. I assure you that any one of us has the power to take you out with ease. The only reason why you're standing here and talking to me now is because we've allowed it."

Red Guardian narrowed his eyes and crossed his arms.

"So what if I took that dumb ass hat off your head and put it on mine?"

"Sorry, kid. Doesn't work that way. The power is tailored solely for me, just like your staff is for you. Even if I took it from you, you would still have to the power to make it appear and disappear however you saw fit. I can't make my hat disappear, but I guarantee you can't get any power from it."

Red momentarily nodded his head in silence, then followed with, "Hmm, then I guess I'll just take it from you and burn that ugly thing!"

The man sighed. "Go ahead and try!"

Red shrugged his shoulders and ran towards Skye in a zigzag formation. Skye immediately lifted his right palm and shifted it from right to left as he struggled to get a lock on his rapidly moving opponent. The close calls of gushes of wind that brushed his left shoulder and right knee only encouraged him as he closed in on Skye.

Red was mere feet away and Skye had unsuccessfully captured him. With a smirk plastered on his face, the dropped his hand and stood still as he carefully watched Red Guardian and his every movement.

As Skye watched Red's movements go from right to middle to left of him then the opposite, he was reminded of a game of ping pong and he was determined not to lose. Red ran past Skye and used to glider to make a quick turnaround as he lunged towards the patiently waiting man.

With a second to spare, Skye hopped backwards to get out of his range, cocked his balled right fist behind him, and pushed forward as his palm opened. As his hand went forward, Red Guardian was lifted off his feet as he was jerked backwards and hit the ground about ten feet away.

Red Guardian immediately stood to his feet, embarrassed and outraged. He was just swatted away like a harmless fly and he did not appreciate it in the slightest. All jokes and threats subsequently went away as he balled up both fists and stared down Skye again. Red bellowed a loud grunt as he hopped on his glider and headed away from him.

Skye flashed a puzzled look until he saw Red Guardian a few seconds later heading straight for him at a high rate of speed. The plan was simple: either grab the hat or run him over in the process.

As he gingerly moved towards the nearest lamppost, Red closed in on him with his right arm positioned by his side. Red Guardian was seconds away from impact when Skye outstretched his right arm towards him and he suddenly lost all ability to function his own body. With complete inability to control his actions, Red's glider took a sharp turn from his intended path and his left shoulder and sternum crashed into the freestanding pole.

Red screamed in pain as he fell to the ground, unable to stand. Skye took his time walking towards him and elevated Red's body one last time, forcing his head against the same pole. Red's screams were silenced as Skye gently laid him back down to get some sleep.

Purple stood before the twins. They seemed identical in height and similar in size, but the female possessed small breasts while the male had a slightly greater muscular build. They both stood a few inches shorter than her with equally slanted black eyes and jet-black hair. Both hairstyles were straight and free flowing, but Ya's was much longer and went down to her shoulders. They appeared to be in their early twenties and maintained a childish grin as they approached her.

"AN-YONG-HA-SE-YO!" the twins yelled simultaneously as they bowed in front of Purple Guardian and greeted her like an old friend.

Regardless of the demeanor of the two, she carefully watched every movement as chaos erupted around them. The duo could've easily been mistaken for harmless tourists that shared a common interest for the same yellow stoned jewelry. Purple watched the two in silence as they spoke in their native tongue, when Yi stopped to address Purple.

"You have boyfriend?"

His sister Ya quickly interjected in her native language and they started to argue as Purple stood in silent amazement. Purple crossed her arms as the twins grew louder, even though neither one seemed truly invested or angry.

Everyone else around her had already started to fight and had taken the moment seriously, but she felt like her opponents had just thrown her into some ridiculously scripted anime. She watched the two go back and forth for a second longer and yelled out: "Hey!"

The male immediately paused and looked up at Purple.

"Hey, baby!" Yi responded as he placed his hands behind his head and rotated his pelvis in a circular motion a couple of times. Purple exhaled a loud breath.

"Look, are we going to fight or are you two going to step aside so we can do our job?"

The twins silently started at her with puzzled looks, and Purple exhaled another deep breath and immediately pointed her index finger at the two.

"You give up? Yes?" Purple asked as she nodded her head.

They both chuckled before Ya crossed her arms flashed a defiant stare.

"No! You!"

"Yeah, right," Purple muttered to herself and she sprinted towards Yi, eager to kick the smug look right off his face. When in striking distance, the twins locked arms and while he rotated out the way, his sister lunged forward and the fluid motion barely gave Purple time to block the incoming round-house kick. Ya wasted little time to follow up with punches and kicks that kept Purple Guardian actively blocking. Yi jumped back in and quickly swept Purple's legs from under her, as she focused on the incoming dropkick by Ya.

As Purple Guardian fell to the ground, Yi rolled out of the way as his sister simultaneously positioned herself to sit on top of Purple's chest the moment her back had made contact. Ya maintained a sadistic grin as punched she the side and elbowed the front of Purple's mask, until Purple found an opening to take hold of her arm and flip her off. Purple quickly scrambled off the ground, and with the help of her glider established a distance between them.

She faced the twins as they stood side by side in a fighting stance, completely focused and ready for her next move. Although they continued to possess playful smiles on their faces, Purple began to understand where all of their confidence came from. The technique was unique and devastating. Even if she had a partner, or all three Guardians with her, there was no level of training that would get them on the same page and truly fight in one accord like the twins.

At the rate the twins were going, adding allies would only complicate things, like adding cyclists to a stock car race. She alternated looks between the two of them as they waited with amused expressions. Purple closed both of her hands and placed them directly in front her, with thumbs touching and knuckles facing outwards as if she was about to operate an invisible standing air pump. As she pulled her fists away from one another, a streak of purple kept them connected. Seconds later her left hand clung onto the center of her 5-foot staff while she beckoned the twins with her right hand.

The look of surprise flashed Yi and Ya as they looked at one another. A moment later, the moment had passed as they cracked a smile and shrugged their shoulders, almost as if they were communicating telepathically and had reached and virtually instantaneous agreement. The twins took off towards Purple and remained side by side.

By random selection, Purple decided to go left and ran towards the male counterpart with staff in hand, prepared to keep her distance. In perfect sync, Yi performed a baseball slide to sweep her legs from under her; at the same time Ya went high and executed a spinning roundhouse kick.

Unable to dodge both, Purple fell victim to Yi as she fell to the ground for a second time. Suddenly, Yi moved out the picture a split second before Ya's knee descended towards her stationary face. With no time left to move or counter, Purple closed her eyes and braced for the impact that would surely put her out for a while.

A gush of wind rushed over Purple's face and she opened her eyes to Ya's surprised yelp as she flew several feet off course. She looked up to find Black Guardian's open hand and extended arm hovering over her as his face continued to stare down the agitated brother.

With the help of Black Guardian, Purple pulled herself up in enough time to see Ya chuckling as she took a knee, blotted off the dab of blood from the corner of her mouth, and licked her bloody finger like cake frosting. Black Guardian stayed focused and prepared to defend himself against the angry brother.

The two appeared to be evenly matched as they mutually dodged powerful punches and kicks around various regions of the body. Aware of the minuscule window of opportunity to gain the upper hand, Purple grabbed her staff and ran towards the both of them. Noticing the inbound assistance, Black made sure to keep Yi busy and solely focused so Purple could sneak on his blindside.

Purple continuously glanced at the sister, but Ya remained perfectly still as Purple closed in on the brother. She figured that she must be more injured then she let on and she moved closer and closer to her target.

With his back turned to Purple, Yi continued to fight valiantly against the man in front of him. Soon Purple stood inches away with her arms cocked and staff in hand. Suddenly Black yelled, "Watch out!" and a split second later, she felt a sharp pain from the back of her thigh as she fell down to one knee.

Both Guardians looked shocked as Ya stood over Purple with a satisfied grin. Even when she was monitored, she had managed to use speed and stealth to sneak up and regain the upper hand. Ya began to chuckle again as she kicked Purple in the kidneys three times and used her knee to drive her body to the ground. As Purple used her energy to fight against the submission, Ya effortlessly flipped and snatched the staff away from Purple's loosened hand. With blinding speed, Ya spun around and managed to strike Purple in the upper back once before she had time to make it disappear.

As Purple screamed in pain and as she laid flat on the ground, Ya and Yi began to laugh, which set Black off. He yelled as he attacked more ferociously then before and connected punch after punch, and knee after knee. With Purple stagnant, Ya jumped into the fight and they began to dominate by attacking opposite directions with pinpoint accuracy.

With every high and low hit, the twins appeared to be more and more entertained. Soon after, Black fell to his knee and he immediately materialized his staff as his hand trembled with rage. As the twins closed in from opposite angles, a familiar voice said, "Hold on a second," and the duo immediately stopped to retreat to the location of the man's voice.

"Sucky position to be in, right?" Skye asked in a casual voice as he strolled to Black. His baseball cap remained perfectly still on his head and his hands were once again stuffed in his trench coat pockets.

Black glared up at the man and used the staff to pull himself up. The big man, Crush, strolled up to rejoin his team and unlike the rest of his amused gang, for a second Skye looked genuinely concerned as Black stood to look at him at eye level.

"Kid, that's really not necessary. I hate to throw salt into your wound, but it's not like I didn't warn you that this very thing would happen."

Crush crossed his arms with a satisfied smirk, while the twins began to mock Black as they took turns to hobble around, pretend to fight and beg for mercy with one leg, while speaking in their native language. However, nothing upset him more than the look that Skye gave him: pity.

"This isn't over yet!" Black Guardian yelled out.

"Hey, you heard the man, Skye! He wants some more! Maybe I should step in."

"Chill out, Crush. And you! Look around you! Look at your team; you failed!"

Black gripped his staff tightly and clenched his teeth as he saw his comrades laid out and realized he was helpless to help or avenge them.

"On the bright side, we were generous enough to leave you all breathing and able to fight another day. I don't expect a thank you, but you're welcome anyway. We are not bad people, and we're not heartless."

Skye glanced at the people around him and muttered, "Well, not all of us."

"All you have to do is stay out of our way, and I assure you that your life will be better for all of us. This starts with Panda. We're going to take him and return him in a few days once we figure out what we need to know. You can do whatever you want to him after that point.

Whenever you think about us, just remember that we took it easy on you all and allowed you to live, just like I promised. However, I can't keep that same promise if we ever meet again, so here's to hoping we don't. I know you're going to get some heat for this. Being a leader is never an easy thing, but there are worse alternatives. Good luck to you, kid."

Skye turned around to head to the van and the rest of the crew followed without saying a word.

Black took one last look of the four members of Nero's crew and watched them drive off as he used his glider to check up on Purple and moved onto Red and Blue nearby.

His heart pounded and his hands began to shake as he called for G4 and explained how he needed a pickup for his team. The agent asked three times for confirmation of the odd request and every time it was harder for him to admit.

"Sir, do you mean you need a pickup for the enemies, because if so you're supposed to call--"

"No, pickup for my team. And make sure the windows are blacked out."

After an awkward delay on the phone Black angrily muttered, "We failed. I need assistance."

# CHAPTER 16

The ride back to HQ felt long and silent as the blacked out windows allowed the Guardians to keep their suits on as the G4 member drove. The suit allowed for an accelerated healing process, and by the time the vehicle pulled up at the facility, the bulk of their pain was internal.

Not only were they dismantled and destroyed as a team, it wasn't even a close call. They had completely failed and every last one of them felt the brunt as individuals. There wasn't even a scapegoat or an excuse they could use; the other guys were simply better in every way, which made them all look like amateurs playing pretend heroes.

The group remained dead silent as the G4 member parked. They all removed the suits as they entered the training room. Chris looked around the somber group and tried to find the right words for the particular moment.

"We obviously have a lot of coordination and planning to go over soon, but I'm sure none of us needs to hear a lecture right now. Let's just go upstairs in the lounge and collect our thoughts."

All three silently followed Chris to elevator and grabbed a spot on the couch of the upstairs level. As Chris turned on the TV, Tyrell grabbed a water for everyone. There was no need for verbal communication as they went through to the motions of sipping the cold drink and watching the reality dating show, allowing their minds to wander and reflect on what had just happened.

Ken would be beyond pissed and rightfully so, but they figured a little time alone could help them at least process the events and articulate them intelligently. As all four watched the overly dramatic female on the screen confront a backstabbing supposed friend, they mentally played back their own versions of the events that led to their demise.

Suddenly, the telephone next to the TV rang and they all nervously looked at each other before Tyrell stood up to answer it. Looks of dread flashed across their faces as all three already knew what would happen next. The phone was only linked to one place, which was downstairs, and all three stood up in preparation for the only one who could be calling.

Thirty seconds later, Tyrell reached for the remote as he unenthusiastically stated that Ken was headed up. They had hoped to avoid this moment a little longer. Maybe with a little more time, they could find a solution or a viable excuse, but as of right then, nothing came to mind. In his line of work, mission failure was unacceptable and nothing could change that.

Ken stormed into the room with eyes wild with rage and deep, heavy breaths. Tyrell's finger was on the remote to mute the TV, but he wasn't fast enough as Ken exclaimed, "Mute that shit, now!" He stood in front of the TV and paced a couple of times before he stood still and slowly glared at each member of his team.

"What...the hell...was that!?"

"What the hell was that!?" he repeated.

All four remained seated and refused to look at him in the eye when he gazed their direction.

"Let me get this straight. You are Guardians, an elite group of highly trained fighters. We give you everything, everything you ask for, and you can't get the job done!? When I heard the news, I thought to myself: okay, there must've been an army of guys that we didn't see coming!

The enemy must have a freaking formula that turns any every day citizen into a mighty warrior and you guys were overwhelmed! But four!? Four!? You couldn't handle an evenly matched fight!?"

Ken paused for a second and continued to scan the room as they remained silent and refused to look at him. The other members wanted to speak up, but not even Tyrell spoke, for there was no excuse good enough. Ken angrily chuckled as he shook his head in disbelief.

"How in God's name do you screw up so badly?"

Silence.

"How!? I want to know!"

"We're trying to figure out the same thing," Ava spoke up.

"No one in here is proud of a defeat like this, so we're trying to figure it out."

"Train!" Ken interrupted. "Train your asses off and work as a team. Obviously, you've all been slacking!"

Chris interjected with a calm and rationale tone. "I respectfully disagree. I know we lost, but I think we all have been training hard--"

"You really shouldn't be talking now," Ken interrupted again. "You're the leader of this group, aren't you!? I'm tired of all this 'I'm the new guy' crap. Man the hell up and get your team in order! You have some mighty big shoes to fill and so far you have been completely lacking!"

Tyrell seemed to be satisfied with the last statement, but dared not to speak up in his own defense.

The room was silent again.

Suddenly Max spoke up while rubbing together the two dog tags around his neck.

"We need to do better! We will do better!"

"Damn right you will! Lucky for you all it was just a person we wanted to extract information from. What if it was something more serious? What if you had to stop a nuke from being detonated? What if you had to stop a madman from going on a killing spree? You can't afford to fail! Do better! In the meantime, get the hell out of here. You all obviously need rest and I'm tired of looking at all of you!"

With those final words, Ken stormed out of the room and the remaining four took heed and scattered from the area.

When Chris had made it home that night, he was mentally and physically exhausted. Although the suit helped his body heal, he still ached from the numerous shots the Minutemen had landed on him. They knew how to work together like the HQ Trainers that he worked with, except there was no established leader and they played for keeps. He had to destroy each Minuteman individually and had barely escaped.

He brushed his teeth and showered, but the stench of failure and embarrassment lingered long after. His team had just been slaughtered, but the featured highlight had to be the infamous knockout blow on the ally he cared about the most.

Ken didn't help matters at all, as he echoed how Chris had already felt: inadequate. As he put on his pajamas, he desperately wanted to sleep it off and start the day refocused and reenergized. He slowly dragged his body to his bed and moved under the covers as he placed his head on the pillow. He closed his eyes and in no time drifted off to sleep.

The first thing he saw as he opened his eyes was sand as he felt the cool breeze on his skin.

"No! Not now! Not now! Not now!" he protested as he balled his fist and pounded against the bed of sand. He took a couple of deep breaths and gripped a fistful of sand as he stood to his feet. As he allowed the grains to slowly slip through his fingers, he looked up at the ancient ruin. He stood at the base yet again, and the light of the archway continued to shine brightly at the peak.

One glance at the light and he narrowed his eyes as he restarted his ascension. He grumbled as he stomped his way up the stairs. He was not in the mood to be in this land, and he definitely wasn't in the mood to deal with the robed trio. He had just had one of the worst days in his life, and yet he wasn't allowed to sleep it off like normal people.

He only made it up a few steps before he heard the familiar voice of the original male robe. "Chris, get back down here for a second."

He ignored him and continued to climb.

"Hey! Did you hear what I just said?"

Chris continued to climb.

"Hey!"

He turned around at gazed at the trio with both sincerity and conviction.

"Look, I'm really not in the mood for this crap and I don't feel like being here. Please just leave me alone; I'm going to go up to the top and see what this light is all about. Let's just continue this next time."

He didn't wait for response. Instead, he turned back around and continued his climb.

"Like hell you are!" he heard behind him.

All three ran up towards him as Chris tightly clenched his fists and turned back around. Feeling bewildered, he looked at the trio with intensity as he gritted his teeth and waited.

Chris made one last plea as the three stopped in front of him. His heart raced and his voice was shaky with rage.

"I don't know what I've done to you people, but just leave me alone! Maybe I'm invading your land, but I didn't ask to come here. Hell, I don't want to be here! Just leave me alone!"

"We can't do that. How many times do we need to tell you to give this Guardian life up? No suit means no visits, and yet you keep being stubborn. So now we don't care about you and your rough day. Things are about to get a lot worse for you."

"AAAAAAAAAGGGGGGGGGGGHHHHHHHHHH!!!" Chris
bellowed out as he tackled the robe that had been speaking
and elbowed the side of his hood. He acted purely on emotion
and was surprised that his hits actually connected to something within that dark void.

Chris saw the other male attempt a punt with his foot to the
side of Chris's head, but he stood up in time to dodge it. Chris
ducked the follow-up punches until he was able to bring him
down with an arm drag and followed up with swift knees to the
kidneys. He waited for him to stop resisting before standing
up and immediately running towards the female.

Anticipating his approach, she attempted a flying kick
when he was in striking distance, but he was already sliding at
her feet instead. As she landed, she was met with a ferocious
spear strike that sent her flying down the flight of steps as she
shrieked in pain.

The two males attempted a coordinated attack, but the
fired-up Chris had managed to continuously separate and attack right before the other had time to provide backup. Within
minutes, the trio was left the same way his crew was left hours
ago: unable to stand.

He had no idea who or what these things were, and frankly,
he didn't give a crap. He was tired of thinking. He was tired of
fighting. All he wanted was a moment of peace, and with that
thought he continued to climb. As he made it to the top of the
steps, a gentle warm breeze caressed his face. The glow made
it feel like a warm spring day and as he approached the threshold, he squinted his eyes from the bright light and walked
through.

He walked a few feet and stood still as he allowed his eyes
to adjust. The first thing he noticed was that the sand was
back, but it was much different. Unlike the on the other side,
the white sand looked groomed and inviting. The sound of
the ocean fifty feet away placed him in a tranquil mood, and
halfway between the arch and the beautiful turquoise ocean lay
an immaculate bed with four palm trees that shaded it inch by
inch.

Besides the bed and trees, the picturesque area was completely empty. The warm weather was ideal and his eyes began
to droop as the waves crashed. With a weary smile, Chris
climbed in the bed and pulled up the silk covers.

Unbeknownst to Chris at the time, it would be months before he would ever have to revisit the peculiar dream world. However, he was fully aware that he would have to bust his ass in the upcoming weeks to become a stronger, faster, smarter, and an all-around better Guardian.

In that moment, Chris didn't care about any of that. With a smile on his face, he quickly closed his eyes and enjoyed the much deserved rest.

# About the Author

Johnny Duncan has a creative soul and from a young age, he constantly fabricated stories mutually for the love of story-telling and to occasionally talk himself out of trouble. He was born and raised in Philadelphia, Pennsylvania and moved to Greensboro, North Carolina at the age of 12. Fascinated with world travel and world cultures, Johnny enlisted in the United States Air Force at the age of 19, and he spent the next 15 years traveling the to include multiple countries throughout Europe, Asia, and Africa. He currently resides in San Antonio, Texas.

www.ingramcontent.com/pod-product-compliance
Lightning Source LLC
Chambersburg PA
CBHW052033020726
47501CB00004B/1391